TILL WE BECOME MONSTERS

AMANDA HEADLEE

Woodhall Press
Norwalk, CT

woodhall press

Woodhall Press, 81 Old Saugatuck Road, Norwalk, CT 06855
WoodhallPress.com

Cover design: Asha Hossain Design, LLC
Layout artist: LJ Mucci

Library of Congress Cataloging-in-Publication Data available

ISBN 978-1-949116-48-9 (paper: alk paper)
ISBN 978-1-949116-55-7 (electronic)

First Edition

Distributed by Independent Publishers Group

To those who face monsters.

Amanda Headlee

CHAPTER ONE

March 1971

Monsters existed.

Korin Perrin knew this was true because his grandmother told him so. Whenever he visited her, she read from her book of folklore, telling him stories of faeries, sea creatures, ape men, and dark creatures that roamed the forests. This information came from her book, so it had to be true.

He sat, curled up on the oversized leather armchair in what used to be his grandfather's study, the scent of old wood and tobacco heavy in the air despite his grandfather having died long before Korin was born. He loved the sea of books that lined two out of the four walls of the study. Each colored spine sparkled like a hidden gem when the light from the giant bay window shone on them.

His grandmother had rearranged the room for him so that the leather armchair now faced the bookshelves, with its back to the door, as opposed to looking dead-on at the large mahogany desk and bay window behind. On the credenza that sat by the door was his grandmother's record player, the one his parents had bought her for Christmas last year, after the one she'd received as a wedding gift had finally died after fifty-odd years. She loved classical music and today, the sounds of Wagner drifted around the room. He didn't know much about Wagner's music, but he loved the sound of the Valkyries charging in.

Right here, on this chair, was Korin's favorite place in the world. It was safe. Today, his grandmother sat next to him, squeezed into the chair with her soft plump thighs pressing against his own bony ones. The giant blue leather-bound book cracked open in her hands as she read to him a story about a changeling, a faerie creature hailing from Ireland.

"And you know what the wee faeries do with their own children?" his grandmother asked in a hushed tone, tilting her head ever so slightly toward him.

"No," he answered in the same hushed tone. "What?"

"The faeries sneak into a human household and swap a newborn human baby with one of their own."

Korin stared at her wide-eyed. "Really? Why?"

"Some say it is because the faerie baby would be cared for better in a human household, or that a faerie may love a human child better than her own. Others say it is because the faeries are seeking revenge on a couple, or . . ." Her voice started to dip.

"Or what?" Korin whispered, hanging on her every word.

"Or they take a human baby as a gift for the Devil, and they don't want the humans to know, so they leave a faerie baby in the stolen human baby's place."

"How do the human parents not know their baby was switched?" Korin asked, shivering.

His grandmother put her arm around his shoulders. The scent of Shalimar enveloped him in a cloud that smelled of safety. No one could ever hurt him while she was by his side.

"This book says it is because faerie babies are shape-shifters and can take on the form and looks of the human baby."

"So there could be a lot of faeries that look like humans? How can you tell who is a faerie-human?"

"Well," his grandmother said, looking back at the pages of the book, "faerie babies tend to act out and misbehave. They enjoy creating mischief. Faerie babies and children also love attention, trying to obtain it in all different ways—especially from their human parents."

Korin went silent and stared at his lap. His thoughts instantly went to his older brother. Korin lived in Davis's shadow and could never seem to get out from under it. He could never seem to get the level of affection he wanted from his parents. That is why he gravitated more to his grandmother. She showed him the love that his parents withheld from him and showered upon his brother. Whenever he was in her house, her entire focus was on him, not his brother. In fact, Korin would go so far as to say he didn't believe his grandmother even liked his brother.

Yet it was his brother's constant demand for attention that got him thinking. Could anyone really be that selfish? A faerie child could be.

"Granma?" Korin asked.

"Hmm?"

Do you . . ." He lowered his voice to a whisper. "Do you think Davis is a changeling?"

His grandmother laughed and swept the hand that had been around his shoulder up through her hair, tucking away a few snow-white strands that had come loose from the bun neatly coiled on top of her head. She was silent for a moment, staring at the door that led out of the study. She looked back at him, her ancient wise eyes shimmering, and she winked.

"Maybe."

Korin sucked in his breath. "If Davis is a changeling, how do I get my real brother back?"

"Granma!"

The door to the study swung open, slamming into the wall behind it. The old cordial glasses that sat on the table near the door rattled from the force.

Korin felt his grandmother's body stiffen, and in response, his did too. No one could ever hurt him while he was at his grandmother's side. No one but Davis.

"Child!" she yelled at Davis. "How many times do I have to tell you not to slam doors open that way? And you need to knock before entering a closed room."

Davis shrugged his shoulders. "I'm hungry."

"Then go to the kitchen and fix yourself something," she said, glaring at him.

A small smile started to prick the corners of Korin's mouth, but he couldn't allow it to come through. If Davis caught him smiling, all hell would break loose.

"But I want you to do it for me," Davis whined. "I like it when you make me a sandwich."

Korin always wondered why his older brother acted more immature than he did. After all, he was two years younger.

"Go." The stern direction seethed from his grandmother. He could feel the anger emanating from her body. She was so mad at his brother that it was actually beginning to make Korin uncomfortable.

"Make me a sandwich, bitch," Davis said. He laughed as he ran from the room, leaving the door wide open.

Korin immediately grabbed his grandmother's arm as she leaned forward to get up.

"Please stay here." While Korin didn't like his brother, he knew things wouldn't turn out well if she went out there. He knew the magic of being tucked away in the study would disappear. As much as he hated to admit it, he didn't like seeing his brother get into trouble—especially with his grandmother.

She sighed and leaned back into the chair, the leather squeaking under her bottom as she readjusted herself. She set the book down on her lap and once again reached up to smooth a few fly-away strands of hair. Her neat bun was always a picture of perfection, and she never allowed a single wrinkle to crease her dress. "Cleanliness is next to godliness," she'd say, and wink at Korin.

Korin pressed his cheek against the top of her arm as she picked up the book to resume reading. He closed his eyes and drifted off into her words, into the world of monsters and faeries coming to life inside his head.

He was in absolute peace. His grandmother was the only person in the world who truly cared for him. She always went above and beyond to show him that he was loved—by her at least. He couldn't say the same about his parents or brother. When he was at home with them, he was invisible. They barely spoke to him or showed him any type of attention.

Most of the time, Korin hid in his room reading his own book of folklore, the one his father had bought for him at an estate sale held at a rickety home near the center of Rachet. The house had been owned by a little old man who died there during the winter. Due to heavy blizzards that year, his body wasn't found until the spring thaw. Korin had heard rumors that the old man's body froze, and had sat preserved on a ratty wingback chair before a long-dead fireplace in a room lined with books. His frozen clawed hands held the Bible.

Early on after receiving the book, he would try to get his father to read it to him. Korin loved his father's deep baritone voice. When he read a story, it was more mystical and mysterious, not light and imaginary like when his grandmother read. The magic of the little bond that he and his father started to build was always interrupted by Davis. Unlike his grandmother, his father would put the book down and walk away, leaving Korin to retreat to his bedroom and finish reading the book on his own.

"Granma, you were about to tell me how to get rid of a changeling."

She frowned, "I'm tired of this tale. Let's move on to the next one."

"Yo, Granma." Davis was at the door again. He just couldn't stay away.

Their grandmother visibly sighed, but she ignored Davis and turned the page to start a new story.

"Hey, I need you now," he said.

Without looking up from the book, she said, "You'll have to wait."

"No—now."

She quickly snapped her head in his direction. "Young man, you will learn patience and go back into that living room and watch TV. Now!"

"Fine," he said, "but I am not responsible for anything that I break in there while I'm looking for stuff."

She sighed again. "Davis, what are you going on about?"

Davis walked over to the desk, hopped up, and sat on it. His grandmother hated it when anyone touched the desk because it had been her great-grandfather's.

"You know, Granma, you're pretty old."

"Davis!" Korin yelled. He couldn't handle anyone insulting his grandmother. She was still quite young in his eyes. He believed she was the same age as his mother, just more wrinkly and white-haired.

"What?" Davis said back to his brother. "I'm just telling the truth."

"What in the world do you want?" his grandmother said.

"Isn't there anything you don't use anymore because you are so old

8

and will die soon?"

Korin inhaled sharply. The spit that was in his mouth hit the back of his throat, causing him to cough uncontrollably. He tasted acid, coughing so hard that bile came up.

"Sweetie, are you okay?" his grandmother asked as Korin choked back his saliva. He didn't want to throw up.

She turned her attention back to Davis. "You know, child, that is very rude of you to say. Whatever is in this house will be willed to you and your brother after I die."

Davis huffed.

"Why in the world are you asking for something, anyway?"

"I need money, so I gotta pawn something."

"What do you need money for?"

"A new pair of blades for my ice skates. Mom and Dad won't buy them for me, and I'm gonna be a bad hockey player because of them."

Korin was about to remind him that their parents had just bought him a new set of blades a couple months ago when his brother gave him a look that made Korin fear for his safety.

His grandmother sighed. Korin knew she would give in. Davis was giving her his pitiful look, complete with big sad eyes and trembling bottom lip. It was how he charmed everyone into getting what he wanted. Korin shuddered as he knew his grandmother would give in to Davis's plea.

Just as he predicted, his grandmother placed the book in Korin's lap and stood.

"Keep the page for me. I'll be right back."

While her voice was sweet, there was an odd cold look in her eyes that Korin didn't quite understand. Her jaw was set tightly.

"Go," she said to Davis, pointing toward the hallway that led to the stairs at the front of the house. She started walking in that direction.

Davis's only reply was a big smile as he followed her out of the study.

Korin was left alone. He listened to them ascend the staircase up to her room. He knew she was going to give Davis money for whatever he wanted. He stayed put because he didn't want to witness his grandmother giving in to his brother—the creature.

Korin turned his attention to the big bay window. Leaves danced on tree branches in the autumn wind. Their colors were beginning to change from emerald green to a brilliance of orange, red, and yellow. Some leaves off the silver birch right outside the window had already fallen. The base of the tree was covered in little yellowish leaf corpses. Korin thought it was sad that leaves were only born in the spring, to live for a summer and then die in the fall. They didn't even get to see their first birthday.

The book was heavy in his lap. He'd never realized the weight of it before, as his grandmother usually held it when she read to him. The pages stood open to the tale of the Bullebak.

Korin turned back to the story his grandmother had been reading. He didn't understand why his grandmother wouldn't tell him how to get rid of his changeling brother. If he could just get rid of Davis and get his real brother back, then their lives could be happy. *His* life could be happy.

Korin fingered the upper right corner of the page and slowly turned it. The final paragraph spelled out how to get rid of a changeling monster: *Throw the changeling into a burning fireplace. Watch the creature jump, and escape up the chimney. By that evening, the human child shall be returned.*

Korin couldn't breathe. This is how he'd get his real brother back.

A sudden crash gave him such a start that he jumped from the chair, dropping the book to the floor, facedown, crumpling some of the pages. In a panic, he rushed out of the study and found a mass lying at the base of the staircase. His eyes wouldn't focus, but he knew that what was lying there shouldn't be there. It shouldn't be there at all.

As if the world had slowed down to a slow reel, his vision focused—although he soon wished it hadn't. A small squeak for help escaped his lips as he realized that it was his grandmother at the base of the stairs. She was on her stomach, her neck bent at an odd angle. Her hair had escaped the bun and was wildly strewn about her. She never allowed her hair to be messy.

Stars appeared at the outer limits of his vision, and for a second Korin wondered if angels were there to help. Unfortunately it was reality crashing in on him. He fought off the urge to faint as he looked up to the top of the stairs to see Davis standing there, no emotion on his face and some dollars clutched in his hand.

Korin knelt by his grandmother and shook her shoulder. She made no sound. He bent his head over her face. No breath tickled the hair that hung over his eyes.

"Granma . . . Granma?" He could barely speak as he continued to gently shake her, trying to get her to wake up. Through his tears he looked up at his brother, but it wasn't Davis. It was something black and hideous. Its eyes were filled with hate. Korin blinked and the tears cleared his eyes, and now at the top of the stairs he saw the form of his brother as he normally looked.

"I didn't push her. I know that's what you're thinking," Davis said, still unmoved.

It hadn't been his first thought. But it was the second.

"Wh-what happened?" Korin stammered.

"Her greedy butt tripped on something and fell. Karma's a bitch. She should have thought twice about giving me only five dollars."

Korin felt like spewing every bad word he had ever heard at Davis, but stopped short, not wanting to do it in the presence of his grandmother. He looked back to her form, laid down next to her, and began to sob loudly. He clutched her arm and curled into her warm body, breathing in her scent and mentally trying to urge her to wake up.

"Guess I will go call nine-one-one while you lie there like a slobbering idiot," Davis said, and he turned and walked back into their grandmother's bedroom.

Amanda Headlee

CHAPTER TWO

Glory Perrin's funeral was small, held at the Methodist church in the center of town. The initial viewing was at ten, with the service at noon. Glory would be put into the ground immediately following the service.

The town itself had no mortician, so Glory had to be taken away to the closest town that had a mortuary, Grand Portage, then returned to Rachet once embalmed. Her final resting place would be in the graveyard behind the church. Nearly all of the town's citizens were buried in this graveyard, which was quite small compared to other cemeteries nearby.

Rachet, Minnesota, ten miles north of Grand Portage, had a population of 279 people—278 now, seeing as Glory Perrin had just passed away. It was crushing for Albert Perrin, to have lost his mother. Both his parents were gone now, his father having died about fifteen years earlier. Now he knew how his wife Natalie felt. Both of her parents had died in a freak car accident when she was seven. Natalie herself had barely survived the accident. She still carried scars from the accident, including a slight limp. Albert hoped his children wouldn't have to feel this grief until they were well into their older years. It was hard to no longer have parents.

Natalie was home when she'd gotten the call from police. Had she not been, neither of them would have known what happened for several hours, as he had been out working, logging trees in the forest. A typical workday had him away from home for 11-12 hours if the job site was local. If the job site were over an hour from home, he'd be away for a week or more. His employer had sites all over Minnesota, the Dakotas, and central Canada. Natalie had originally planned to be in Grand Portage, shopping, not returning until the evening, but after she'd dropped the boys off at their grandmother's house she felt a migraine coming on and went back home to take a nap. She was awakened four hours later, still with a blasting headache, by the ringing phone. She told Albert that she'd forgotten to take it off the hook. The only time she had ever forgotten.

Albert felt guilty about being happy that the boys were there when his mother fell down the stairs. He hated that they had to live through that horror, but the happiness came from knowing she wasn't alone when she passed. Still, he knew his children would be scarred from this event, Korin more so than Davis. Korin had had a closer relationship with his mother, something else Albert had always been thankful for. He and Natalie struggled to find a balance between the two boys, as Davis just demanded so much attention. Korin was usually content to sit alone and read, which they allowed him to do most of the time. It was Albert's mother who had intervened, saying that Korin couldn't grow up alone and ignored; he wouldn't develop good communication skills. She had stepped in to provide the social interaction that Korin needed.

Davis, on the other hand—well, she didn't have the time of day for him. It should have been love at first sight when he was born, seeing as he was her first grandchild. Yet she refused to connect with him, observing him from afar. Once she told Albert that Davis had ugly eyes. Albert thought Davis had his father's pale blue eyes, and never understood why she thought they were ugly.

As Davis grew older and started to talk, she began to show contempt for his attitude. She would tell Natalie and Albert that they allowed Davis to get away with murder. Glory said that they gave too much to Davis and never set any boundaries for him. Albert and Natalie often talked about Glory's comments, concluding that she just didn't understand what it was like raising a child in the 1960s. She had raised her own just after the Great Depression, and didn't have the opportunity to give her children what they wanted.

Although Albert was often angry at his mother for insulting his parenting skills, he realized she had a point. They were terrible at finding a balance. Davis was honestly so damn demanding, and as his parents, they definitely struggled to say no to him. And now he was worried about his youngest. Albert and Natalie needed to change how they raised their boys. Korin was seven, very soon to be eight, and Davis ten; they needed to learn how to act a little more maturely. He would speak with Natalie when they lay in bed later tonight on how they could help their boys grow and be more responsible.

My god, they put the worst color of lipstick on her, thought Albert as he walked up to the casket and looked at his mother. She was painted in makeup—stuff she rarely wore. They had given the mortuary a powder-blue dressing gown to bury her in. Korin really wanted her to be buried in a flowered dress that she wore for Easter Sundays, as he had such fond memories of her wearing it. He told Albert that he loved seeing her stand outside in the sun with the dress on as they ran around the snowy yard in the cold, still-wintry air, finding hidden Easter eggs. But Albert had always thought it was a hideous dress and had no desire to see it again, so he ignored his son's wishes and pulled the dressing gown from the closet instead. He handed it to Natalie with a murmured "Good enough." He was satisfied with the way his mother looked when the mortician had shown them last night.

Now, he, Natalie, and Davis stood at the casket, taking a final look before the doors opened and those wishing to pay their respects filtered in. Korin was nowhere to be found. He was probably hiding in the organ loft; he'd never liked crowds.

"Anything else before we start?" asked the mortician. He was a wiry man with a receding hairline and a creepy demeanor. Albert got the shivers when the man looked him in the eye. The life of a mortician suited him well.

"No, I think we're all set," Albert replied.

Pastor Barker stood next to the mortician, nervously sliding a bulletin of service between his fingers. He wouldn't make eye contact with Albert; he'd stopped doing so several years ago. He may have looked pious in his robe and sash, but you couldn't let the white collar fool you. The pastor's puffy red eyes and chapped nose solidified in Albert's mind that this "man of God" had been screwing around with his mother.

Albert had begun to get suspicious right after his father's death, when the pastor suddenly started showing up unannounced at his mother's house. It soon became habit for the pastor to be at Glory's house for every holiday. Then there were the times the boys mentioned that the pastor was visiting while his mother was watching them. Albert couldn't help but wonder if she may have been having an affair with the pastor even before his father passed.

Albert used to tell Natalie about his suspicions, but she was so pure-minded that she would continually brush Albert off, saying that Barker was just doing his righteous duty and helping an old, lonely woman cope after the death of the only man she had ever loved in the world.

Albert would roll his eyes. "Sure, he was just helping."

She'd smile, completely missing the sarcasm in his voice, and go back to whatever task she was doing in the house. He would always walk away, dwelling on his suspicions.

"It's lipstick on a pig," Davis said aloud when he looked into the casket. "Look, Dad, that wasn't on her face last night." Davis laughed.

"Hush," Natalie whispered to her son, swatting him in the arm with her bulletin.

Albert said nothing, but saw anger growing on Pastor Barker's face. The mortician was unmoved.

"Guess we should let everyone in," Albert said as he walked over to the head of the casket. Natalie and Davis walked over to his side, Davis still laughing at his own comment. Pastor Barker stood at the end of the line next to Davis, a look of anger still on his face. The mortician went to open the sanctuary doors.

Albert looked up to the organ loft. Through the slats of the railing he could see Korin looking down on all of them. He felt pity for his youngest. The kid really loved his grandmother. Albert knew that seeing his grandmother's body at the bottom of the stairs would haunt him for the rest of his life.

Davis was much stronger. He may have watched her fall, but he would've known there was nothing he could have done to help her. Korin, on the other hand, would make himself feel guilty. Albert didn't know how he was going to help his son through this.

When his father stood to give the eulogy, he pulled a small round candy from his pocket. A "bull's-eye" is what his grandmother called it, because of the white cream center surrounded by a thick layer of soft caramel. She had told him that these little candies always made her think of the center of a dartboard. They were her favorite, and she always had a candy dish full of them. It sat on a green enamel table in the middle of her kitchen. These caramels were Korin's favorite, too, and on the day she died, before he left her house with his mother, he scooped a handful of them from the dish and hid them in his pocket, eating one every day since, in her honor.

He only had a few left, and he'd saved today's for the funeral. It was the only way he felt he could be with his grandmother one final time. As his father spoke, Korin took the soft little candy out of its clear cellophane wrapper, being ever so cautious not to crinkle it and draw people's attention up to the loft.

He held the candy in his hand and looked through one of the slats at his grandmother. Tears welled in his eyes as he put the candy in his mouth and bit down, relishing the rush of sweetness that filled his mouth. He chewed slowly, feeling the tougher texture of the caramel against the softness of the cream center. Once the candy was mashed down into smaller bits, he swallowed hard, a heavy lump forming in his throat. It was the last caramel he would ever enjoy with his grandmother.

His father looked up to the loft after he was done speaking, no emotion etched on his face. After a few final prayers, his parents and Davis stood next to the casket and talked with all of the guests who wanted to share their condolences before leaving the church for the graveyard.

Korin couldn't look at his grandmother anymore. He didn't want to see the lid closed and her trapped within a box for all of eternity. Instead he focused on his family. His father, still stone-faced; his mother's face red, streaked with tears. And Davis . . . Davis stared up at him from the front of the church with a sickening sneer on his face. A sneer that told Korin that Davis had in fact pushed their grandmother down the stairs, killing her. A sneer that said he was proud of what he had done.

Korin slid away from the railing and curled up in the corner behind the organ. He laid there crying for what felt like hours, still tasting the faint sweetness of the caramel in his mouth, until his mother finally came to get him.

"Come on, sweetie—time to go," she said, appearing in the doorway next to the organ. She held out a hand to him.

"Is she still down there?" he asked, not wanting to see the casket any longer.

"No, honey, they've taken her outside. She's already resting in the ground."

In the ground, he thought.

"Granma will be in the ground forever," he whispered to himself.

"Sorry, sweetie, I didn't hear that."

"Nothing," Korin said.

His mother said nothing more, merely took his hand and helped him to his feet.

Korin breathed in deeply through his nose as they walked toward the stairwell. The last smell he would associate with his grandmother would be the musty scent of the organ loft.

He and his mother walked hand in hand down the stairs and out the front of the church. The contact with his mother made him feel good, and he rubbed the back of her hand on his cheek. She looked down and smiled at him.

As soon as Davis saw her holding his hand, he started to cry and rushed up to their mother.

"Mommy, I'm so sad," he cried.

Korin felt his throat constrict as his mother loosened her grip on his hand and reached out to Davis, pulling him in close to her. He buried his face in her shoulder.

Korin just stood there.

Davis slightly turned his head and looked at Korin, dry-eyed. Once more, a sneer appeared on his lips.

Dejected, Korin walked toward his father who was standing on the sidewalk near the front entrance to the church. He was looking at his wife and Davis, not paying attention to Korin walking up to him. Natalie, her arms still wrapped around Davis, approached them. Albert patted Davis on the back and the three turned to walk home, Korin following behind.

For once the Perrin household was quiet. Albert and Natalie sat in the kitchen staring absentmindedly at the cold cups of coffee in their hands. Davis was watching a hockey game. Korin was sitting in the living room. Although a cozy fire burned in the fireplace, he was freezing. No matter what he did, he couldn't get warm. He felt so alone, so empty. His face hurt from crying, and now his eyes were dry.

While Korin had never felt truly happy during the short seven years of his life, today was the first time he'd ever felt hate. Hatred raged through his little body as he stared into the flames. It caused his heartbeat to quicken and his mind to wander back to a few days ago when he'd been sitting on the old leather chair in his grandfather's study, moments before his grandmother fell to her death.

The last words that he'd read in her book of folklore whispered from the flickering flames before him. He knew what he had to do. Yet as much as he hated his brother—that is, the creature that had replaced his *real* brother—he wondered if he could handle inflicting harm on the changeling that sat on the floor behind him? If he followed the instructions in his grandmother's book and pushed the creature into the fire, what would happen if the fire killed it before it had a chance to climb up the chimney? If the changeling died, would his real brother be returned? His parents would hate him because their eldest—changeling or not—would be dead. And it would be his fault.

Korin knew that he was never going to have a happy life with his family as long as the changeling existed. He needed to get rid of the creature today, despite the risks. Korin hated that the creature needed to be constantly attended to—that it had ultimately pushed his grand-mother down the stairs. He knew she hadn't tripped like everyone said.

The changeling had pushed her because he hated the fact that she loved Korin more.

Movement out of the corner of his eye caught his attention. He looked down to see a small spider crawling along the hearth, which gave Korin an idea.

"Yuck!" He jumped up. "A spider!" He pointed at the little arachnid making its way across the front of the fireplace.

Davis broke his concentration on the game long enough to look over at Korin. Davis loved squishing spiders and other bugs; it was one of the few things that could break him away from the TV. He jumped up, ran over to the fireplace, and pushed his brother out of the way. Davis knelt and put his face close to the hearth, ignoring the heat of the blaze.

"Oooo, I am going to make you burn, little bug," he said as he prepared to flick the spider into the flames. Just as he was about to do so, there was a push from behind, and Davis's right arm went into the fire.

"You killed Granma!" Korin yelled. "Bring back my real brother!"

Korin pushed his weight into his brother's back. Davis screamed at the top of his lungs and swung his elbow behind him. His elbow connected with Korin's head, knocking him away.

As Davis pulled his arm out of the fireplace, the smell of burning flesh filled the room, and there was a sizzling sound like bacon frying on the stove. His right hand and arm came away raw, red, and glistening. Some skin was starting to bubble and peel.

Korin clawed at his ears as Davis continued to scream. He had failed— he failed! The creature writhed on the floor in agony, still inside the house. From his own throat, Korin echoed the creature's wail.

Natalie and Albert came running to see Davis lying on the floor, his right arm in the air, shrieking in pain. His shirtsleeve was singed, and his arm was badly burned. Korin's high-pitched screaming never stopped, tears streaming down his face.

Albert tried to get Davis to his feet while Natalie ran to the kitchen and started filling up a hand towel with whatever ice was in the ice trays. When it wasn't enough, she grabbed bags of frozen vegetables. She came out and wrapped the icy bundles around Davis's right forearm and hand. The contact of the cold against the fresh burns made Davis screech even louder.

"Natalie! I don't think you're supposed to do that with burns!" Albert snapped, pulling away the ice packs. "Help me get him into the car, and hold his hand up."

Natalie frantically grabbed her son's arm and lifted it high in the air. Davis's cries still filled the house. Albert grabbed the keys and the coats from the closet and ushered Natalie and Davis out of the house and to the car. The door slammed shut and Korin sat there in the middle of the room, with a hand to his throbbing head where Davis's elbow had connected.

They just left him there. They left him there alone.

CHAPTER THREE

The sterile white walls with a single seven-inch-wide pea-green stripe painted four feet above the speckled linoleum floor indicated to those who walked the hallway that they were in the residential wing of Duluth Asylum. Built sometime in the 1800s initially to house those who were caught up in the spread of tuberculosis that ransacked the United States, the state of Minnesota took over the buildings to house those who struggled with mental health issues, accepting its first mentally ill patient in 1942.

Korin thought himself to be the sanest person in the facility. Even as a seven-year-old child, he knew that Duluth Asylum was not a place he was supposed to be.

In the administration office, it was explained to him that he had a routine that varied only on Sunday, when the number of staff was at its lowest. Every day for him, for the most part will be the same. The goal was to get him into a routine...to get him compliant.

When Korin awoke on the morning of his first full day of being committed at the asylum, the sun filtered through the barred windows, illuminating the crisp white room. Korin would never get used to the bright dawn shocking him awake nearly every morning. The room was barren except for the steel bed frame, a flimsy stained mattress, and white cotton sheets. He wasn't allowed to have a pillow. No one was. Suffocation was a risk.

Once awake, he sat on his bed until eight a.m., when the orderlies made their rounds.

The first brought him clean clothes—simple white fabric, scratchy, and, of course, stained.

The second came in with medication after he was dressed. Korin didn't know why he was taking the pills. He wasn't sick and refused. A burly female nurse with a faint mustache held him down in his bed while a wiry older one had come in with a hose and a cup of water. They opened his mouth, shoved the hose down his throat, and washed down the pills with a cup of water. The burly nurse made two threats once she'd confirmed the pills were down: One: If he threw up the pills, they would do this again. Two: If he refused to take his pills tomorrow, they would do this again.

The third orderly brought him breakfast. Congealed or runny scrambled eggs. Burnt or raw bacon. Cardboard toast with no butter. Everything was laid out on a plastic tray that had dividers separating the food. There was only a metal spoon provided. The orderly gave him exactly seven minutes to eat—not a minute more or a minute less. Korin never understood why the number had to be seven, but that was all the time he had. If he didn't eat everything in seven minutes, the "food" would be taken away and he wouldn't see anything to eat again until 12:30 p.m. About an hour after he ate, someone returned with a cup of water, which he had to immediately drink, because once taken away, he wouldn't get another drink until after lunch.

Korin jolted when the fourth orderly, the nerdy one with the thick coke-bottle-bottom glasses, walked into his room without knocking. "Time to go," he barked. Time to be ferried around to his daily appointments. Korin's stomach churned from breakfast. The routine had him slated to see Dr. Barrister after breakfast every morning.

"Can't I have thirty minutes?" he said, rubbing his stomach. "I just ate."

The orderly moved so fast his body was a blur, and before he knew it, Korin was facedown on the cold linoleum with his arms chicken-winged behind him. The fingers of the orderly dug tightly into his wrists with a strength Korin had not expected. A gasp escaped his mouth when the orderly leaned forward and whispered harshly into his ear. "You know what happens to little kids who misbehave. They get locked up with the monsters in the basement."

Korin squirmed and tried to get out of the man's grasp.

The basement was where Dr. Barrister housed those who were truly insane, and beyond help. He feared being surrounded by these patients, locked in their own nearby cells, screaming and crying and bellowing.

He never wanted to be sent to the basement.

"I'll go," he whispered and stopped squirming.

"Good boy."

The orderly released his grasp and allowed Korin to get to his feet. Once standing, the orderly ruffled Korin's mousy hair. "Now let's go," he said, pointing down the hall toward the administration wing.

As Korin tentatively took a step into the hallway the nerdy orderly promptly shoved him from behind. The man's fingers were now digging into Korin's shoulder as he led him down the hallway to the administration wing of the asylum.

Korin shivered. Buildings like this, like all hospitals, never seemed to be warm places. When he was about five, Davis pushed him off the porch of their house, and when Korin hit the ground, his forehead hit a rock, splitting the skin at the hairline. Stiches were needed and Natalie rushed him off to the hospital while Davis stayed behind with their father who just returned from a week away at a job site across the border.

All he could remember of the waiting room was the cold. The same of the Emergency Room bay they were put in. An icy grip followed him the moment he stepped foot in the building, it were as if the death had hold of his shoulder, ready to take him at any moment.

"Mommy, am I going to die?" He asked her several times. She'd laugh and pat his hand, telling him no. He just needed stiches.

When the doctor came in to speak with his mother, Korin didn't follow much of what was being said, but he did hear the word "shot". He would have to get a shot in the head. Korin hated needles and promptly started having a fit. He tore the gauze that was placed over the cut to slow the bleeding, releasing a torrent of blood. A nurse appeared with a small backboard and she strapped him to it, the nylon straps bit into his skin as she tightened the straps.

A linen cloth was placed over his face. He couldn't see. He screamed. The doctor slid the cloth and a hole appeared over his right eye. He could see the doctor and nurse looking at him. His mother was nowhere in sight. Then the cloth moved, covering his eye. He couldn't see. Again, Korin screamed.

The hole appeared again.

"Peek-a-boo," the doctor said, looking at Korin through the hole. This cycle continued repeatedly until Korin's throat went raw from screaming and he could no longer make a sound . Eye covered once more. He felt a sharp jab on his forehead and whimpered as his head flushed warm then cold. He shivered again.

The halls of the asylum stirred up that memory every time he stepped foot in the hall. While the feeling of pain from the fall and subsequent stiches were a vague recollection, he never let go the memory of feeling so cold while being terrorized by a game of peek-a-boo.

Though, the feeling of the cold hallway was the least of Korin's worry. The patients on his floor, while mentally unstable, could roam freely during the day, as they were not deemed to be dangerous. Most ignored him as he passed, but there were a few who tried to touch him—his arms, his face, his legs. The older ladies especially liked to coo at him, combing their fingers through his hair and whispering, "My precious little boy is growing up." The orderly seemed to enjoy seeing Korin uncomfortable and slowed down as they passed a small group of ladies, allowing them to pinch his cheeks.

It was not the elderly ladies who bothered him, but the man at the end of the hall who sat in a wheelchair, staring at the floor. As Korin approached, he observed that the man ignored everyone else that passed, keeping his head bowed. Something about the man unnerved Korin and he tried to put his escort between him and the man. His attempt was thwarted, and the orderly pushed him forward toward the man.

"Oh there is no need to fear Quintin," the orderly said, squeezing Korin's shoulder, pushing him even closer.

Quintin's head snapped up and he stared Korin down. With a crazed glaze in his eye, he began to mutter "Burner, burner, burner" the whole time Korin walked by. Korin gasped and side stepped, his heel crushing the top of one of the orderly's feet.

"Watch it!" The orderly pushed Korin into the wall next to Quintin, who by now was screaming "Burner, burner, burner" at the top of his lungs. Flecks of Quintin's spit landed on Korin's face. The orderly grabbed Korin's shoulder and steered him firmly down the hall.

"Quintin has water on the brain, preventing him from functioning as a person normally did," the orderly laughed. "He's a simpleton, not understanding anything that anyone ever said to him. He usually ignores all of us, but boy, does he like you!"

Korin was scared. Even though it was his first day in the asylum, this simpleton Quintin somehow knew why Korin was locked in the halls of Duluth Asylum.

"Come in!" The voice on the other side of the large oak door was baritone and sharp. The orderly pushed open the door.

A large man sat hunched over a massive oak desk. Any normal person would look dwarfed in the chair sitting at the desk, but not Dr. Reginald Barrister. His shoulders were broad and hunched, much like a vulture looming over a carcass, ready to pick at the dead flesh. Korin wondered if Dr. Barrister would prey on his body, should he die in the doctor's presence. What didn't help in the matter of Korin thinking the doctor looked like a vulture was that he had a long sharp nose, bald head, and tiny dark eyes.

Dr. Barrister didn't look up from his paperwork when Korin entered the oak-encased office, just gestured with an upturned hand to a leather-clad seat in front of his massive oak desk. The nerdy orderly steered

Korin to the seat, pushed him down, and left.

Dr. Barrister still didn't look up. When he'd finished looking over the last page in front of him, he shuffled the papers into a neat stack, shoved them into a brown folder, set it aside, and reached for another folder from a stack to his right.

"Korin Thomas Perrin. Age seven. Soon to be eight here I see. Your birthday is next month," Dr. Barrister looked up from the paperwork to the nerdy orderly standing behind Korin. "That is all." And he waved his hand, shooing away the man. Dr. Barrister returned his attention to the paperwork, not once making eye contact with Korin.

"Yessir," Korin answered in a low voice.

"What's that, boy?" The doctor snapped his head up and glared at Korin, the darkness in his eyes stirred a quaking sensation in Korin's chest. "Speak up when you are being spoken to by an adult."

"Yessir," Korin said a little louder.

"Better," Dr. Barrister said as he shuffled the paperwork. "So you are here because you tried to kill your brother."

Korin flinched at the accusation. A small smile crept across Dr. Barrister's face.

"I didn't try to kill my brother. I was trying to get the real Davis back."

Dr. Barrister scribbled something onto a writing pad on his desk.

"Let's start somewhere else first, because I think you are a little too delusional right now to address what you did to your brother."

Korin opened his mouth to say something, but the look on the doctor's face caused him to clam up.

"Tell me about your parents."

"I love my parents," Korin responded.

"Such an interesting response," the doctor mused. "I asked you to tell me about your parents, and you immediately told me that *you* loved them." He paused for a moment to scribble again on his notebook. "I wonder, do they love you? Do you think your parents love you, Korin?"

Korin just stared at Dr. Barrister, unsure of what to say. He should be loved by his parents. They are his parents after all, and parents are to love their children. They should love all their children. Yet maybe his parents didn't love him. He clearly was the last thing they ever thought of at home, giving their attention primarily to Davis, the television, or taking care of things around the house. To Korin, he always seemed to come in last place to everything else in the household.

"I don't know," he whispered.

"Come now, boy," Dr. Barrister barked. "Speak up and out with it. Tell me why you think your parents don't love you and why you think you love them."

"I don't think anything, I know."

25

"Well then, what do you know?"

"I love them because they are my parents and kids are supposed to love their parents. I know they don't love me because they have to give their attention all to my brother and other things that are more important than me, I guess."

"You guess? Boy, that is a heavy accusation there for you to just *guess.*"

Korin went silent. He had nothing more he could tell the doctor because he had no words for what he wanted to say. Deep down he was frustrated, lost, and didn't understand why his family dynamics were the way that they were, yet he didn't know how to tell this scary man in front of him. He feared whatever he said would be repeated to his parents, making them dislike him even more.

"Child, I am talking to you. Answer me."

Korin ignored him and stared at the brass name plate that sat atop the desk which declared the desk as the doctor's property.

"Your silence leads me to believe that you tried to kill your brother to get rid of him, which would make you the only child, leaving your parents to only love you."

Heat coursed through Korin's body and all around him radiated a brilliant white. He felt himself stand and swipe out his arm toward the doctor. When his vision cleared in the next moment, he saw that he had grabbed Dr. Barrister's name plate and threw it across the room, shattering the glass of one of his bookshelves.

"Well, now." The doctor was unfazed by Korin's action and calmly reached over and picked up the receiver of an ebony rotary phone. "Please come in here now and take our newest patient to our... special place."

Korin breathed heavily, but the moment that Dr. Barrister mentioned the "special place", he started to shake. All the rage subsided from his body as quickly as it ignited, and before he could gather his bearings, the nerdy orderly returned.

He turned to look at the orderly who just returned a glare. Roughly grabbing Korin's shoulder, he dragged him out of Dr. Barrister's office. As he was being forcefully pulled from the room, he looked back at the doctor who just smiled and waved.

The "special place" turned out to be the asylum's basement. Despite it being Korin's first full day in the facility, right after he was dropped off at the asylum's front steps and registered by the head nurse, he started hearing about the horrors of the basement. And it was a place he never wanted to see.

Yet, nearly twenty-four hours after being admitted, he found himself locked up in a solitary cell with only a rough wooden bench to sit on and a small window in the door to let in light.

"Please, let me out!" Korin yelled, banging his fists against the door. Down the hall, he heard his calls echoed by other patients.

"Enough!" A voice roared from the other side of the door. Korin skittered back, falling onto the bench when he collided with the far wall. The voices outside the door ceased as heavy footsteps headed his way. The light was blotted out in the door as someone—a guard possibly—looked in.

"First day and already find yourself down here." The man's laugh sounded evil. "You are going to be a special case."

The man walked off, allowing the light to shine back in through the small window. Korin couldn't make out the man's face, but he'd remember the voice as from someone he never wanted to meet in person.

Korin curled up on the hard bench and gagged a little as he breathed in, smelling the wood that pressed against his cheek. The smell was putrid, as though someone had died on this bench and their body was left here to decay for a year. He sat up and aggressively wiped at his cheek, disgusted that his face touched the bench. Pulling his legs up into his chest, he leaned against the wall. He began to cry, allowing the tears to freely flow. No one could see him here so he couldn't be made fun of for crying. He didn't know what was going to happen next or for how long he'd have to sit down in this dank and dark room while the screams and cries of the insane surround him.

Amanda Headlee

CHAPTER FOUR

Korin hated his nearly daily walk to Dr. Barrister's office. It had been nearly three weeks since he was admitted and after his terrifying first day, Korin remained on good behavior by listening to the orderlies, nurses, and Dr. Barrister. After spending most of the afternoon of his first full day in the basement, he realized that he'd have to play along with their game if he wanted to survive and never be put down in the hellish basement again.

He especially hated the walk today—the day after his eighth birthday. He held on to excitement yesterday that his parents would come visit, or at least call and wish him a Happy Birthday. Korin spent the entire day trying to be positive, even having an okay session with Dr. Barrister where the doctor had barely said a word to him due to being preoccupied with the documents on his desk, allowing Korin to speak about school and his interests. The doctor never made mention that he knew it was Korin's birthday. When Korin casually mentioned it, Dr. Barrister replied, "Is that so?" and continued reading his paperwork. Korin was hurt, but pushed the feeling down, continuing to rattle on about school and how good his grades were.

He tried to tell himself that Dr. Barrister is just a mean and grumpy person. He is not the kind of person to wish people Happy Birthdays. But then no one else throughout the day wished him a Happy Birthday. They all continued as they normally do, only noticing Korin's existence when he is needed to be somewhere or doing something wrong. As night descended, that is when he realized there was no one who genuinely cared that it was his special day... not even his family.

The pain and anger from feeling unimportant and forgotten carried heavy on his heart that morning. Without fail, the orderly that walked Korin down the hall, ensured that he had a run-in with Quinten. As per the usual protocol, Quinten sat in his wheelchair, slack jawed and drooling, until Korin came into view. Life ignited in Quinten and the ritual chant of "Burner, burner, burner" began and continued as he walked past the wheelchair-bound man. Hearing Quinten's chants normally put him on edge. As he passed Quinten, Korin felt empty. Not even the accusations of burning someone nearly to death rattled him today.

"Hmm . . . Korin ," he said gruffly and, as usual, looking at paperwork on his desk versus making eye contact with Korin. "now that you are now eight years old. Time to start acting your age and better understanding the consequences of your actions. I think we are ready to get to the meat of why you are here. You pushed your brother into the fire because you thought he was a demon."

Korin stared at his feet. For the past few weeks, they had ever talked about was his parents. He had been spared having to speak about Davis up until this point, except for what was discussed on his first day. He felt his face flush hot. Dr. Barrister had it wrong.

"No, Davis is a changeling, not a demon."

"Hmm, a changeling . . . Is that so?"

"Yes, sir."

"And what is a changeling, may I ask?" Dr. Barrister lifted his head and looked at Korin, who shifted uncomfortably in his seat. It always felt like the doctor's eyes were able to pierce his soul.

"Well . . . uhh . . . ," he started, struggling to find the words.

"Out with it," barked the doctor.

"Well, the faeries replaced my real brother with the creature that is my brother right now. I was trying to push this creature into the fire so that it would jump up the chimney and bring back my real brother." He took a breath. "My current brother is a bad thing, and I want my real brother back. Can you help me? He killed my grandmother." The words rushed out of him, and he found himself shaking with fear.

"Hmm."

Korin looked at him with pleading eyes. He needed help, whether the doctor scared him or not.

"Well, young boy, that's quite an imagination you have there. Where did you learn about changelings?"

Korin looked at him, perplexed. He wasn't imagining anything. It was real.

"My grandmother told me a story about them, and I immediately knew Davis was one."

"And?"

Korin's breath rattled from his mouth as his body shook, the leather seat creaking under him. He clamped his hands together.

"Granma told me the story of the changeling right before she died. I was actually reading about how to get rid of one when Davis pushed her down the stairs."

The doctor ignored the accusation thrown at Davis.

"Changeling or not, you do know what you did was a bad thing, don't you?" The doctor crossed his arms in front of his large belly and leaned forward. "You are a very bad boy."

Korin sat back in his chair. He didn't think he'd done anything wrong. His temper boiled inside him. He was furious because no one believed him. He was furious because no one—including his family—remembered his birthday yesterday. He was furious because he now knew with one-hundred percent certainty no one in the Perrin family household cared about him. They only cared about the monster that abducted and replaced the real Davis.

Korin stood up and screamed at the doctor, "Shut up! I just want my real brother back! I'd set the creature on fire again if I knew it would bring Davis home!"

Dr. Barrister leaned back in his chair and *hmm*ed again, then pulled out a small white pad from his desk and began writing on it.

"What are you writing?" Korin leaned forward, trying to read the words. He noted to himself that it looked like a prescription pad.

"It's none of your business," said the doctor. He picked up the black phone on his desk and said "Now."

A different orderly, one Korin had never met before, walked in. The man's face was rat-like, and Korin knew immediately he couldn't trust him.

Dr. Barrister tore off the page he'd written on and handed it to the rat-faced orderly, who cast a glance at the paper, then Korin, then the doctor.

"This boy is still trouble," the doctor said with a chuckle.

Ratface glared at Korin, roughly grabbed him by the shoulder, and hauled him out of the doctor's office.

"Hey!" Korin slapped at the man's hand.

"Hit me one more time and I'll drag you down to the basement," Ratface seethed.

The orderly's black hair hung in long bangs and equally dark eyes peeked through the strands. Black stubble peppered his face, and the rank stench of cigarettes came from his mouth when he spoke. It took everything Korin had in him not to gag.

The man continued to pull Korin down the hallway toward his room.

Quintin was still sitting outside his room in his wheelchair, staring at the floor. A silver thread of drool leaked from his sagging lower lip onto the small blanket covering his lap. As they neared, Quintin raised his head, eyes locked on Korin. Even from down the hallway Korin could see Quintin's lips moving and hear the word *burner* being repeated. The volume increased with each step he took, until by the time they were nearly next to him he was shouting.

"Shut up!" Ratface snapped at Quintin. He kicked at the wheelchair, twirling Quintin so he was facing away from them.

Ratface was the first person to stick up for him. Despite his gruff manner, Korin began to think that maybe the man had a kind heart inside.

"Thank you," Korin said to him.

"You shut up too," he glared at Korin. "None of you noisy idiots know how to keep quiet."

They continued on in silence until they got to his room. Ratface opened the door and pushed him in, slamming the door behind him.

"Hey!" Korin pounded on the door. "I get TV time before my next appointment. Hey!"

The little window in the door opened and Ratface glared in.

"Shut up, you little brat! No TV, no appointments, no food, and no coming out of your room for the rest of the day." He stood so only his mouth was visible in the tiny window. "Doctor's orders." His thin smile revealed tobacco-stained teeth, several ending in jagged points, some missing entirely.

Korin kicked the door.

Ratface's eyes appeared in the window again. "Oh, bit of a temper, have we? I warned you."

Korin backed away from the door, panicked. He looked around the room for a weapon, and seeing the bed, grabbed it and tried dragging it over to the door to hold it closed. It was bolted to the floor.

Outside the door there were multiple voices, and Korin knew he was going to be taken to the basement. Ratface, Nerd Boy, and Mustache Lady all entered the room, arms raised to chest height, fingers splayed to grab Korin. He tried to duck and head for the door, but there were too many of them. There was the heavy smell of body odor that came from whoever's armpit was near his face. Mustache Lady grabbed his foot, and the iron taste of blood seeped into his mouth when his jaw connected with the floor.

Shaking his head to dislodge the pain, he tried to get up, but a weight on his back held him down. There was much yelling from the orderlies as he screamed, all of it suddenly silenced when he felt a sharp pain in his shoulder. The pain turned to a warmth that spread throughout his body and the world tilted on its side as his vision faded to black.

Korin woke up to a wail, followed by maniacal laughter. He couldn't tell if his eyes were open or not. If they were, the room was pitch-black.

He was alone in a tiny solitary holding cell. Despite how mean the staff was at Duluth Asylum, they weren't evil. Putting another patient in the room with Korin could be fatal—for him.

A wet drip fell from his nose onto his hand, and he sniffed. His eyes were open. He was crying. The floor was soft beneath him. Whoever had put him here had at least had the decency to place him on a thin mattress rather than the filthy floor or the wooden bench that smelled of death. A hiccup escaped his lips and he clamped his mouth shut. He didn't want the others in the basement to know he was here. If they did, they would say awful things to him and make him cry even harder. Best to be silent.

Korin leaned back against the cool wall and shifted his weight. When he moved the smell of pee wafted from the mattress. Curling his legs to his chest and wrapping his arms around them, he cried silently into his knees. He just wanted to go home. Back to his own little bedroom away from everyone. He'd promise to never hurt anyone ever again, even the creature that now existed in place of his real brother.

He bit his lip and started rocking back and forth, tasting blood. "I'm not insane, I'm not insane," he whispered to himself as quietly as possible. No one outside the cell heard him. His arm throbbed where one of the orderlies had jabbed him with a needle to sedate him. He had no idea how long he'd been out, but he hoped that he'd been asleep for several hours. They wouldn't keep him down here for very long . . . at least, he didn't think so.

Korin closed his eyes and leaned his head against the wall. This place was alive and its heart was evil. He imagined he could hear the heartbeat behind the stone wall, breath whooshing down the hallway. It fed off all the lives trapped within its walls. He'd heard people that entered Duluth Asylum died here. There were moments when Korin feared he would do the same. And maybe he should. Maybe he should allow the asylum to take him into its heart, to feed off the badness that everyone thought he has inside of him. Only bad kids get sent to terrible places like this. Maybe he shouldn't be allowed to go home.

The warmth from the wall at his back was soothing. Inviting. The heart of the building wanted him. It would take care of him.

Laughter from the next cell over merged with the wails from a woman somewhere down the hall to his left. Combined with the sound of the wind and what he believed to be the heartbeat within, it was enough to send Korin off to sleep.

His whole body felt electrified. When he tried to open his eyes, all he saw was stark white.

Korin turned his head away and his eyes adjusted. Someone knelt in front of him, shaking his shoulders and shining a flashlight in his face. Hoots and hollers echoed up and down the corridor on the other side of the now-opened cell door. Everyone knew he was here.

"Get the fuck up."

It was Ratface. Korin squirmed as he grabbed his shoulder, yanking him to his feet. He bit back any smart comment that might have formed on the tip of his tongue because he didn't want to be shocked again, but he did pull away from Ratface. Korin wanted to stay in the cell. This is where boys like him belonged.

"I said, get up!" Ratface yanked harder, so hard that Korin thought the man would pull his arm out of its socket.

The pain forced him to comply and tried to balance on feet that felt like they were hanging in midair. He couldn't sense the floor underneath him as he was pulled forward. The beam from the flashlight was now cast out in front of Ratface, and from where he stood, he was plunged into darkness.

Hands reached out through the bars of the cells next to him, trying to grab hold of him as he passed. They wanted to keep him in the basement. He tried to walk closer to the grabbing hands, hoping for one to rip him away from the clutches of Ratface, but the orderly drew

Korin in closer to himself. Korin tried to pull away again. Ratface put him in a headlock and dragged him towards the large door that led to the stairway. Stars sparkled in the periphery of his vision as he struggled to breathe. He tried to hit Ratface in the side, but the man was built solid. Korin's punches had no effect.

The steel door glistened. There was a small leak in a pipe above that dripped down the door's surface. Ratface slammed Korin up against the door and leaned into his back. Being released from the headlock, oxygen whooshed into Korin's lungs but was immediately expelled from being sandwiched between the cold metal and Ratface's hidden brute strength. Fear triggered in his mind that he was going to suffocate to death, but the emotion dissipated when he realized that meant if he died here, he could be where he was truly wanted. Korin didn't struggle.

With his free hand, Ratface fished out a clump of keys from his pocket. Korin guessed he had to have twenty to thirty keys on the small key ring and it would take him forever to find the correct one. Somehow, the orderly managed to quickly find the right key and unlock the door. The steel door swung open, spilling Korin onto the cold concrete floor. Ratface grabbed him by the back of the shirt and dragged him toward the staircase.

"Get upstairs." He pointed to the metal staircase leading back up into the residential wing of the asylum.

Korin turned to look back at the entry into the basement. The steel door slammed shut on its own. Ratface jumped then pushed Korin quickly up the stairs. Korin complied, the heart of the asylum didn't want him either.

Amanda Headlee

CHAPTER FIVE

Natalie Perrin's kitten heels clacked as she walked down the sterile hallway of Duluth Asylum. She should have worn flats. The awkward, unrhythmic sound on the linoleum signaled that she was damaged. A limp she carried with her throughout her life since the car accident that took her parents away. The constant reminder of how her childhood was stolen from her. She hated how places like this made her feel. It was the same feeling that hospitals gave her. The smell was awful, something she could never quite put her finger on. Disinfectant mixed with the scent of chemicals and medication, and a hint of death. The air was thick, and when she inhaled it lodged at the back of her throat. Natalie stopped walking and leaned against the wall and placed her hand to her head. The temperature was set at a point where you should feel warm enough, but somehow you could never quite shake the chill. It was just like that day when she woke up in the hospital as a child. The room smelled and felt like this when a doctor told a seven-year-old Natalie that her parents were dead and that her shattered leg would never fully heal.

She hated leaving her baby in this place, because being in a place with this kind of smell and temperature meant something bad was happening. But she needed to do what was best for her family.

Natalie and Albert had argued about it almost daily since Korin was admitted.

Davis needed constant care and attention. Although most of his badly damaged arm had been salvaged, he would still be scarred for life and have mobility issues. The fact that Korin was away did help. Having someone else deal with what he had done to his brother was even better. She couldn't handle caring for Davis and Korin at the same time, and with Albert gone in the forest all day, she most certainly could not do it alone.

While she was at peace with the situation, Albert was not. He wanted both his boys home, and at the same time, he wanted no one home. Davis's constant demands for attention wore on him much more than her. She was the mother, after all, and could handle it. Albert could not. She knew there were many nights he slept in his car out on the job site, or at least that's where she hoped he was. She shook her head to clear her wandering thoughts. Today was a happy day. Korin would be released and coming home with her.

She tightened her grip around the leather strap of her purse that hung from her shoulder and picked up the pace as she mentally put back the awful memories of her childhood back in its box. She was ready to bring her baby home.

Natalie rapped her knuckles against the door of Dr. Barrister's office.

"Come in," a gruff voice beckoned from the other side of the oak door.

Natalie turned the brass doorknob and pushed open the heavy door to find an office outfitted in the same wood as the door, a blur of oak that was quite boring and drab. Diplomas and certificates decorated the walls, along with photographs of the doctor at various functions. Bookshelves spanned the left side of the office.

In front of her sat the good doctor, behind a massive desk, two aged leather chairs perfectly placed in front. He signaled her to take a seat, and she chose the one on the left, as it was closer to the window and the sunlight. The chair on the right seemed to morph into the confines of the room, fading into darkness.

"Mrs. Perrin, wonderful to see you again."

A shiver shot up her spine at the sound of his voice. No warmth found its way into his monotone delivery, and for a moment Natalie felt concern at the knowledge that Korin had been dealing with this man on an almost-daily basis. She had not seen a speck of warmth within the facility yet.

"Hello, Doctor. It's good to see you again," she lied. "How is my son?"

The doctor's thin lips tightened to the point where they were almost invisible.

"Your son is a troubled young fellow. Fanciful. Head in the clouds."

"He just turned eight. He's allowed to have an imagination," she replied dryly. *It was a mistake to have brought him here.* She wrung the strap of her purse in her hands.

"An imagination, yes. Fantasies about killing, no. Those are the marks of a serial killer," Dr. Barrister said, in a self-satisfied tone. He sat back in his rich chocolate leather chair, folded his hands across his plump belly, and looked down his nose at Natalie.

Heat radiated through her body, and she suppressed the tremor in her hands by tightening her grip on her purse straps. She had hated this man from the moment she'd first met him three months ago. Surprisingly, even though he wanted Korin home, Albert was the one taken by him, saying the doctor would whip Korin into shape.

"My son is not a serial killer," she said in a low voice, narrowing her eyes at the man.

"Hmm . . . says every mother of a serial killer."

He reached over to a brass container on his desk and withdrew a cigarette. Without asking if she minded if he smoked, he lit the cigarette and inhaled deeply, exhaling in her direction. She suppressed a cough and continued to stare him down.

"I know we said that we would evaluate Korin's diagnosis and mental state in three months, and consider releasing him. I feel the boy needs more time here. He has been lashing out at everyone, including me. Until I know he is in a stable condition, I won't release him." He shrugged his shoulders as though everything were out of his hands and smiled thinly.

Natalie returned an equally cold smile as she pulled some paperwork out of her purse. Flipping open the packet, she quickly found the paragraph she was looking for, and read aloud: "Pursuant to a three-month evaluation, the legal guardians may decide on the next steps of the patient's care, regardless of the outcome of the evaluation period." She looked at the doctor, whose face had now gone slack. "See, I am the kind of person who reads the fine print. And don't think it was lost on me that the font size here is smaller than the rest of the document."

"Mrs. Perrin, where is your husband?" Dr. Barrister asked.

Natalie, caught off guard, took a moment for her to reply. "He... um, he's away for work."

"But one would think he would take off to pick up his son after being away from him for so long. Where is your eldest?"

"Albert..." she paused and shook her head. She didn't need to tell this awful man that her husband, while he won't admit it, is too guilty to face Korin. Albert deliberately took a job that started yesterday and would have him away for six days. Despite being conflicted on having a quiet home for once, there is a heavy guilt within Albert (and her) for sending Korin away. "Davis is staying at his best friend's house while I am here. That's all there is to that matter."

Dr. Barrister coughed, taking the hint returned to the original topic. "So you want to take the boy home with you today, then, even though it is my educated prognosis that his mental condition is not strong enough to warrant this step."

Natalie narrowed her eyes at him. He coughed again and avoided eye contact with her. *Good,* she thought.

"Mrs. Perrin, your son's imagination is beyond that of a typical eight-year-old. He has this fantasy world in his head that he escapes to, where there are no consequences for his actions." He tapped the glowing ash of his cigarette into an amber glass ashtray. "He doesn't understand the difference between right and wrong."

"Are you saying that he was never properly taught how to be a good kid?" Natalie's voice seethed from behind clenched teeth, her heart pounding. This man was basically claiming that she and Albert were terrible parents—that they had never taught Korin how to behave.

Dr. Barrister smiled smugly at her and took a drag from his cigarette, once more exhaling in her direction. She didn't flinch. "Mrs. Perrin, the child is staying here."

"Absolutely not. It's bad enough that you denied Albert and me from seeing Korin on his birthday, turning us away after we drove over three hours. Then you didn't even allow me to speak to him over the phone once we returned home. He probably thinks that we forgot his birthday and is now even more traumatized. God knows what else you are doing to my child."

"As I told you over the phone *before* you left your house to drive the whole way down here, visiting with Korin—even without your eldest in tow—would interrupt the progress in his treatment. The child is terribly damaged. Some of that caused by you and your husband."

"My son is leaving with me—*today*," she snapped. Then, shifting her voice to make it sound as sweet as she possibly could with a hint of venom, she added, "I have a lawyer on standby, and he'll be interested to hear how you are disregarding the terms that we agreed to for Korin's medical care." She didn't care that this was a lie.

Dr. Barrister reached for the phone on his desk and pushed a button. "Please gather the release paperwork for Korin Perrin and have him readied for release. Hmm. Yes, I'm sure." He slammed the receiver down and pulled a document from one of his desk drawers.

"This is a non-disclosure agreement. You will sign one and Korin will sign one. His release is contingent on these signatures."

"Why do we need to sign an NDA when he was here for treatment?"

The thin smile reappeared on Dr. Barrister's face. "I don't want anyone speaking of my rehabilitation methods or sharing the secrets of my success. Now, if you will, please go sit in the hallway and wait for your son," he said, taking another drag of his cigarette.

Natalie stood and withdrew from the vile doctor's presence before he could exhale the smoke in her direction again. She slammed the door with such force that the sound echoed down the corridor. She sat on a nearby bench to wait for her son.

Two hours later, a woman carrying a stack of paperwork in one hand and gripping Korin's shoulder with the other walked down the hallway toward Natalie.

Natalie stood, her entire focus on her son. He looked ragged, with dark circles under his eyes and a bruise on his lower jaw. His hair was lank and the clothes he wore hung off his thin frame. The woman, dressed in a white blouse and black skirt, stepped between Natalie and Korin and thrust the paperwork in Natalie's direction. Korin stared at the floor, avoiding all eye contact.

"You need to sign these release forms where indicated, including the NDA," she said, passing the stack of papers to Natalie. "I will have Korin sign his copy. We'll be waiting for you in the canteen at the end of the hall."

Natalie stared, openmouthed, as the woman led Korin down the hall, away from her. She hadn't even had the chance to hug him or say hello.

"Wait! Can I not come to the canteen too and sign the paperwork there?" Natalie called after the nurse.

The nurse stopped and Korin followed her lead. Turning, the nurse looked at Natalie without any emotion or further explanation, said "No".

Natalie plopped back down on the bench, took a pen from her purse, and started signing the mountain of paperwork. She barely absorbed the words. She just wanted to get her son out of this place.

After she'd finished she walked quickly to the canteen. The room was empty save for Korin and the woman, who was pacing around the perimeter while Korin sat at a table, head hung low, staring at nothing.

"Finally," the woman said, walking up to Natalie and taking the paperwork from her. "Take him."

And with that the woman exited the canteen through the swinging doors, back into the heart of the asylum.

Natalie walked over to her son.

"Time to go, sweetie." She smiled and held a hand out to him.

Korin slowly raised his head and looked at her.

Natalie's heart sank as she looked into his hollow eyes. The spark that usually lit his expression was gone. While he still looked like Korin, deep down she felt like she was bringing home a different child.

CHAPTER SIX

March 1986

Surrounded by a sea of old books, their fragrance dancing in the air, Korin searched for his white whale. Legends of American folklore were splayed open on the table under the fluorescent lighting of the Kelton University library. Tales lost to modern man swirled about as he paged through a heavy red-bound tome laid open on his lap. It was quiet, as this long-forgotten section of the library held but one soul this day.

Year of Sasquatch was several years old, and held a full account of sightings collected by a journalist named John Green. Many billed it as a joke when it was first published, calling it a work of fiction. Perhaps that's why a copy of it was included in the folklore section of the university's library. Korin noticed the crisp pages and pristine cover. He was probably the first student to ever look at the book, let alone crack it open.

Korin desperately tried to find a muse among the monsters. The books strewn about in front of him ranged from terrestrial creatures to the aquatic. The kraken, the Loch Ness Monster, El Chupacabra—all of these monsters were thrilling, but he was struggling to find one that had truly existed as opposed to being simply a tale of lore.

"My thesis is dead before I can even begin," he muttered.

Even though he didn't need to begin his thesis research until the autumn, Korin wanted to get a jump start on having his topic nailed down. His plan was to have completed all research by September so that he could spend the whole school year writing and editing the document before defending it prior to his graduation next May. He had submitted his application yesterday morning, ten minutes after the doors to the Academic Center opened. His preliminary topic was to find a tangible truth behind cryptic legends. He wanted to prove that at some point in antiquity, actual monsters had existed. A true vile life form that wreaked havoc on humans.

"I figured I would find you here."

Startled, Korin turned and saw his academic adviser standing at the end of an aisle of old wooden bookshelves, his slim frame and short stature dwarfed by the towering columns of literature. "Already stressing about your thesis?"

"Have been stressing about it since my first undergrad semester," Korin grumbled, looking back to his notebook containing the list of monsters.

Dr. Elliot Maynard had been a professor at Kelton University since the late 1950s, teaching anthropology to a student body that grew larger each year. Despite being out in the middle of nowhere in Minnesota, throughout the 1970s the popularity of the school had increased, mostly due to its football team, whose performance was beginning to rival the more well-known and costlier universities.

Korin knew that Dr. Maynard was proud of his school, and even more proud of his students, especially his graduate students. Maynard had told him that he was particularly proud of Korin's graduating group. An extremely hardworking lot, each of his thirty-two graduate students was exemplary, dedicated to their education, yet Korin was the star who shined brightest. When Maynard told him this, Korin had struggled to digest his words. No one had ever been so pleased by his work.

It was a Saturday morning, when most students were still in bed, sleeping off their hangovers. And here sat Korin, working on his thesis, which he really didn't have to begin until the following semester. Korin knew he tried too hard sometimes. Yet he had something to prove, something that he needed to show the world—to show that he was worth something.

"Why so frustrated?" Dr. Maynard asked tentatively.

Korin's brow furrowed. "I have been searching for the past four months for a true account that proves a legend actually existed," he said in an irritated tone, "but all I keep coming up with are stories, secondhand accounts—not one shred of factual evidence." His hands trembled with either fear or anger.

Dr. Maynard shook his head. "You are on a ghost hunt," he said. "Have you learned nothing from me over these past few years?"

Ashamed at the thought that he had let his professor down, Korin kept his focus on the book in his lap.

With a sigh, Dr. Maynard said, "Why don't you try looking at the influence these legends have on culture rather than trying to determine what stories might be true?"

Korin's head shot up and his wide eyes looked at his professor. "But I want to prove that these legends are based on reality."

"Korin, you are well aware that these stories are called legends for a reason. They are stories designed to teach people something about how to live their lives—illusions that exist within the context of reality. Besides, most of them are downright horrific. Do you really want to discover that some of these horrors are real?"

Dejection overtook Korin's face. "But that means I have to change the entire outline of my thesis."

"Well, that happens. I had to change my thesis topic four or five times when I was at grad school."

Korin stared at the pages of the book in his lap. He was losing ground on his goal; the desire to make an impact on the world was slipping from his grasp. He wanted to prove that there was some lost legend out in the world that physically existed within this modern age. A legend that was walking and breathing.

He had to prove himself, too; he just had to. If he failed at this, there would be no way to salvage his relationship with his parents. Their full hearts and attention had always been focused on Davis. The son who could do no wrong in their eyes. Korin believed he would fade into non-existence with his family if he didn't do something that brought attention to himself.

All through his school years, Korin had devoted himself to being the perfect student, getting perfect grades. He had graduated from Kelton University with a BS in anthropology, at the top of his class. When he was named valedictorian and offered the honor of giving a speech to the class of 1985, he had turned it down. His parents had initially told him that they would not be attending the graduation ceremony because Davis had a hockey game that day. His team was in the local league playoffs. Amateurs. Davis wasn't anywhere close to pro and was mostly a bench warmer due to his arm.

When they saw the look of sorrow on Korin's face, Albert and Natalie said that one of them would go to Davis's game and the other would attend Korin's graduation. Though it would only be one parent attending, Korin was still overjoyed. After all, this was a once-in-a-lifetime achievement for him, and his brother had a hockey game nearly every weekend, fall through spring. Korin decided to give his valedictorian speech.

On the day of his college graduation for his undergrad, Korin was up early, pacing his room as he recited his speech to himself. Outside his room, both parents were hustling Davis to get ready to go to his game. Korin rolled his eyes. Davis was old enough to get himself ready without his parents' help.

There was a knock at his door and his father poked his head in. Albert, dressed in his only suit, was ready to go. A lump formed in Korin's throat as he looked at his dad, wearing the same suit he'd worn fourteen years ago to his grandmother's funeral. The navy fabric had faded after all these years, and Albert could no longer fasten the buttons on the jacket. Korin smiled warmly at his father and Albert put an arm around his son's shoulders as they walked out of the house together.

A calmness overtook Korin as he spoke to his graduation class at Kelton University. Nearly five hundred people sat in front of him, a mixture of students and family members. His speech was fifteen minutes long, and at the halfway point, he felt his confidence surge—until his eyes found his father in the audience, fast asleep. Korin's voice began to falter.

He had failed to hold his father's attention back then. Grad school was his last chance. If he could prove to his parents that he was an academic scholar—if he was able to establish that a legend truly existed—there was no way they wouldn't be proud of him. Giving up his original thesis topic would weaken his chances; who really gives a damn about how legends influence the culture? The world wants proof that monsters really exist. If he were able to find this proof, he'd be famous.

Dr. Maynard broke into Korin's thoughts. "I recommend that you put your thesis aside for a while—take a break from it."

Korin's head snapped up and he glared at his professor.

"I am serious. As your adviser, I am telling you to take a break. You are in your early twenties. You've been pushing yourself too hard lately and haven't really been living. Take a break from the academics. Trust me; it will all be here when you get back."

"But my research—"

"Does not technically need to start until next semester," interrupted Dr. Maynard. "Get away from the books and the stories and do something else for a change. Sometimes doing too much research clouds your ultimate goal, what you're trying to achieve."

Korin chewed on what Dr. Maynard had said. Could taking a week off really affect his thesis? He hadn't taken a break from anything since he was in grade school. He considered his possibilities. He could go home for the week of spring break and talk to his parents about what he was trying to do. If they took an interest, then he would continue his hunt, to follow through on his current thesis topic. If they had their usual air of disinterest . . . well then, he wasn't sure what he'd do.

With a ragged exhale, Korin looked at his adviser. "Okay."

CHAPTER SEVEN

"Hello?" Natalie Perrin's voice crackled through the phone's receiver. Korin jiggled the cord to help fix the static. "Hey, Mom."

"Hi, honey, how are you?"

"Fine."

"Oh, that's so good to hear. How—"

"Ma!" a gruff voice bellowed in the background.

"One second, Korin," his mother said.

Korin could hear her place the phone down on the table in the hallway.

Not even on the phone with his mother for ten seconds and Davis had already pulled her attention away. Korin seethed. It never failed; the second Korin had an ounce of his parents' attention, Davis stole it away.

He could hear Davis whining to his mother about the TV reception, how it was interrupting the game. His mother calmly replied that there was nothing she could do to fix it. It was probably the ice that was messing with the antenna on the roof. Surprisingly, there hadn't been any major snowstorms this Spring, but there had been an onslaught of ice storms.

After about five minutes of babying Davis, she finally returned to the phone.

"TV reception is so bad this time of year. Poor Davis has missed three games because of it. Someday we must get him cable. Hopefully, it will come up into these parts. It's no fun living out here in the boonies, is it, sweetie? We've never been able to enjoy modern conveniences. Oh my, just think how happy Davis would be if we could get him cable . . ."

His mother yammered on and on about how poor Davis hadn't had anything that he enjoyed growing up, how hard his life had been. Korin stared hard at the wall as she talked, his jaw set tight.

"Oh, but you were always the lucky one. You never had to worry about being bored. You always found a way to keep yourself content with your books, or by going outside to play. We never had to worry about you."

He could hear her smiling on the other end of the phone as the illusion of the life she thought her youngest son had led swirled about in her mind. She deluded herself into believing that his life was so good, that their entire family was simply perfect These thoughts were her way to avoid worrying about him; she and dad could just keep giving Davis the attention he needed without having to figure out how to split it between two boys.

"So, sweetie, why are you calling?"

"Uh . . . yeah . . . well, I wanted to see if I could come home next week."

"What about school?"

"It's spring break. The school will be closed."

"Oh . . . but you never come home over spring break. This will be the first time . . . ever," she said and through the pause of silence, he knew she thought back on his undergrad years, trying to remember if there had ever been a time when he came home that wasn't over Christmas.

"Yeah, well, I'm working on my thesis and need a little time off from it all."

"Ah, okay. A thesis. I didn't know you were working on one of those."

"Yeah."

"I will have Davis get his stuff out of your room, then," she said, completely changing the subject and asking Korin no other questions.

Korin was speechless.

"Davis needed a place to store his hockey equipment, so I told him to put it in your room. It's not really taking up that much room, but I'll have him get it out anyway."

Korin still said nothing.

"The boys and your father will be going out to trap beavers on Monday. If you're coming home, I think it would be good for you to go with them."

A sickness grew in his stomach.

"Mom, you know I have not gone hunting or trapping since I was twelve. Since that time Davis tried eating that deer's heart—raw."

"Oh, Korin, that's just a story. You know Davis did no such thing. I would ask that you never bring it up again."

"Fine," Korin whispered. As always, let's forget about all the weird or bad things Davis has done.

"You could just go with them and stay in the hunting cabin while they are out trapping."

Korin could hear Davis yelling for her again in the background.

"Okay, see you in a few days," his mother said quickly, then hung up the phone.

Korin slowly replaced the receiver, his vision blurred by tears.

Nothing would ever change.

CHAPTER EIGHT

Natalie untangled her index finger from the phone cord and replaced the handset into the cradle on the wall. Her hand stayed on the handset as she heard her eldest call for her again. Korin sounded so sad on the phone. Davis's yelling distracted her and she cut Korin off. She didn't mean to. She always immediately reacted when Davis called for her.

"Just give me a minute." She choked back tears. She needed to clear her head.

The long-coiled cord made a tapping sound as it hit the floor after she removed her hand from the phone and lightly brushed against its cord. The coils were stretched out after years of use, the beige color a bit grimy from being swirled around fingers during countless calls. Everyone in the family did it, a trait passed down through the Perrin family bloodline. She fondly recalled watching Glory Perrin do the same thing at her home, years ago.

Natalie had been sitting at the old oak dining-room table watching her mother-in-law as she fretted about the kitchen, making a peach pie while chatting away on her old rotary phone. Glory's phone cord, too, was stretched almost beyond its limits. Glory stood on the opposite side of the small green enamel-top table that sat in the middle of her kitchen, where she would often be found mixing together some lovely baked good.

As Natalie sipped her Earl Grey tea, she could see Glory becoming further involved in conversation, not focusing on the pie crust in front of her. To Natalie's satisfaction, she saw Gloria start to twirl the cord around her left index finger as she chatted away. She secretly hoped Korin had been twirling his phone cord as they talked. Maybe she misread the sound of his voice and he was happy to be coming home.

She let out a long slow breath. Her moment of emotional upset dissipated. Natalie needed to focus on Davis right now because in a few minutes they would be driving to Grand Marais for one of Davis's bimonthly therapy visits. Although he would be grumpy on the trip out, he was usually quiet and reflective on the way home. Those were the times she believed he was a good and balanced boy. She would have enjoyed being able to take him weekly, but the commute was just too much. Since Davis's license had been suspended—for the second time, due to multiple moving violations—it was up to her to take him everywhere. Over the years they had tried many different therapists for Davis, but the best one they'd found who had an actual effect on Davis was two towns away.

Natalie now hummed with happiness. Korin was coming home. She would make his favorite meal, venison roast and mashed potatoes, for the night he came home, so that it would make him feel homesick, and maybe want to return one day. Not that she wanted him to move back in. No, he needed to be an adult. But she would like to have him live closer so she could see him more often. They didn't have a super-close relationship. This was mostly because she didn't know how to relate to him. He was smart and well-educated. Sometimes when he would call to check in on how she was doing, she would ask him how his classes were going. He would start talking about some long-dead philosopher or an ancient tribe with reverence, and she would have to feign interest in what he was saying. She oftentimes found herself saying "You don't say," or "Wow, that is interesting," without knowing what he was talking about. He was a very bright boy and on a different level than the rest of the family.

Now, Davis—she could relate to him on a simpler level. He only had one interest, and that was hockey. While she didn't follow the sport, at least it was something tangible, something real that she could see, whereas Korin's interests were beyond her, somehow. She tried at one point to read some of the same literature he was reading. She had borrowed *Moby-Dick* from the library, thinking it was something she could speak to her son about. It was very high-brow and literary, one of those books that intellectuals discussed. She struggled to even get through the first chapter, and often found herself falling asleep and forgetting what she had just read. In the end, she gave up.

For someone who lived in Minnesota and had never seen the ocean, the initial pages, obsessed with the sea and whales, failed to capture her interest. She found it all quite boring, and gave her youngest son a lot of credit, not only for being able to read through these dreadful books, but for being able to discuss them with his fellow academics.

The clock in the hallway struck noon. It was time to get Davis and head out to Grand Marais. The drive would take over an hour, and she didn't want to be late for his two p.m. appointment.

Natalie made her way over to where Davis sat on the recliner, staring away at the television, the fuzzy picture barely visible.

"Come on, sweetie, we need to head to Dr. Sanderson's."

He grumbled something indistinguishable, stood up, and walked over to the TV to shut it off. "I'll get my shoes," he spat at her as he walked back to his bedroom.

Well, today was going to be a good day! Natalie thought. She was happy that she hadn't had to bribe her son to leave his precious television.

She'd have to remember to tell her husband later tonight how well it had worked to loosen the connection between the wire on the back of the television that led to the antenna on the roof. Watching an incredible grainy television would drive anyone to distraction, and their little trick had worked like a charm to pull Davis away from the TV without a fight.

She chuckled to herself. There was nothing wrong with playing a little joke on her child every now and again.

Amanda Headlee

CHAPTER NINE

"So, Davis, how does it make you feel to realize you are twenty-five years old, have no paying job, and still live at home with your parents?" Dr. Sanderson asked as soon as he was settled on the beige chaise in her office. She sat facing him, a legal pad in her lap and ballpoint pen in her hand, a list of questions scrawled in her oh-so-elegant handwriting across the paper.

Natalie Perrin had told her that Davis had seen many therapists since the childhood accident that had burned his arm, leaving it disfigured. None of them had been able to elicit any reaction out of him. When Natalie had heard about Dr. Annabelle Sanderson and her nurturing healing approach, she'd decided to take a chance on something different. Where his prior therapists had been men with a focus on snapping Davis out of his neurosis, Dr. Sanderson's approach was more coaxing. To an extent it was working as Natalie had remarked on several occasions that after the first few sessions, she had seen a slight change in his demeanor at home and he became motivated enough to return to school to obtain his EMT certification, allowing him to currently volunteer for the Rachet EMS community. However, the progress made did not reach the goal that Dr. Sanderson hoped for after working with him for two years— breaking down all his barriers. Davis only allowed her into his world to a certain point, which was superficial, and he still had not obtained a *paying* position at the Ambulance Corp. So she'd decided it was time for something different: She was going to be blunt as opposed to asking her usual delicate, roundabout questions.

"Davis, you're not answering."

Dr. Sanderson leaned forward in her chair to look him squarely in the eye. When he didn't return her gaze, she sat back in her chair, smoothing her jet-black hair that was pulled into a perfect chignon. While the tight hairstyle pulled at her temples and gave her a slight headache, it did provide the illusion that she had straight hair as opposed to her natural curls. Women with straight hair want curly hair, and women with curly hair want straight. We always want what we don't have.

That's it! she thought. *Davis wants something he doesn't have.* A smile crept across her face. She knew exactly what he wanted: success.

"Davis, I'd like for you to answer my question," she said, dropping her voice an octave.

Davis finally met her eyes, then casually looked at the wall to his right.

"It makes me feel fine. I'm not living with my parents; I am staying home to take care of them."

Dr. Sanderson looked down at the notebook in her lap, took up the pen, and jotted some notes. *Why does he feel like he is taking care of them? Does he feel responsible for something in some way?*

"You say you are home taking care of them, but what are you actually *doing* for them?" she asked.

He continued to look at the wall, keeping the back of his head turned toward Dr. Sanderson and absentmindedly rubbing his scarred forearm.

"They would be alone if I wasn't there, seeing that my brother abandoned us."

"What do you mean by that, Davis?"

"Someone just needs to stay at home with them."

"Okay, Davis, I understand wanting to be close to them to take care of them, but from what I've heard, you don't do anything specific to take care of them."

She paused to see if he would jump in to defend himself. He didn't.

"All you do is sit at home, eat, and watch TV. On occasion you do some volunteer work at the local ambulance corps or visit your friend Tate, but outside of that, you don't do anything. You once told me that you wanted to be an NHL player, yet you dropped out of your amateur league. You also said that you wanted to be a surgeon. What happened to those dreams?"

Davis remained silent for a moment, but Dr. Sanderson knew something was ticking away in his mind. His silence showed her that her new approach was working. He was thinking of a response.

Dr. Sanderson felt further strengthened in her resolve after witnessing what happened when Natalie and Davis had entered the waiting room of her office this afternoon.

Davis had walked in first, not even holding the door for his mother, allowing it to slam back and hit his mother in the forehead as she was looking down, trying to put her keys in her purse. When the door hit her, he just kind of looked back and snickered, not even attempting to grab the door or apologize to his mother.

Natalie had readjusted herself and entered the waiting room with a big red welt on her forehead. She'd looked at her son and tried to laugh it off, but Annabelle knew all too well that there were tears hiding in those eyes. Natalie avoided eye contact with everyone else as she sat down.

The doctor had had enough of this young man's arrogance and

selfishness. Those were the masks he wore to hide the years of hurt and rejection that he carried with him.

"Davis, I need you to answer me. Why are you not doing more with your life? Volunteering as an EMT—when you feel like it—is not going to get you anywhere in life. You should be getting paid for your work, committing to it, not just volunteering occasionally. Why don't you go back to school for nursing? You earned your EMT certification—why not expand on that?"

Davis's head snapped toward her and behind his eyes she saw something that gave her a little start—an angry, hellish fire seemed to burn in his eyes. She worried she may have just pushed him a bit too far. For a brief moment, she felt a wave of fear, but she wanted to push him further.

"So, Davis, what is your answer?"

"Nursing is for women."

Dr. Sanderson disregarded the misogynistic comment, brushing it off as a defense, and instead turned the focus back to his dreams.

"You believe your arm and hand prevented you from playing in a professional hockey league or becoming a surgeon?"

No response. He just continued to stare at her, and she returned his gaze, challenging the anger.

He rubbed his scarred forearm again. The skin was redder than the rest of his body, and there were pits where flesh had been lost and poor attempts at grafting were made. His hand had received the worst of it. The skin was severely disfigured, tight and pink. Dr. Sanderson knew that Davis constantly experienced some level of pain, but the hand and limb were still usable. It would have taken patience and discipline, but dexterity could have been relearned, at least for possibly following his hockey dream. Sadly, she had to admit that his dreams of becoming a surgeon could never come to fruition with an injury like that. Regardless, she knew Davis was unmotivated, and Natalie had indicated that at the time, they couldn't afford physical therapy, so Davis had had to heal as best he could on his own. As a result, his hockey skills had suffered. She felt this was at the root of Davis not standing on his own, allowing his parents to take care of him.

"Davis," she said gently, "why are you not being more productive? Why don't you strive for something more?"

She could see him begin to shift on the chaise—a reaction. He sat up and looked her in the eyes. Something broke within his gaze. As if realizing that she'd seen something he didn't want her to see, he cut off eye contact and looked down at his scarred arm, turning his hand palm up, palm down, palm up, palm down. The barrier that had stood between then had finally come down.

She was elated. All of the nurturing methods that she had used up until this point to understand how Davis ticked had been forgotten in a matter of seconds. The moment she'd broken out the tough questions, forcing him to face his own resistance, he'd broken, no longer able to maintain his tough exterior.

"I feel lost," Davis said in a soft tone. "Like something is missing . . . like I am broken."

"What's broken?" Dr. Sanderson asked.

"My future." He sat in thought for a moment. "Korin stole something from me when he did this," he said, indicating his arm. He raised his eyes and looked deeply into hers. "He never apologized to me for what he did."

"What did he do?" Dr. Sanderson asked. Although she knew full well the details of the accident, this was the first time Davis had opened up about it.

"He tried to kill me because of his delusional belief that I was evil."

"Davis, I'm going to ask you something you may not like, but I truly want you to tell me the answer, with honesty."

He gave a slight nod of his head.

"Why did your brother think you were evil?"

Davis thought for a moment. She took his silence as an indication that he'd never really considered why his brother had attacked him.

"Jealousy," he replied, but the way he said it sounded more like a question.

She jotted this in her notes.

"He was jealous. How so?"

"I told you he was delusional. My stupid grandmother read him all of these storybook tales when he was a kid. I never wanted to listen to that shit because it's all lies, but my brother ate up every word. I always tried to ruin story time because I didn't want her making Korin even more delusional, living in that fantasy world."

"To satisfy my curiosity, can you explain to me why you believe your brother was delusional?"

"Lady, he pushed me into a fire because he thought I was some monster that faeries left on the doorstep. Doesn't that sound delusional to you?"

"More misguided. Davis, do you feel like you did anything to Korin that might have made him feel that way?"

He snorted but stayed engaged. "I told you—he was jealous of me."

"Davis, based on what you've told me, I'm not seeing what would have made him jealous."

He smiled at her in a way that sent shivers down her spine. While his lips were upturned, his teeth were bared in a threatening way, as if he were asking if she really wanted to travel down this road.

There's something more than just the accident that made him this way, she thought. For the first time, she became incredibly uncomfortable in his presence.

"Korin is a fucking mistake. He isn't supposed to be here. Mom and Dad were stupid one night. They never really wanted him and were going to get rid of him before he was born, but then their morals kicked in. I guess he picked up on the fact that he was almost destined for the trash can," he said smugly. "He is jealous that I'm the one they wanted."

And there it was, she realized. The truth behind it all. Davis was putting the blame on his parents' unplanned pregnancy, which truly may have been an accident, but it was Davis who didn't want Korin. He wanted to be an only child and command his parents' full attention.

"Davis, I can see how that could potentially spawn jealousy, but I still don't understand why he thought you were a monster and pushed you into the fireplace. What made him do that?"

His look was deadpan, and a darkness returned to his eyes. The sinister smile spread across his face again. She was very unsettled by it and broke the connection first by looking down at her notepad. She would have liked to explore this further, but honestly, fear was overriding her rational thoughts.

"Let's get back to the topic of your dreams and talk about what we can do to get you back on track toward success," she said.

The look in his eyes didn't change and he stood up, towering over her in her chair.

"I'm done talking to you today."

"No, Davis, wait," she said, standing to meet him eye to eye. "I really want to know why you lost hope in your dreams."

He took a step closer and put his face next to hers. She inwardly shivered at their proximity. For a moment she thought he was going to hurt her.

"I can't hold a fucking hockey stick right anymore; I can't even cut up vegetables properly, let alone cut into someone's body, because my hand is all fucked up. My brother stole that from me."

He turned sharply and walked to the door.

"Wait," she called out to him as he grasped the doorknob.

Despite her fear, she wanted to continue their discussion. They had about twenty minutes left, but the look he gave her put a stop to that thought.

"Umm, this was a good session today. Thank you for opening up to me. I appreciate your honesty."

He sneered, opened the door, and slammed it on his way out.

She collapsed back into her chair and held her head in her hands, mentally and emotionally exhausted. This was by far the most progress she had ever made with him. Yet, she worried that she was starting to uncover something within this man that she truly didn't want to see.

CHAPTER TEN

Davis didn't like to be questioned. He just did as he pleased. He wanted an easy life because he was royally screwed over as a kid. What was the point of living if it all had to be such a struggle? Life should be about being happy. And for the most part his parents made him happy—his mom, more specifically. His father, he did not care for. As he'd told Dr. Sanderson, it was his grandmother and father's fault for making Korin so delusional.

He grunted and crossed his arms across his chest as he sat in the passenger side of his mom's car, his mom chatting away incessantly.

It was his father's fucking fault for making Korin in the first place. Despite these feelings, however, Davis acknowledged that his parents did take care of him, just as he took care of them in return. It was a symbiotic relationship.

Everyone apart from his parents and Tate thought he was dumb, even though deep down Davis knew he was quite intelligent. His grades may have been poor, but he'd paid attention in class. Especially in biology. He'd always enjoyed the idea of being a scientist. Anatomy intrigued him. He was curious about how the body worked. Which was why he loved to hunt. He loved gutting animals. He liked to see how their insides connected together, how it all worked. He was interested in how it all smelled. And he had always wondered how everything tasted. A true scientist should use all of his senses in experiments.

His arm tingled and he was brought right back to the memory of the pain when his arm caught on fire and his flesh boiled. While the recovery had been unbearable, the fact that he still had his arm at all was a miracle. If the doctors hadn't been able to perform skin grafts using tissue from his thighs and his butt, he most likely would have had his lower arm amputated. He had never let on to anyone that some of his butt skin was on his arm and hand. He knew this would get him ridiculed even more. While no one was stupid enough to say anything to his face, he'd always heard the whispers behind his back. He was a freak. He was scarred.

And it was his brother's fault.

Korin and his stupid imagination, believing there was a monster inside of his older brother. He had wanted to pulverize that little shit—and still did to this day. But his parents had intervened and shipped Korin off to some nuthouse right after the incident, to give them time to help Davis rehabilitate.

Except rehab had been a joke. He was supposed to do exercises. Actually, Natalie was supposed to remind him to do his exercises, but she'd felt that they had stressed him out too much. He had constantly forgotten about them, so his mobility had never fully returned to his hand. Because of this, he couldn't grip a hockey stick well enough in his right hand, especially through the padded gloves. His formerly perfect stick work turned sloppy, and he believed that he'd only been allowed to play through high school and the amateur league due to pity. Mostly from his best friend, Tate, begging the coaches to keep Davis on.

He caught himself rubbing his scarred arm again.

Fucking Korin. He gets to achieve his dreams while I get left behind.

Davis didn't want to tell Dr. Sanderson why he believed Korin had pushed him into the fire. She already knew too much about him—at least, to the extent he allowed. He liked her, despite not fully trusting her. Honestly, he loved her voice. It was sweet like honey, light, fragrant, and musical, lulling him into a sense of calm. Not at all like his mother's voice, which, although loving, always sounded kind of condescending, and brassy.

Dr. Sanderson talked to him with genuine concern, as a human being. Something no one else did, other than his best friend, Tate, and, to an extent, Tate's younger sister, Addy. His parents *should* talk to him this way, with true concern. His mother showed her concern through coddling, and his father—well, the man didn't give a shit about him.

As much as Davis liked Dr. Sanderson, he kept her at a distance. He'd started to feel that she didn't really have an accurate picture of him, especially based on the questions she'd asked him today. Yet somehow he couldn't bring himself to tell her the truth about certain things. He didn't want her to think even less of him than she did, which would definitely be the case if she found out that Korin believed Davis had killed their grandmother.

The car came to a sudden halt and Davis crashed forward, hitting his forehead on the dashboard. A bright light flashed and for a moment he thought he was dead. A wave of annoyance washed over him when he realized he wasn't.

"Oh my gosh, honey, are you okay?" Natalie said, tightly gripping the steering wheel. She was staring at him, too afraid to move. She hadn't been paying attention to the road, talking away since the moment they'd left Dr. Sanderson's office. He had completely tuned her out, immersed in his own thoughts, only returning to her when she'd almost run a red light, slamming on the brakes at the last second.

"What the fuck," he spat at her, then reached over and put on his seat belt. Had he been wearing it, he would not have hit his forehead. Her lack of awareness for his safety burned within. "You know, sometimes I really hate you."

"Oh honey! You can't mean that. I'm so sorry. I am just so frustrated with how Dr. Sanderson treated you today."

His comment had hit a nerve, and that made him happy. As much as he loved being with her, he also enjoyed punishing her. She held some level of fault in all of this.

"It just isn't fair that we can't seem to find you a therapist who can help you."

"Sanderson is okay, Mom."

"No, no—no she isn't." Natalie chewed at her lip.

He hated when she did that. It was a sign of weakness, and also signaled that she was about to start whining.

"She costs us so much money, and every time we leave her office you are in a funk for a few days. I think we should find you someone else to talk to. It's been two years and you pretty much feel the same way you did the moment you first walked into her office."

"You don't know that," he muttered quietly.

"What? What was that?" She turned in her seat to look at him.

"Pay attention to the fucking road. I don't need you wrecking the car and killing us both," he snapped. "Sanderson is fine. I'm not going anywhere else."

"But it's not working. I am not seeing a change in you. You are just not happy . . ."

Davis tuned her out, looking out the passenger side window while lightly rubbing his scarred arm, trying to ignore the pain in his head from where he'd hit the dashboard. Sometimes he liked to think he had some sort of secret treasure map that was burned into his arm, the scar tissue forming mountains and valleys and riverbeds and plains. He had an imagination, too; he just didn't let anyone know. Unlike his brother. His idiot brother who always had his head in the clouds, searching for answers for why things were the way there were. Things were the way they were because Korin wasn't supposed to be born.

He heard his parents discussing it years ago when they thought he was in bed. They were sitting around the kitchen table. Davis remembered the smell of coffee but never saw either one of them take a drink from their mugs. His parents were discussing how they couldn't fathom having to balance two children, with Albert always working. They'd only ever wanted one child.

Davis would have always been the best if he'd been an only child. But then Korin had to show up. Davis wasn't about to be upstaged by someone who was weaker than him. He'd planned to make sure his parents wouldn't have to worry about balancing their attention between two sons, because as the eldest, he rightfully should have all their attention. After all, Korin was just an accident.

An accident who had tried to kill him.

CHAPTER ELEVEN

"You honestly have no relationship with your brother, or with anyone in your family?" Maeve asked Korin as they headed toward the campus cafeteria. The way she asked the question made it sound like she didn't believe him.

He breathed in heavily. Korin had only been dating Maeve for a little over six months and wasn't yet ready to introduce her to the perils of the Perrin family. He kept his family secrets close.

Maeve had been one of his first friends at Kelton. He'd met her when he was an undergrad, and over the years, their friendship had grown. She'd always been aware that there was a strained relationship between Korin and his family, and to his relief, she had never pressed for more information. That all changed when their platonic relationship turned romantic, however, and if he wanted it to develop into something that would last, he was going to have to start allowing her into his life.

He looked over to her, giving her a slight smile. The air was bitterly cold, and Maeve wore a purple wool cap pulled down over her thick and curly raven hair. She wore a matching scarf around her neck, tucked into the top of her parka. Her glasses couldn't hide the sparkle in her green eyes, filled with curiosity or sympathy—Korin could never tell the difference. He loved the way her eyes and her purple scarf popped against her dark complexion.

"Correct," he admitted, offering no additional information.

A few moments passed as they walked toward the cafeteria, leaving footprints in the freshly fallen snow. Kelton's campus was nearly deserted, not unusual for mid-March, just days before the school closed for spring break. Classes had already wound down—most midterms had been scheduled for this past Monday—and students tended to depart for break early. The snowfall was one of many over this past winter. Even sitting on the cusp of spring, the winter refused to relent. While today's snow was only a dusting, the clouds above threatened to let loose a blizzard in the coming days.

"Well . . . why is that?" she asked.

Fresh snow dusted the top of her wool cap, and for a moment Korin thought about licking it, because it looked like powdered sugar. But then his stomach soured at the thought of his brother.

"Because the world revolves around Davis," he replied.

"Do I detect a twinge of jealousy?" she kidded.

Korin stopped and locked eyes with her.

"Korin, I'm—" she started.

"Davis was born first," Korin began, ignoring Maeve's comment. "He is almost three years older than me, giving him a head start to completely dominate my parents' attention. When I was born, that was it. I was born. I just existed. My parents cared for me enough to keep me alive. As for caring for me as their son, well, that was never in the cards." His voice trembled as he spoke.

Maeve looked at him with a pained expression. She didn't say anything.

"I had to teach myself almost everything after they'd provided me with the basics—how to eat, how to dress, how to tie my own shoes. Though at school I learned how to read and write, at home I was an outcast in my room, alone, to work on my homework. Science projects, reports, all of that was completely on my own.

"Davis commanded every ounce of attention from my parents. If at any point their focus would shift to me—even for a second—he would throw a tantrum or do something that would pull their attention back to him, and I would be forgotten."

"That can't be completely true," Maeve whispered.

"You have no idea how many times I was forgotten at department stores. The worst time was when I was five. My parents drove us to Grand Marais to see Santa at the Ben Franklin five-and-dime. Davis had to be first to sit on his lap, and the moment the elf plopped him on Santa's knee, he began jabbering about everything—and I mean everything—that he'd ever wanted. He expected all of it to be under the Christmas tree that year.

"Santa tried pushing Davis off his lap but he wouldn't stop talking, until finally this elf girl, who was probably just a teenager at the time, tried to pick him up. Davis punched the girl right in the eye."

Korin held his fist up to his right eye. Maeve gasped.

"Next thing I know, Mom and Dad are pulling him off Santa's lap and dragging him toward the front of the store. The girl Davis punched was being walked away by some guy and suddenly I was lifted by another elf to sit on Santa's lap. No one realized that my parents were mine. No one called out to them that they forgot me."

"Wow, your brother was a brat," Maeve said. "What happened after that? What did your parents do to him?"

"I watched my parents walking away from me with my brother. They actually left the store. It took them until they got into the car and were about to drive off to realize that they forgot me. Dad stayed in the car with Davis while my mom returned to get me. I told Santa that I wanted my parents for Christmas."

"How do you know they didn't remember until they left the store. I'm sure you couldn't see them exit the store or get into the car?"

"Because Davis told me. He came into my bedroom that night and woke me up to rub it in my face that I was forgotten."

Maeve said nothing, but by the quizzical look on her face, he knew she was digesting and analyzing what he had said.

"They never apologized for forgetting me," Korin said.

"Sweetie, you were so young. You may not remember them apologizing to you."

He shook his head in disagreement.

"Korin, that sounds like it was just a momentary lapse on your parents' part. They were probably horrifically embarrassed and maybe afraid that someone would call the cops. Sounds like they wanted to get away from there quickly; after all, Davis had technically assaulted someone."

He bristled. Even his girlfriend was siding with his family.

"You really believe your brother has that kind of power over your parents—enough to make them just forget about you, or bend them to his will?" she asked. There was still a tone of disbelief in her voice.

"Yes," he snapped. "When Mom and I got into the car, the look on my brother's face said it all. Davis was smug. He knew he'd made my parents forget about me. I was very alone. Davis was the golden child."

"I am so sorry," she said.

Korin knew she realized that she'd crossed a line that she shouldn't have, especially if she wanted him to continue to be open with her.

Korin linked his arm with Maeve's, pulling her in close. He accepted her apology and kissed her forehead. She was only trying to help him.

Maeve was the first person he'd ever really connected with, although he remained wary of letting her see the hateful side of him—the side that kept the ugly truth about his family a closely guarded secret. But now, he felt compelled to share. He needed to share. There might be some healing that could come from sharing these emotions, this pain.

"You see now why I'm not overly excited to go home over break. No one will notice that I am even there." He stopped for a moment and contemplated the thought.

"It may not be a bad thing," Maeve said. She picked up on what Korin was thinking. "You will be able to focus on your thesis."

"Yeah, that crossed my mind. The others will be out in the woods, hunting and trapping beavers." Dread filled his voice.

"And that is bad because . . . ?"

"I've never told you about the one and only time I ever went hunting."

"No. You never tell me anything about your family life."

Korin went silent at the jab. He knew she wanted their relationship to be a lot more serious. He just had such a hard time opening up to her. There was so much damage in his past. Too many things that his brother had done had scarred Korin. Scarred him to the point where he'd stopped trusting people. He couldn't trust his parents and he couldn't trust his brother. If you can't trust your immediate family, who can you trust?

Maeve gave him a warm smile as he pulled open the door to the cafeteria building. She unhooked her arm from his and took his hand, leading him up the stairway to the second floor, where it was quieter. Students tended to congregate on the first floor where there was coffee, premade sandwiches, and more comfortable seating.

"Let's get our food and find a quiet corner to talk," she said.

He nodded in agreement as he fought back tears. Maeve was the only person in the world who had ever shown him love aside from his grandmother.

Maeve looked over at Korin, who was staring at his tray of grilled cheese and tomato soup. Since they'd entered the building, he'd stayed silent. She had never pushed him to reveal more about his family, but he knew she was curious. She was a grad student in psychology, after all. As much as he wanted to tell her everything right away, part of him struggled with the fear that she would disconnect and not talk to him as her boyfriend, but more like a patient.

"Korin." She reached out and placed her hand on top of his clenched fist.

It took a moment for his eyes to focus on their hands.

"I don't even know where to start," he whispered.

Not meeting her gaze, he looked around the cafeteria. There weren't many students in the room; in fact, the two of them were sitting alone on the far side of the room.

"I think you need to talk about this, to get it out in the open—to let it go," she said.

He raised his hand to his mouth and coughed, his throat suddenly dry. He took a swig of Coke before speaking.

"Remember, I'm your boyfriend."

She winced.

Although he knew the comment had stung, he wanted to be sure she wasn't going to put him under a microscope. He just needed her to listen.

"It was not just Davis's selfishness and control over my parents that led me to despise him. There is something deeper in him that I absolutely fear."

She looked shocked when she heard the word "fear."

"He's evil. There is something completely evil within him that terrifies me to my core." His voice trembled and began to rise in volume.

"Shhh," Maeve said.

He watched as she nervously looked around. She was probably having second thoughts about having this conversation in a public place. Then she returned her focus to him, reaching around her bowl of chili and grabbing his hands.

"Korin, I don't understand your fear of him. Why do you think he's evil?"

Korin let out a long steady breath, trying to collect himself. He let go of the tension in his hands and held hers firmly.

"I only went hunting with Dad and Davis one time. Davis was the one who killed a deer on that trip. It was an awful thing to watch. I was about twelve years old and really had no desire to kill another living thing. Davis, on the other hand, relished each moment. I'd never seen him like that."

He patted her hand as she shivered.

"His eyes glowed and he was antsy. Anxious to kill something. My father joked that Davis had a natural hunter's instinct. When we had finally tracked down and targeted a deer, Davis took her down with ease. A single shot through her lungs and heart. Pretty much instant death. My father was ecstatic, and kept telling Davis how proud he was of him. Meanwhile, I just stood behind the two of them, looking at the dead carcass."

Korin paused and reached out for his glass of Coke, taking a sip. His hand trembled.

"This wasn't his first deer, but it was the first one I'd ever seen him take down. Davis gutted the doe with no help from my father. Dad just stood back and watched him work. My brother enjoyed tearing out the insides of that deer while I just stood there, doing my best not to throw up."

Maeve squirmed in her seat, and she pushed away her chili.

"But that's not the worst part." He paused for a moment, feeling his mouth go dry again, trying to find the words to describe what happened next. "Davis . . . Davis cut out the heart of the deer and . . . oh god." Korin started to breathe rapidly and his hands shook. Across the table, Maeve gripped his hands tightly. He knew she was trying to calm him down, but it wasn't working.

Korin cleared his throat and leaned in closer to Maeve, whispering, "He started eating it. The heart. Raw, bloody, fresh out of the body."

Maeve pulled away and made a gagging sound.

He instantly felt terrible about telling her, but at the same time, relieved to have told someone.

She coughed, tried to regain her composure. "And your father—he just let him eat it?"

"For a few moments. Then Dad said that was enough and pulled it out of Davis's hand, throwing it into the woods. But that was only after Davis had offered to share the heart with me. I'll never forget the bloody smile on his face as he held it out to me." Korin's face was white.

"That is absolutely disgusting! How could your father allow him to do that—and why would Davis even want to?"

So many questions. He gave her a look that made her stop asking.

Korin shrugged. "I told you. He's evil."

He picked up his grilled cheese, which by now had cooled. The cheese that had melted out of the bread had started to congeal on the plate. He bit into it and started chewing methodically.

Maeve never took a bite of her chili, just sat there silently, staring at the table.

CHAPTER TWELVE

Maeve Alders stared out the large second-floor window of the classroom. She always tried to choose a desk that was near a window so she could look out at nature whenever she found herself bored in class. Most of them moved too slowly for her, as she was apt to read ahead in her textbooks according to what was outlined in the syllabus.

She liked to be challenged, which was why she had chosen the field of psychology. There was nothing more challenging in the world than the human mind. Each one was unique and posed its own intricate puzzle to solve. She wanted to find the keys to unlock the myriad of mental, behavioral, and emotional challenges that affected others. She had carefully honed her education, starting in middle school when she'd first discovered the field of psychology. Her dream was to help those who were institutionalized, her inspiration coming from *One Flew Over the Cuckoo's Nest*, which she'd read when she was thirteen. She had kept it hidden between her mattress and headboard, where her mother would never find it. It was on the list of banned reading materials in her home because it wasn't the Bible.

Aside from reading contraband books, Maeve had found school quite lackluster. She was consistently among the students who earned the highest grades, and was valedictorian of her high school class. AP courses had littered her annual schedule, and when the time came to apply to universities, they sought her out as opposed to the other way around. She could have attended any medical school of her choosing. She checked out the University of Pennsylvania's curriculum for psychology and saw that through their program, she could work her way toward getting a PhD and become a psychologist. On the East Coast between Philadelphia and New York City, there were several well-known institutes that she could work for.

Yet her dream was not to be, because her mother became gravely ill with breast cancer and died during her senior year of high school. She didn't have the heart to leave her brother and father so soon after her mother's passing, so she had accepted a place at Kelton University, thinking that she could eventually transfer to the school of her dreams.

Kelton University was small and homely. Eighty percent of the students were education majors. Fifteen percent majored in literature and the arts, and a lowly five percent made up the math and science sector. She was a rare breed at the school, which consisted of maybe a thousand students in total. Korin reveled in this small school. He had grown up in the middle of nowhere in a tiny logging town, so this was big-city living for him.

Maeve had grown up in Kelton. Spent her whole life in the house she was born in. She yearned to escape to a bigger city, and one day she would. Until then, she was stuck sitting in her advanced ethics class, contemplating what it was about Korin's brother that made him such a . . . well, such an asshole. Maeve shook her head. While she dearly loved Korin, she knew she'd heard only half of the story—Korin's half. It may be close to the truth, but she didn't take everything he had said at face value. It was just his perception of a situation. One day she would have to visit his family and meet the real Davis in person.

"Survivor's guilt!" Professor Alan Sable said in a voice louder than his usual tone, capturing everyone's attention and indicating it was time for class to begin. "Today, we will discuss survivor's guilt and the moral dilemma that some survivors of tragic situations suffer when others do not survive."

Maeve perked up and she put thoughts of Korin and Davis aside. For some reason, she was morbidly fascinated with tragedy and the macabre. There was something alluring about the taboo of death.

"When one survives what is deemed to be a tragic situation and others do not, a mental condition can occur in the survivor. Sometimes a survivor believes that he or she must have done something wrong to survive the situation when others did not. Now, there are varying degrees of survivor's guilt, starting with someone feeling guilty that another perished while they lived, all the way up to someone who may have survived because they focused only on saving themselves, perhaps pushing another person out of the way to escape and dooming that person in the process. Now," he said, picking up a piece of chalk to write on the board, "give me some examples of those who may suffer from survivor's guilt."

"Batman!" a boy called out.

A collective groan emanated across the classroom, along with some giggles.

"Real-life scenarios, Mr. Harper, though you're technically on the right track," Professor Sable said.

A girl next to the Batman guy raised her hand, and Professor Sable nodded to her.

"Holocaust survivors."

"Ah yes, very good," he said, and turned to write it on the chalkboard.

"Pearl Harbor," said another student, and the professor added it to the list on the board.

"The Civil War."

"World War One."

"We'll combine those under 'War,' " Professor Sable said, erasing the items and making a new heading.

"Uruguayan Flight 571," Maeve said. Her mind was on the hunting trip story that Korin had revealed earlier, and this horrific event popped into her head.

"Ah, very good, Ms. Alders," Professor Sable said. After writing this on the board, he turned and wiped the chalk dust off his hands. "That is a very good example. Not that all of these examples aren't good, but there is an extra layer of complexity in this particular situation. We all know about this ghastly plane crash in the Andes that happened in the early 1970s. What isn't spoken about much is what the sixteen survivors had to do to stay alive until help arrived."

Maeve tentatively raised her hand and Professor Sable nodded.

"The survivors had to resort to cannibalism in order to survive."

"Yes, that's right. When the surviving passengers realized there was no food, and no guarantee help was on the way, they resorted to eating the bodies of the dead."

Squeamish looks spread across most students in the class, except for the one that Professor Sable called Mr. Harper. He leaned forward in his chair, hanging on every word. "They actually ate each other?" he asked.

"Relatively speaking, yes," Professor Sable answered, now leaning against his desk, eyes focused on the class. "A lot of the survivors were devout Catholics. They struggled with the thought of eating their fellow passengers and members of the crew, despite the fact that they were already dead. The survivors thought that eating their remains would essentially mean eternal damnation for their souls. One way they came to terms with eating the dead was not just based on their will to survive, but also out of believing this was a sort of Eucharist—essentially, much like Christians partaking in Holy Communion, eating the body and drinking the blood of Christ. They compared what they had to do with what was done during the Last Supper."

He stood to pace in front of the classroom.

"Now, all the survivors struggled with a massive amount of guilt once they were rescued, and initially they didn't tell the public that they had had to resort to cannibalism. When questioned about how they had survived starvation—as you know, they were stranded on that glacier in the Andes for a little over two months—they stated that they had eaten cheese and preserved meats that they'd had in their luggage at the time of the crash. When those foods ran out, they said they had turned to eating local flora—even though anyone who had any knowledge of the desolation of the crash site would have known there was no local flora there. Eventually the survivors admitted to what they'd had to do to survive. Initially there was some backlash, as many believed that the survivors had committed murder. However, at a press conference attended by all sixteen survivors, they said that they had never killed anyone, only consuming the remains of those who were already dead."

There was a collective silence as everyone took in what Professor Sable had said.

Harper seemed to enamored by the subject, making some in the classroom uncomfortable. "Did the survivors keep eating people after they were saved?" he asked.

The girl behind Harper smacked him on the back of the head. "What's wrong with you?"

"No, they did not retain any cannibalistic tendencies after they were rescued," Professor Sable answered. "Why would you ask that?"

"Well, I've heard that some people, once they get a taste of human flesh, continue on with cannibalism," Harper replied.

"Historically when someone commits the act of cannibalism, they are eating another person because there is something within the victim that they need," Professor Sable said. "For example, we know the Aztecs performed ritualistic sacrifices according to the dictates of their religion, but what is lesser known is that they were also cannibals. One of the reasons they committed this act was to gain the power of the person they were eating. Essentially, if you ate the biceps of a person, you would gain their strength. Eat their brain, and you would gain their knowledge. Their heart, maybe their compassion or empathy. Cannibalism was used as a power play in these cultures."

He paused to allow this information to sink in.

"So no, Mr. Harper, the survivors of the plane crash did not continue to eat people after they were rescued."

"Professor Sable?" Maeve asked, raising her hand. The mention of eating a heart had stirred something in her mind. "Apart from certain tribes partaking in cannibalism in the past, are there any situations in current day where someone might decide to commit the act?"

"Well, we are getting a bit sidetracked from today's topic, but essentially, the answer is yes. There are instances of people today who commit this act in solidarity with others, but typically the reason behind the act is the same. There is something in the victim, a trait or a strength, that the person wants. The way they can rationalize consuming another person is that they will get what they seek. As I mentioned, this has obviously been seen as taboo across the world. But it's important to note that cannibalism has not been relegated only to other countries. It is deeply rooted in our own American history. Have any of you heard of a wendigo?"

The room was silent, filled with blank stares.

"The legend comes from the Chippewa, Ojibwa, and Cree tribes," the professor continued. "They believed that if someone committed the act of cannibalism, that person would be infected with an evil spirit—the wendigo. That person would turn into a monster who would grow in proportion to the meals it consumed—meaning that the monster's body would grow larger with each meal, eventually leading to the monster never being satisfied, continually committing acts of cannibalism to satiate its hunger—or maybe in an effort to regain its humanity."

"There is an evil spirit that makes people eat each other?" the girl behind Harper asked.

"No." Sable chuckled. "It is just a psychological event. It is called wendigo psychosis. It's honestly quite horrifying." He clapped his hands together. "Now, back to survivor's guilt."

When class ended, Maeve closed her notebook and quickly packed up her bag. She wanted to get to the library quickly so she could read up on this wendigo psychosis. There was something about this disorder that resonated with her. It didn't sit well.

And she kept thinking about the story Korin had told her.

CHAPTER THIRTEEN

Maeve had always felt that libraries had a certain Old World charm. She attributed it to the musty smell of the books, which seeped into the pores of the building that housed them. The Temperance Tabor Library was quite large compared to other buildings on campus, and filled to the brim with books from a benefactor. The Tabors were an old family whose lineage could be traced back to the earliest days of Kelton, when it was established by emigrants from England. The Tabors were in the lumber business, and one of the wealthiest families in the state of Minnesota. Mr. Aloysius Tabor had owned one of the local logging companies, and his wife, Portia, had been a lover of literature. Upon her death in the 1930s, all of her beloved tomes, which had filled up the north tower of their mansion estate, were donated to the Kelton Library. Since she died before her husband, he had bequeathed, on her behalf, a million dollars to Kelton University to build a library in her memory and to house her entire collection.

The library was Maeve's favorite place to escape to, and she often found herself buried deep within the stacks. Typically she haunted the psychology section, which, despite the low number of psychology students at the university, proved to be quite extensive. After the discussion in Professor Sable's class, however, she found herself in the folklore section with a thousand thoughts running through her head. She was looking for the monster that would help her to better understand wendigo psychosis, and maybe along the way, it could also help Korin with his own research, as there was a hint of truth surrounding the legend.

She was also feeling a link between the psychosis and Korin's brother. The story he had told her about Davis eating the heart right out of the deer he'd just killed would not leave her head.

As she wandered the aisles, Maeve started thinking about sacrificial rituals. The survivors in the Andes plane crash had eaten the flesh of the victims in order to survive, believing it to be similar to the Eucharist. The Aztecs had eaten the flesh of their sacrifices in order to obtain some sort of power.

While she certainly didn't believe Korin's brother was a cannibal, the circumstances of what Davis had done led Maeve to believe that he was trying to obtain something—perhaps a kind of connection with others? It seemed he had no idea how to do so, and had gone about it in very odd ways, like offering to share the deer's heart with Korin. Maybe it was a way to share love? If Maeve could suggest that Korin research the wendigo and how the myth was culturally ingrained, perhaps she might be able to show him that his brother's neediness and greed was due to Davis not being whole.

Within the folklore section, she found only one book of Native American tales that referenced the wendigo. It was a start, but not very helpful. She pulled the book and made her way to the circulation desk at the entrance of the library. As she was coming out of the stacks, she ran into Dr. Maynard, dropping the book she was carrying.

"Maeve!" Dr. Maynard exclaimed, bending down to pick up the book.

Maeve's glasses had slid down, and she pushed them back up the bridge of her nose.

"I am so sorry, Dr. Maynard," she said, taking the book from him.

"No worries," he said with a chuckle. "I wasn't paying attention to where I was going either." He looked at the book she had in her hand. "Native American folklore? Interesting. Not something I would have expected you to be interested in. Helping Korin figure out a topic for his thesis?"

She smiled. "In a way."

"Well, hopefully you can give him some inspiration. He seems to be a bit stuck right now, and he doesn't like any of the suggestions I've offered. Honestly, I don't think he will be successful with his chosen topic."

"I hope I can help him."

"Good luck, and take care." He took a step, continuing toward the library's grand staircase that led up to the second floor.

"Oh, Dr. Maynard, before you go—have you ever heard of a wendigo? I can't seem to find much on the topic."

He grimaced. "A vile creature of myth, certainly not as popular as, say, dragons or phoenixes. There are only two books I am aware of on the topic. One is Algernon Blackwood's novella, *The Wendigo*, and the other is Milton Parker's journal, which detail his personal experiences of his many scientific expeditions for the University of Minnesota. The last set of entries will be of interest to you as they detail his encounter with the creature while exploring the wilderness of Grand Portage. The former is in the fiction section and the latter is in nonfiction, even though no one knows for sure if Milton Parker's experiences actually happened or not. Regardless, he and his fellow explorers had a run-in with what they believed was a wendigo, and the event was quite horrific. This is certainly true for readers like us, since we live in such close proximity to where the events took place."

"I'll go look those up now. Thank you, Dr. Maynard!" Maeve said.

She dashed off to pull Blackwood's novel from the shelves, then made her way over to the nonfiction section to grab Parker's journal. Both were on the small side, but nonetheless, she hoped the information contained in each would help Korin.

Finally, before she left the library for the afternoon, she went to the psychology section. She remembered reading a book called *Extraordinary Psychological Disorders*, and wanted to see if it was on the shelf. She recalled the book being large with a blue leather binding and the title embossed in gold. It jumped out at her right away, and she pulled it from the shelf. She sat down and cracked open the book, placing the other books on the floor beside her. Flipping to the "W" section in the index, she found *wendigo psychosis* and turned to page forty-seven. She had a sinking feeling in her stomach but passed it off as hunger; it was dinnertime, and she hadn't had a chance to eat yet.

A curl of long black hair fell from behind her ear as she started to read. She pushed the hair behind her ear and readjusted her black-framed glasses on her nose. She took a deep breath when she saw the section on wendigo psychosis was about ten pages long. It included information on the disorder's history and its ties with the myth. Then it delved into some actual case histories, along with why psychologists believed people suffered from it. Labeled as a social disorder, those who have suffered from it often lacked a healthy connection with society. They stated that something was missing from their lives, and they found that this missing element existed in another person. Oftentimes, those afflicted went to devastating lengths to resolve their plight.

One such case was Robert Leyton. In the 1950s, he lived in a small apartment in San Francisco, a recluse with no friends. All of his family members were dead. Leyton made money by traveling around the city as a handyman. When he had a heart attack at the age of forty, doctors told him he had a very weak heart and he should no longer do any sort of manual labor; instead, he should just stay home and rest. But Leyton had bills to pay, so he continued his work as a handyman.

One day, while working on the plumbing of the kitchen sink at the home of a well-known politician in the area, Leyton experienced a severe fluttering in his chest and asked the politician to drive him back to his apartment. He knew he didn't have the energy to walk home. The politician, not wanting to be responsible for this man getting sick, agreed, and took Leyton home. On the way, Leyton bemoaned his cardiac problems and said how incredible it was that the politician had such stamina and strength, remarking that the politician must have had a very healthy heart. To which the politician agreed, boasting that he was in top health.

Upon arriving at Leyton's apartment, the politician helped Leyton out of the car and up to his third-floor apartment. Suddenly filled with jealousy for the strength the politician had, Leyton somehow summoned the power to swing his toolbox around and hit the politician in the head. The politician's head began to bleed profusely, and his eyes rolled back in his head as he fell forward, unconscious. Leyton pulled the man into his apartment, closed the door, and bound the man so he could not escape or scream.

Exhausted, Leyton sat there and stared at the unconscious politician. He wanted to be as strong as this man. He wanted to be healthy. He wanted his heart to be normal once again. And that was when he heard a whispering in his ear. It told him to kill the politician and eat his heart. Once he'd eaten the man's heart, Leyton's own would be restored—healthy and whole.

The politician groaned. Leyton retrieved a large butcher knife from his kitchen and tore open the politician's shirt to expose his bare chest. The man tried to thrash about, but Leyton had him bound too well.

Leyton turned on his radio and increased the volume. With the politician's mouth taped shut, he wouldn't be able to scream, although he could make a certain amount of noise. This he did as Leyton started cutting into his chest. Blood bubbled from the wound, running in rivulets across the skin and pooling on vinyl floor underneath the politician. When the butcher knife proved fruitless at getting through the ribs, Leyton pulled out a small handsaw from his toolbox and sawed through the cartilage that connected the ribs to the sternum. Just a dull moan emanated from the politician as Leyton pulled the ribs apart with a sickening crack. A portion of the politician's left lung was visible, and it inflated and deflated as jagged breaths came from his nose.

Then Leyton saw the heart, pounding away in the man's mauled and bloody chest cavity. He picked up the butcher knife and pulled away the thin viscera that connected the organs together. Then he cut away at the large vessels that connected the heart to the whole body. Blood seeped out of the severed arteries and vessels. The politician went into convulsions and Leyton had to kneel against the body to steady it as he separated out the beating muscle. Then with a swift tug, it was in his hand, and the politician bled out onto Leyton's floor. Leyton's hands shook and exhaustion threatened to consume him. He didn't hesitate as he bit into the tough, warm heart that spasmed as it died.

After consuming most of the heart, Leyton claimed that he felt full of energy and vigor. He was strong enough to carry the politician's body down to his car. Driving the car with the body inside, Leyton drove it off an abandoned pier, jumping out at the last moment before the car fell into the waters of the bay. After a few moments it sunk heavily to the bottom, where it would not be discovered for ten years. This was after Leyton had been captured, when his kill count had reached twenty-seven. He attributed the cure of his cardiac disease to all the human hearts he had eaten over the past decade.

Maeve was absolutely disgusted by the account of Leyton's crimes, but at the same time there was something intriguing about his psychosis. How was this man, who'd been on death's door, able to survive the hard manual labor involved in killing these people? Before he'd killed and eaten the heart of the politician, he'd barely been able to get out of the car. Once he ate the heart, he was able to carry the body out of his house to discard it. Was this confession from Leyton completely true? Or had some of it been fabricated?

Maeve was too disturbed to continue reading. Later that evening, she'd give these books to Korin and talk to him about this. It would be interesting to see what he'd make of all this—if it sparked any theories about Davis and his behavior. Maeve could see the correlation, and hoped Korin would, as well.

She stood up and stretched her legs, picking up the books and making her way to the front desk to check them out.

Then she headed to the cafeteria to get something to eat, since she'd never touched her chili at lunch. This time she'd choose a salad.

CHAPTER FOURTEEN

There was a slow-moving, chilling wind that made Korin zip up his jacket. While the sky was clear, he sensed a storm brewing. A thin crescent moon started to rise out of the purplish horizon as Korin walked across Kelton's DMZ toward Maeve's dorm.

The DMZ was a funny little place, a strip of land between the boys' and girls' dorms that served as a meeting place between the sexes. Some jokester had come up with "the demilitarized zone" a couple years ago, and the shortened form of the nickname stuck. Boys were not allowed in girls' dorms after four p.m., so this communal area had become a shared hangout for everyone. During warmer weather it was nearly impossible to see the grass due to everyone sitting around on blankets, hanging out and talking, sneaking a joint. Now it was mostly barren, aside from a couple trying to make out on the benches in the freezing weather.

One of the maintenance doors to Maeve's dorm was broken, and that was how every guy snuck in after hours. The resident staffing the front desk never noticed because she usually had her nose buried in some romance novel.

As Korin neared Maeve's room, he couldn't shake off the annoyance he'd felt with Dr. Maynard that morning. He felt like his trusted professor wasn't providing him any support, sending him off on break with a family who didn't understand him and would mostly ignore him. Was there really any point in going home? Especially when he didn't really feel like he had a home to go to.

The girls' dorm at Kelton was the old main hall, appropriately named Old Main. Once the sole building on campus, it was now flanked by numerous others used for either academia or student housing. This revitalized Old Main was the only building that served two purposes: a combination of academic classes in the basement and on the first floor, with the top three floors used for student housing. There were two other all-male dormitories on campus. There had been talk of building more student housing that would be co-ed, as the school was growing and they were seeing an uptick in the female population. However, as with all things at Kelton, things moved very slowly.

Korin lived at Lakes Hall, named in homage to the Great Lakes of the northern part of the country. He was diagonally across the DMZ from Old Main, flanked by the arts building and one of two education buildings. Although Kelton was small, somehow it needed two buildings to house all of the education majors. Those classrooms were almost always packed, while the classes in the arts and sciences buildings were never full. Korin hoped that one day the school's student body would be more equally balanced between the education, arts, and sciences students, believing that would make the school more successful. Although it wasn't one of the biggest schools in America, it could be the biggest in Minnesota.

Korin knocked at Maeve's door, the sound of his knuckles echoing down the hallway.

She smiled when she opened the door, and motioned for him to come into the room, which was fresh and vibrant. The walls, like all dorm rooms on campus, were a generic white; however, Maeve had hung posters of her favorite bands and singers, adding a touch of neon color and flair. Cyndi Lauper, The Bangles, and Sade all graced her walls.

She was one of the lucky students who'd been able to secure a scholarship, and as part of the deal for a graduate student, she had her own single room. Without this room, she would be twenty-three and still living with her father, since his house was only a few miles away. Tonight, Van Morrison's *Moondance* album played on her small tabletop record player, a sign that Maeve was in a mellow and "thinking" mood.

"I have something I need to show you," Maeve said as she walked over to the books that lay on her desk.

Korin coughed, interrupting her, and she turned to look at him.

"Actually, before you show me, I need to discuss something with you first."

Her face went dark. "You're breaking up with me," she said, a frown etched across her face. Tears began forming in her eyes.

"What?! No! God, no!" Korin grabbed her hand and pulled her over to the little sofa that she had wedged in between the door frame and the foot of her bed. "No, I need to talk to you about what happened today. You really think I would break up with you?"

She sighed. As usual, she always jumped to the worst conclusions.

"No, no—I would hope you never would. Sorry, I have a lot on my mind at the moment."

"So do I," he said. "I forgot to tell you at lunch."

There was a pause as they both looked at their hands, clasped together tightly as they sat side by side on the couch.

"I had an interesting talk with Dr. Maynard about my thesis this morning. He wants me to change the topic," Korin said, looking dejected.

Maeve feigned surprise.

"He thinks my focus can't be achieved, that I won't be able to uncover any factual evidence that may prove a legend to be real. There is no way that *all* these stories across antiquity are made up stories to provide a moral lesson. Something *real* had to happen at some point to birth one of these stories."

"So he wants you to change your overall thesis because he thinks you're essentially on a ghost hunt? What does he suggest as an alternative?"

"He didn't say. Actually, he wants me to take some time off from the thesis and not focus on it until next semester." His voice rose. "It's so frustrating! You know that I want my thesis to be incredible. I want to prove to my parents that I can do something amazing and that I have become someone!"

Maeve didn't say anything right away, just looked at her desk.

"You shouldn't be doing this just to prove your worth to your parents," she said finally. "Your thesis should be something that you yourself believe in—that you want to be known for. Why are you so desperate for their acknowledgment, anyway?"

Korin gave her a look that told her she'd crossed a line.

"Because they are my parents." He let go of her hand and leaned forward, head bowed.

Maeve stood up and went over to her desk, picked up the books, and returned to the sofa.

"I think I may have something here that could help you." She opened Blackwood's book and started flipping through the pages. "I know this is a work of fiction, but I think it could help you find a new direction for your thesis. Algernon Blackwood wrote this book after hearing many accounts of a creature called a wendigo."

"A wendigo? I've never heard of that before."

"It's a creature found in Native American folklore. In fact, it comes from some tribes in this state. It's quite a horrendous legend, a tale of gluttony and selfishness."

Korin looked intently at her, wanting more information.

Maeve continued. "There is a belief that cannibalism is based on one human desiring to obtain a trait from another human. For example, intelligence; one person, subject A, wants to be more intelligent and sees another person, subject B, with that level of desired intelligence. In subject A's view, the only way to get that intelligence is to take it from subject B."

Korin scrunched his nose, not quite following her. "Intelligence isn't tangible. You can't just take it from another person."

She smiled. "That's the crux of the matter: Subject A believes that they can. So subject A kills subject B and eats their brain, believing that he will become more intelligent by ingesting it."

"Well, that's disgusting. But that doesn't make them a wendigo, right? That makes them a cannibal."

"Essentially you are right, but the wendigo is born from the act of eating. Let's say both subjects are college students and have the same level of access to education, where subject A could apply himself and become as intelligent as subject B. The wendigo spirit is born out of that greed. Subject A would commit the moral sin of eating subject B as opposed to taking the time to learn on his own. In Native American folklore, they equate this to someone committing cannibalism during a time of plentiful harvests—"

"But what *is* the wendigo, exactly?" he said, interrupting her.

"I'm getting there," she said, glaring at him. "The wendigo is essentially what the cannibal physically transforms into—a great beast who continues to feed upon human flesh. The most appalling part of this monster is that its body grows in exact proportion to the meal it just ate, so it is constantly hungry and never satisfied."

"Okay—cool monster, I'll give you that—but how does this help me with my thesis?"

"Wendigos could potentially be real."

"No way. If they are real, why have I never heard of them before? How are they not on the news? These monsters would have eaten themselves through the world's population by now if they were real."

"That may be part of the myth—the transformation from human into something inhuman. It's possible that part was embellished, but people *do* transform when they are on a downward spiral in their life. They become something different from what they were before. Mannerisms, attitudes, and sometimes appearances change, becoming grotesque." She shook her head. "We never know how far we have fallen until we become monsters."

Maeve set down Blackwood's book and pulled the massive *Extraordinary Psychological Disorders* book into her lap. She opened to a page that she'd bookmarked and began to read: "Wendigo psychosis is a disease of the mind that causes a psychological disorder in humans that gives the afflicted a craving for human flesh. The cravings are something that is never satisfied, as the afflicted are trying to consume something in their victims that they feel is missing within themselves."

She closed the book and handed it to Korin.

"So while a terrifying creature may not be real, there is a real psychological disorder out there that affects humans, and forms the basis for the wendigo legend."

Korin looked at the book thoughtfully. He was considering how he might pull all of this together to show that both the accounts of the legend and the monster itself were real.

"I saved the best for last." She smiled and picked up the final book, *The Journal of Milton Parker*. "There is a section in this journal toward the end that may help. It is written by a gentleman who explored the Grand Portage area with his research party. Essentially, they were on a mission in the early 1900s to establish whether mountain lions still existed in the area. His account provides eyewitness testimony of a real wendigo attacking his group. Dr. Maynard directed me to it; it's from the nonfiction section."

Korin looked at her. "Dr. Maynard?"

"Yes," she said. "I ran into him at the library—it must have been after you'd talked to him. I learned about the wendigo psychosis in my ethics class today. When I saw Dr. Maynard, I asked him about it. He pointed me to these two books. For a guy who wants you to take a break, he did just stir the pot."

Korin smiled. He was starting to see how he could salvage his thesis project. Best of all, he had the week of spring break to focus on his research. There was no way he was going to stop now. Spring break at home would be an ideal opportunity. He knew he'd be invisible there, left in peace to read and write.

Amanda Headlee

CHAPTER FIFTEEN

Korin slid his bag into the trunk of his junker car, the 1971 Datsun 510 sedan he'd inherited from his mother. After paying off several debts, his dad had bought the car for his mother with the remaining inheritance money from Korin's grandmother. The family had required two cars as the boys grew older and needed to be driven around more.

Beige may have been all the rage back then, but the paint was now tainted with ugly rust patches, and the car was going bald on its roof and hood. Every time he looked at the clunker, he secretly thanked whatever god was listening that his parents hadn't had enough money to afford a roof rack. He always imagined driving down the highway and the rack snapping off, flying through the windshield of the poor soul behind him.

The interior still smelled like his mom. Her Oil of Olay essence had seeped into the worn leather seats, permanently marking her territory. The sill of the driver-side door had small markings from where his mother used to set her left hand while keeping the right on the steering wheel. When a song with a good rhythm would come on the radio, she would start to sing and tap her hand on the sill, her wedding ring marking the beat. He would sit in the backseat on the passenger side and watch her. In his head he would hum the tune, and oftentimes, the sound would reverberate in his throat. He would try to keep up with Davis, who always sat in the front passenger seat, singing the song at the top of his lungs, filling the whole car with his vibrato. Korin didn't like to admit it, but his brother had an incredible singing voice.

He also didn't like to admit that those hours spent riding in the car together when they were teenagers had been some of the best times in his life. It had been several years since Granma's death, which Korin, at thirteen, had come to believe truly was an accident. His time in the Duluth Asylum and his years of therapy had helped him to heal and look for small moments of peace like these. Nightmares were the only things that plagued him now, which he brushed off as the product of an active imagination. Though he had moments where he thinks back on that dreadful day, about what really transpired between Granma and

Davis that resulted in her death.

The car symbolized those moments when his family worked in harmony. Whenever the song on the radio would end, a tickle of despair fluttered in Korin's chest. He wished that these times could last forever.

"Davis, you have a good singing voice," Korin would often remark. "You should join the choir." Earlier on, the retort was always "Choir is for sissies." As they grew older, Davis would go quiet and just turn his head to look out the window. Everyone would remain silent until they got home or until the next jaunty tune came on the radio.

Nothing inside the car really screamed "Korin." Once it was his, he'd tried to put his touch on it by hanging a set of blue fuzzy dice from the rearview mirror, but they didn't suit him. He had thought hanging the dice would show he was lucky—at least, lucky to have inherited the car—but in reality, he'd gotten it by default, as Davis's license had been suspended again.

Korin was not about to take the car for granted, and graciously accepted it from his parents. This was the biggest gift he'd ever received from them; he could feel excitement surging in his chest. He was finally getting the attention from his parents warranted by his good grades and academic success. However, as they all stood in the driveway for the ceremonial handing over of the keys, Korin could feel Davis's jealous eyes on him, and he had to push down the troubled realization that he'd actually come in second when it came to "winning" the car.

"You have a big responsibility now, son," Albert Perrin said, lowering the keys into Korin's hand. When his mother started to speak, everything moved in slow motion. Suddenly the world was disjointed, and everything was wrong. Korin saw his brother's faint smile grow and stretch almost ear to ear as his mother happily announced that during the summer of 1982, before Korin returned to Kelton for his sophomore year, it would be his responsibility to drive Davis wherever he needed to go, including weekly hockey practice.

Nothing ever came to him without a price.

He slammed the trunk closed, eliciting a yelp from Maeve. "Be careful with that classic there," Maeve said. "This car has survived a lot."

The family singing sessions were the only good times the car had seen. Mostly it had witnessed fifteen years of arguments, fights, crying (either him or his mother), threats (from his father or brother), and the occasional suicidal thought (from him). A wish to just disappear. He tried to hold on tightly to the memory of those songs and let the other bad times fade away, but the pain always lingered.

"Right." He turned to Maeve and gave her a small kiss on the lips. "Time to go." He pushed past her and got into the driver's side. He felt that he had opened up to her too much over the past few days, and

88

feared she would leave him. Really, who would want to be part of a family like his?

He turned the key in the ignition and cranked the window down.

"Call me when you get home," she said. "And let's chat every day, even if it's only for a few minutes." She reached her hand into the car and smoothed back his chestnut-colored hair. "I'm worried about you."

"I'll be so focused on my thesis that I'll barely have time to pay attention to my family. I'm good at being invisible there. Plus, the hunting cabin is so remote it doesn't even have a phone. We're lucky to have electricity." He gave her a reassuring smile even though he didn't feel sure about anything—except for the fact that he'd be called a wimp the whole time they were up at the cabin. If his mom were there, she might intervene and ask Davis to back off. But his father allowed bullying. He thought it would make Korin manlier, or, as Korin believed, it was his father allowing Davis payback from being disfigured in the fire.

"Okay, so you can't call me from the cabin. Maybe I can take a trip up to see you, in Rachet?" she asked.

"We get back on Friday, if I survive. We'll see how it goes," he said, exhaling heavily. "Maybe you could come up for the weekend and meet the family."

"See you later then . . ." She paused.

"What?"

"Sorry," she laughed. "Suddenly I just had this weird feeling that I may never see you again."

"Please." He rolled his eyes and put his car in reverse. "I'll call when I get back to Rachet. Have a good break."

He backed out of the parking spot and headed out of the lot. He could see Maeve in the rearview mirror, waving until he was out of sight.

The drive to Rachet was uneventful. A few weeks ago, the radio in the car had died, so Korin had to travel in silence. He wished he could put on a good tune that would have him tapping his hand like his mother used to do. His thoughts momentarily drifted to Maeve and the future, but he didn't want to go there yet. He was too young to be thinking about marriage. Thesis first—one step at a time.

There were still some things he needed to tell her, but he just couldn't bring himself to do it yet. The fact that she was a psychology major definitely gave him pause. He had severe reservations when it came to telling her about all the events surrounding his grandmother's death, what he'd done to Davis, the time he'd spent in Duluth Asylum. While he didn't believe she would use him as a guinea pig, he didn't want her asking questions about the months he'd spent in the asylum. That was a time he'd prefer not to remember.

Maeve had said something the night before that had been rolling through his head all morning.

We never know how far we have fallen until we become monsters.

The words had unsettled him. How does one know that they have become a monster? Is it through an act of self-realization, or does someone tell them?

"I've done bad things," he whispered to himself as he thought of the flames licking Davis's arm. He'd been so young then that happened. Too young to have been tainted by society, right?

What if some people don't become monsters but are born that way? And if that's the case, how would one realize it, if they had been that way from the start? Maeve hadn't elaborated on what she'd meant by "fallen," but Korin assumed it meant that the person had become evil in some manner.

Was *he* evil?

Korin couldn't have ever anticipated the outcome of the situation with Davis and the fire. Besides, he wasn't born with anger in his heart toward his brother. It was his brother's fault, making Korin feel the way that he did. If his brother had been loving and shared their parents' attention, Korin never would have imagined that Davis was a changeling.

Korin gripped the steering wheel tightly. *He* was the one who had fallen, even though he wasn't a monster, then or now. Davis was the one who contained something sinister. Something that taunted Korin, and brought out the worst in him. Davis wanted to see Korin fail, or disappear, yet his older brother had not fallen. No, Davis was skating through life, having everything handed to him, not aware of the ugliness inside of him.

The driver's seat squeaked as Korin shifted uncomfortably. The trees outside whizzed past in a blur as Korin's mind shifted to autopilot for the duration of the trip. He was focusing on how he could use his life's experiences to influence his thesis topic.

Maeve wasn't entirely correct. It's not that we don't know how far we've fallen until we've become monsters—it's actually how others perceive the person once they've become one.

Charles Manson was a prime example. No one knew the depth of his grotesqueness until he and his "Family" had committed the murders at Sharon Tate and Roman Polanski's home. Once he was captured, everyone saw that Manson was a monster. No one came forth indicating they had seen this sinister side of him prior to the murders. Maybe Manson was a changeling, or worse.

"That's it!" he yelled out loud, pounding his hand on the steering wheel in annoyance. *How could he have not seen this before?* That's what his thesis could focus on—the monsters that reside *within* humans. A smile broke out on his face. That was the basis for all the lore in antiquity, was it not? Dr. Maynard was wrong. Folklore wasn't about keeping people safe, but about telling people the truth. Those humans who are seen as evil, as monsters, are truly born that way. Each one is tainted at birth, a little black speck on their heart that spreads like a cancer as they grow, leading them down the path of wickedness. If someone is destined to be evil, they are born that way, they don't become it.

Korin wondered whether this was something that could be detected early on—whether a treatment plan could be established to essentially rehabilitate someone, to prevent them from becoming evil, something beyond what religion could provide? He needed to talk to Maeve about this, but wanted to do it in person. Until he could get back to Kelton, he'd have to write all of this down. That would give him time to ponder and reflect.

He had the perfect life experience to draw from; while his stay at the asylum had been short, Korin had witnessed scenarios with other patients that made his blood run cold. Madness that would spring forth, unprovoked, as though something otherworldly resided in the person.

The books Maeve had supplied him with earlier in the week had proved to be valuable—especially the specific excepts Maeve found in Milton Parker's journal. The tale of the wendigo was intriguing, and he felt that there was some merit of truth to this legend. He had read Parker's gruesome account twice; it was alluring, like a bad car accident you can't avert your eyes from.

In 1923, Milton Parker had gathered a team of scientists and hunters for an expedition into the forests of Grand Portage, Minnesota, to determine the population of mountain lions existing within the territory. The most intriguing aspect of the book is that it shows the descent of one of the party's members into madness, detailing his mental and emotional decline, and leading to the climax, when everyone's life was in danger due to being stranded in a blizzard. The wendigo unleashes the darkness in his heart, physically transforms into something inhumane, and attacks everyone on the expedition. The author survived the attack and recounts what happened in those final journal entries.

The wendigo's story really intrigued Korin. He'd read the entire Parker journal the night Maeve gave it to him. He couldn't tear himself away from it for anything. It was the most realistic account of a monster story that he had ever read, and thus, there had to be some fact around it—didn't there? Obviously, the Ojibwa and other local tribes had experiences that led them to conjure up such dreadful tales . . . or warnings. He needed to find out if there was any link between the monster and reality. If he were able to prove that monsters are humans who experience either a level of extreme trauma or find themselves drawn to the darkest evils, he might have something truly revolutionary for his thesis.

He had found no other documentation that so tenaciously detailed an account of the wendigo. He hoped that the details found in the journal were true. In the novel Maeve had given him, Algernon Blackwood attempted to write a story about a wendigo. While it was deliciously macabre, the "facts" Blackwood provided about the wendigo monster were so out in left field that Korin couldn't use the text as a reference in his thesis. He still thought he might have the bones of something strong here, especially if he could tie in Parker's journal with the psychology behind wendigo psychosis.

The uneasiness he felt about his thesis no longer centered on whether he had materials and references; it was more the unsettled feeling that there was something too familiar about the topic. Something that was hitting a little too close to home. He just couldn't put his finger on what it was.

Korin exhaled as he drove over the gravel in the driveway. He was home. The Perrins lived in a ranch-style home in the northern area of Rachet. Over the summer, his mother had repainted the shutters and the door a bright pea green. Against the darkness of the wood shingles that covered the exterior walls, the color combination was hideous. The house immediately stood out as soon as someone pulled onto Forest Brook Road. He had no idea why on earth his father had allowed his mom to use such a bright color. Albert Perrin was all about having his house merge into the forest that edged the backyard. He never wanted it to stand out against the trees.

No one came out to greet him as he climbed out of his car and opened the trunk. His stomach hurt. With a groan he pulled his suitcase out of the car. It was going to be a long week. His mother must have had the window cracked in the breakfast nook to let out the heat from the old stove. He could hear the hockey game playing loudly inside. Davis would be in a terrible mood tonight if the Minnesota North Stars lost. From the sounds of the sudden yelling, things were not looking good.

As Korin walked up on the deck, he could hear his mom yelling at Davis to keep it down. While their words were incomprehensible, he could hear them bickering. He stood outside the front door and listened just as his dad was getting in on the fight. He was not happy to be home, and for a moment, he thought about returning to his car and escaping back to Kelton. It would only be another three hours in the car to drive back—totally worth it.

Before he had a chance to pick up his suitcase, the front door opened. His father stood there, red-faced and fuming.

"Oh, you're here," Albert said.

It had been only three months since Korin had last seen his father, but in that short time, Albert's face had changed. He looked even older and more tired than he'd looked at Christmas break. Living with an adult Davis was clearly pushing him to his limits. When you added the stress of his job on top of that, Korin was surprised his father hadn't been committed somewhere. Albert was still employed by the same logging company he worked for when Korin was a kid. Though now he had more job sites to travel to, most being further up North. Albert would be gone for weeks on end in the wilderness in Canada. It was a dangerous job, as he was the one who rigged the logs up to the crane in all variations of weather. Combining that with not being at home or seeing your wife for weeks, it would surely age a man.

"Grab your bag and come on in," his father said, turning away and walking into the kitchen.

No *"Hi, son—how are you doing? Good to see you."*

Korin sighed, picked up his suitcase, and stepped over the threshold. The house smelled of venison roast and mashed potatoes. He was a bit taken aback because it was his favorite meal. He allowed himself a little smile.

Natalie popped her head out of the kitchen.

"Hi, honey," she said, and then disappeared. A typical welcome home from his family.

He walked in through the living room on his way back to his old bedroom. Davis sat on the old leather recliner that was cracking with age, a beer in one hand, the other clutching the thick gold chain around his neck. He stared intently at the TV screen, on the verge of breaking out in screams again. He didn't even acknowledge that Korin was in the house.

Korin observed that the opposing team, which he had no idea who they were, led the way against the Minnesota North Stars. A silent prayer was said that Davis's favorite team would lose the season.

He continued to smile as he walked back to his bedroom.

CHAPTER SIXTEEN

Korin unpacked the few necessities he'd need for the night. Tomorrow he'd be heading to his grandfather's old hunting cabin. Even though it was only about ten miles southwest of Rachet, this area of Minnesota, near Grand Portage, was like a no-man's land. Getting lost in the forests out there could mean a death sentence. Especially this time of year.

While the weather was becoming warmer, it remained unpredictable, which was typical for northern Minnesota. Although they hadn't the typical amount of snow for this early into the start of the year, the threat of freak snowstorms were always on everyone's mind despite the warming weather.

Korin went to his dresser and pulled out the heavy weather gear he'd left at his parents' house and shoved it into an empty duffel bag. Better safe than sorry.

His room was small. A three-drawer dresser, a twin bed, and a desk big enough for him to sit at, crammed in the corner. Two windows were set in the corner so he had a ninety-degree view of the forest. He had no closet, so whatever he couldn't fit into the dresser went into totes slipped under his bed. His bedroom was the smallest room in the house, next to the bathroom. True, it was tiny, but it was his. Davis respected that and tended to avoid his room—except when he stored his stuff there while Korin was away at school. Korin was quite surprised to hear that Davis hadn't made much of a fuss about moving his things back to his own room. Maybe something was changing.

A deep furrow creased Korin's forehead. No, Davis was greedy when it came to getting everyone's attention. Since Korin's room was at the back of the house, away from everyone else, it felt like solitary confinement to Davis. He could never be alone. For Korin, on the other hand, it was a sanctuary.

"Dinner!" his mother hollered from the kitchen.

His parents never came to his room, either.

The smell of roast and mashed potatoes grew stronger as he walked toward the kitchen. Davis still sat on the recliner, staring intently at the TV. The beer bottle was gone, and Korin watched as his brother sat there rubbing his scarred forearm.

A moment of guilt swept over Korin. According to Davis's therapist, when his brother rubbed his forearm, it was a sign of calm anxiety. The fire was the most traumatic thing that had ever happened to him in his life, and rubbing his arm was a way of soothing the hurt. Davis did it a lot. Korin wondered if his older brother was absolutely terrified inside.

A clatter of dishes slamming on the dinner table made Korin disconnect from his brother and hurry into the kitchen. His mother was jumping between setting the table and stirring the gravy on the stove. Worry lines creased her face.

He offered a smile, taking glasses from the cupboard and adding them to the four place settings.

His mother returned to her gravy in an irritated huff.

"If your brother could pay me a quarter of the attention he pays to that moronic hockey, I'd have no complaints!" She banged the spoon on the lip of the pot, slopping gravy back in. "Good enough." She dumped it out into a gravy bowl and pushed it into Korin's waiting hands. Looking into the bowl he saw that it was lumpy, not his mom's normally silky-smooth gravy. Before he could turn back to her, she was already pushing the small platter of venison roast at him.

"Mom, slow down," he said.

"I'm sorry," she said, pointing toward the living room. "Davis is pushing my buttons today. If he was even a little bit of help in keeping this house running, I wouldn't feel like I'd given birth to a lump of flesh that does nothing but hound me for food and money."

"Whoa, Mom, what is going on? You never talk about Davis like this."

His question was dismissed with a wave of her hand. Something was wrong.

He heard a loud knock at the front door and before anyone could answer it, the door opened and Davis's best friend Tate Michelson stood there, taking up every square inch of the door frame, and then some. As he stepped into the house, a little girl peeked out from behind Tate's leg, auburn hair hiding her eyes like a curtain separating her from the rest of the world.

"Evenin', Perrins." Tate bobbed his head toward Korin's mother.

She smiled his way. "I hope you can stay for dinner. I made extra just in case you two stopped by. We were just about to eat."

"That would be great, thanks," he said with a toothy grin.

"Hi," six-year-old Addy whispered from behind his leg. The curtain parted and green eyes peered out, surveying the room.

"Well, Miss Addy, look at you hiding there behind your big brother. Why don't you come here and we'll get you some water?" Natalie said, gracing Addy with a loving smile. Living in a house of men, Korin always saw something shift in his mother whenever she saw Addy. She lit up, and he suspected it was because she'd always wanted a daughter.

"Can I have chocolate milk?" Addy whispered. "Please?"

"Now, Addy, what have I told you about asking for things?" Tate scolded her.

She pushed her hair even further out of her eyes and looked up at her brother, her big eyes brimming with tears.

Korin had to look away and suppress a chuckle. This kid was learning young how to manipulate men.

"Oh, hush now, Tate," Natalie said, kneeling at Addy's level. "Now, sweetie, I would love nothing more than to make you some, but we are just plain out of milk."

"Tate!" Davis said finally from the recliner, without looking at his friend. "What's shakin'?"

"Not much. Mama's passed out, so I figured we'd come over for dinner. Ain't nothin' better than hanging out with y—"

"Shut it, Tate!" Davis yelled, slamming the footrest of the recliner down. "The damn Nordiques just scored." He leaned forward, cursing at the television and rubbing his arm.

Addy turned away from Natalie, walked over to Davis, and stood next to him. Korin just stared as she reached out and petted Davis's arm. Korin cringed, anticipating that Davis would either smack the girl's hand away or yell at her. Neither of those actions occurred; instead, his brother gently pushed her hand away and just pointed to the TV.

"What the fu—," Korin started to say.

"How's school?" Tate interrupted.

Korin looked at him, perplexed. Tate hadn't reacted at all, either to Davis's outburst or the uncharacteristically gentle response Davis had just had to Tate's sister. Something had definitely changed while he'd been away from home.

Turning to Tate and giving him his full attention, Korin responded, "Struggling with my thesis."

"Thesis?"

Korin sighed. "It's a long research paper. I've had enough of school-work today. I'm hungry."

He slapped his hand on his Tate's meaty shoulder and they walked into the kitchen together, Tate ducking as he walked through the doorway. He was as tall as he was thick, standing at six-foot-five and weighing almost 230 pounds.

Natalie pulled out two more place settings and got two more chairs. "Wait, I want to hear more about what you're writing."

Korin turned, a small smile tugged at the corner of his lips. Someone here at home was interested in what he was doing. He began by telling

Tate about his thesis objective and then went into detail about the Wendigo legend. As he spoke, he moved around Tate, situating himself so that he faced where Davis sat in the living room. His brother, still on the leather recliner and gripping his arm, rocked back and forth in the seat with eyes fixed on the television screen. Anyone who saw Davis would think he was absorbed in the game, but Korin knew differently. Davis was eavesdropping, jealous Korin was receiving attention from his best friend. Plus, Korin had the bonus of upsetting Davis by speaking of folklore. The anguish that he currently caused his brother was satisfying.

Korin continued speak of his work as he turned to the kitchen table and pulled out his chair, sitting with his back to the living room. Tate never once interrupted; his eyes shone with curiosity as he listened to Korin's every word.

Addy wandered into the kitchen, over to Tate, and crawled up into his lap. She broke the spell, and Tate's attention was now on his sister. Annoyed, Korin sat back in his chair and shut his mouth.

"What is that?" she asked, pointing to the venison roast.

"It's deer meat, sweetie," Natalie replied.

Addy's mouth closed tight, and she slipped from Tate's lap.

Curious, Korin turned and watched her walk into the living room and crawl up on the couch, turning her back to the kitchen.

"Oh my," Natalie said. "I don't have any other meat that I can fix for her."

"No, ma'am. It's okay," Tate reassured her. "Addy doesn't like the taste of meat anymore. She says the flesh is evil on her tongue."

Natalie's honey-colored eyes opened wide. She shook her head and then looked back toward the living room.

"Davis Albert Perrin!" she yelled. "Get in here now and eat your dinner!"

"Aw, Ma, there's four minutes left in the period!"

"You better get in here now. I'd just as soon let Tate eat it all and not leave you a scrap."

Korin watched Davis stand in a huff and go over to the TV, slapping the power button to turn it off. Addy didn't move from the couch and kept her back to everyone.

Davis stomped into the kitchen and jerked his chair out from under the table so hard that it slammed back into the refrigerator.

"What are you looking at, dingus?" he snapped at Korin as he dropped himself into the chair.

"Oh, Lord, why did you bless me with these boys and such a small kitchen?" Natalie said.

Tate and Korin snickered. Davis cursed under his breath as he took half the roast and most of the potatoes onto his plate.

His mother stared at him, aghast.

"Davis! You can't take all that food—this is all I have for everyone!" In the next breath she yelled out for their father. "Albert, get up here before all the food is gone."

Albert had been hiding in the basement during the dinner preparation ordeal. Korin assumed he was getting their gear ready for tomorrow.

There was no response, but this was not unusual. His father typically just appeared when he was ready.

"Ma, you're being such a drama queen," Davis complained.

Korin gave his brother a hateful look.

Natalie walked up next to Davis and took his plate. Davis glared at her as she divided up his food to split between him, Korin, and Tate.

"Next time you make dinner, make enough so that I am not starving afterward," Davis said as he started to cut into his roast.

"Do you always have to be such an asshole?" Korin asked under his breath.

"What did you say?" Davis paused to glare at Korin, a hunk of roast speared on his fork and hovering near his mouth.

"Nothing."

"That's what I thought."

It was at this moment that Albert walked into the kitchen. "Hello, Tate. Where's Addy?"

"On the couch. She ain't hungry," Tate answered.

"Ah," Albert said as he sat down at the end of the table, opposite Natalie. He started to scoop into the mashed potatoes. "Dinner looks good, honey."

Natalie smiled at him. "Do you think you'll all be able to trap anything tomorrow? With it getting warmer out and the snow melting, won't the streams be flooded? May not be that safe."

Korin started to seethe. She was trying to deflect attention from the Davis situation rather than correcting his behavior.

Before Albert had a chance to answer, Davis snapped, "Give it up, Ma. We ain't going to have any trouble tomorrow." He turned to Tate, "What say you?"

"Whatever you want, Davis," Tate replied.

"That's right," Davis said, grinning pointedly at Korin, then his mother.

"Davis," Albert said without looking up from the food on his plate, his tone filled with warning.

"Oh, Davis, you are twenty-five years old. When—" his mother began.

"Cut it, Ma. We men need to discuss the plan for tomorrow."

"Enough!" Albert said, slamming his fork down on the table.

Korin and Tate flinched even as Davis continued to shovel food into his mouth.

"You boys hurry up and finish eating so we can go downstairs and get everything together," Albert said, turning to his mom. "We'll be fine, Nat. We'll get the traps set tomorrow morning and then we can do the necessary repairs to the cabin's roof."

"Wait, what?" Korin asked. "I thought you guys would be away all day tomorrow, hunting."

Tate and his father laughed, while Davis sneered. "You are such an idiot. We set the traps and they do all the work. We just check them once a day."

"But I need to work on my thesis. I was going to stay inside the cabin while you were all out doing whatever to catch beavers." His voice sounded whinier than he'd intended.

"Oh no you're not. You came home to spend time with the family, and you're not going sit inside the whole time. We need you to help us fix that roof," his father said.

He knew he shouldn't argue with his dad, but he did it anyway.

"But Mom won't be with us, so how is that spending time with the family?"

He knew he shouldn't have said that. The table was silent, and his father's face changed to such a dark shade of red that it bordered on purple. Davis smirked, the "You're in trouble" look written all over his face.

"You can stay in the cabin while we check the traps, I don't care, but you *will* be helping us fix up the place."

Korin said nothing more, and the rest of the meal was eaten in silence.

After dinner, his father, Davis, and Tate went to the basement. Korin didn't care to join them, since he was going to be forced to spend the entire week with them.

He stayed in the kitchen to help his mom clean up, despite feeling like he'd been duped by her. She'd never mentioned that they were going to have to fix the cabin's roof. She'd made it sound like they would just be out hunting and trapping all day. As if Korin really knew anything about it. His one hunting trip with Davis had been enough to put him off the idea of traipsing through the woods with his brother ever again.

After they were done drying the dishes, Korin watched his mother put some leftover mashed potatoes on a dish. She walked into the living room and placed it on the coffee table, saying, "Here, sweets, for when you're hungry later. If it's too cold, just call me and I'll heat it up for you."

He felt himself grow cold with jealousy. Natalie bent down and gently touched Addy's shoulder. The little girl was fast asleep.

CHAPTER SEVENTEEN

From the living room floor there was a rustle and a loud yawn. Someone else was walking down the hallway toward the bathroom.

Korin pulled his blanket tighter up to his chin as he pushed his himself deeper into the crack between the back and seat couch cushions. It was warmer there. The morning already had a chill in the air. It was going to be a cold and windy day.

Despite his back being warmer nestled between the cushions, it was sore. Natalie didn't want Addy sleeping on the couch and woken up by everyone during the early morning. Tate moved her to Korin's bed before they all fell asleep for the night. Natalie said that was okay because Korin hadn't slept in his bed since he was last home, and it isn't like he missed it. Korin remained silent, knowing how he truly felt didn't matter.

Suddenly, his entire body felt like it was being throttled. Tate was shaking him.

"Hey, buddy," he whispered, "time to get up and get going."

Korin yawned and wiped the sleep out of his eyes. "Seriously, dude, all you had to do was say 'hey.' I didn't need to be shaken to death to be woken up." He yawned again. "It's too damn early."

"The beavers don't think so," Tate said.

Korin saw that Tate was already dressed. "Wow, talk about eager beavers."

"I fell asleep in this. Wanted to be ready early, because you know how hard it's going to be to get Davis up." Tate went to Davis's bedroom door, pushed it open, and disappeared into the darkness.

Just as Korin sat up, his mother came out of her bedroom, hair tangled and sleep in her eyes. She smiled and whispered, "Good morning."

Korin just nodded his head as she disappeared into the kitchen to start the coffeemaker. He figured it was his father moving about in the bathroom.

He pulled the blanket over his head. He was still angry that she tricked him.

He felt someone shaking his shoulder. He peeked out from under the blanket and saw his mother. Her face was stern. As if she read his mind, she said, "Get up. You are going. You are spending quality time with your father and brother."

Addy woke up in Korin's room. Someone must have moved her there from the couch. She listened to the movements around the house. The sound of her brother waking up and then trying to get Davis out of bed. Mrs. Perrin in the kitchen, and someone else in the bathroom. She knew she shouldn't be awake yet, but she couldn't help but listen to the sounds of the Perrins' house in the morning. It was busy. Not like her home, where it was always quiet, unless Mama was mad. In her own bedroom at home she would hear only silence, or Tate snoring from his room down the hall. Her mom was always dead asleep at this time of day, often sleeping until lunchtime.

Addy wanted to go with the others to the cabin so she could hear these same sounds tomorrow morning. She could stay inside and color, or read. She told Mrs. Perrin as much—that she wouldn't be a bother—but Mrs. Perrin told her it would not be a good idea. The men needed to have some time alone together.

"Guy time," she said, winking at Addy.

Addy didn't understand what she meant, but she faked a giggle. Addy didn't want to be alone. She didn't want to be without Tate. It would be the first time since their daddy died that she would be separated from him overnight. The thought of a few days without him terrified her.

She snuggled deeper under the blankets and pulled her knees up to her chest. She wasn't changed out of her clothes when she was moved to Korin's bed. It was not uncommon for Addy to spend the night at the Perrins' once or twice a week with Tate. When their mother was drunk and acting crazy, Tate would bring her over to the Perrins' where they would sit and laugh and eat yummy food. Once she'd overheard Mrs. Perrin say to Mr. Perrin that a child as young as Addy should not know what the word "drunk" meant. Addy felt like she knew a lot, even though she was only six, going on seven. She knew what drunk was. Drunk was her mama.

When the thought of her mama entered her mind, she started to cry. Their lives were so much happier when Daddy was alive. He had died when she was five. He had gone out on a trip one day and never returned. It was probably her fault that he died, she thought, and tears started to flow down her face.

Her dad was a scientist, and had traveled a lot. He was the kind of scientist who liked rocks and had to go to different places to study them. He was either far away on a trip or was in Duluth where his office was. When Daddy had to be in the office, he'd stay there during the week. Addy rarely got to spend time with Daddy since he was always away, so when she was able to see him, she tried to spend as much time as possible with him, which was easy because Tate was usually working and Mama was sleeping.

One time after a trip he brought home a bracelet for her that was made of small pearls. Daddy always told her that she was the pearl of his life. She didn't understand what that meant, but the little pearls were pretty and shiny. They were like little white bubbles that encircled her small wrist. Bubbles that she could never pop and would always stay with her. Since her father had died, she'd never taken the little bubbles off.

His last trip had been to Hawaii, to look at volcanoes and collect rocks. Before he left she had begged him to bring home more little pearl bubbles for her. She wanted a necklace this time. Her daddy told her before he left that he would find her the most beautiful pearls in the world so that she could make a necklace. But he never came home after that trip because he died in the ocean.

After that, her mama became meaner and was drunk all the time. Tate started to take care of her just the way Daddy used to. Daddy and Tate have always been the ones who loved her. Her mama never did. She once heard Mama say to Tate that Addy was a burden on the family—nothing but a mistake. Addy was the reason Daddy had to work so much and was away all the time. Then Mama had started to yell at Tate that if Addy never existed, they would all be happier, and their daddy would still be alive.

As she continued to scream at him, Tate picked up Addy and carried her out of the house, whispering in her ear, "I'll keep you forever."

Albert Perrin finished getting ready in the bathroom and went down the hall to his bedroom to get dressed. Before he walked in his room, he smiled at his youngest who was sitting on the couch with unkempt hair, lazily yawning over a cup of coffee.

"Up and at 'em, kiddo," he said.

Albert was unusually jovial this morning, ready to spend time with his three boys. Biologically he may have had only two, but in recent months his family had sort of informally adopted the Michelson kids. He thought of Tate and Addy as his own, and would always think of them as such. They had no one else. Besides, Tate seemed to be the only human on Earth who could control Davis.

The thought of his eldest soured his mood as he walked into his bedroom and shut the door. From the other side of the bedroom wall he could hear Tate trying to rouse Davis, quietly so as not to wake Addy. Davis was stubborn and lazy. Albert felt like he'd never done enough to motivate Davis to stand on his own two feet. He was their firstborn. As new parents, they really hadn't known how to raise a child. They did the best they could, but he saw now how they had failed. Failed horribly, as their child-rearing for the first son ended up affecting the second. They were so focused on Davis and trying to make him "perfect" that they hadn't provided enough support for Korin. Perfection, that was Natalie's dream for this family. She had such a sad childhood that she wanted her parenthood to be different. He sometimes thought Natalie was disillusioned with the dream of perfection, which is why she was never the one to punish the kids. Their lives were far from perfect, but she acted like it was not.

Although Korin wasn't planned, he was still a joyous surprise. Sadly, growing up in Davis's shadow, he'd never received the proper amount of attention. Natalie always reassured him, saying that Korin didn't really need it. He was an independent child and refused to be held back by anyone. They gave him the room he needed to go in the direction he wanted, and as his parents, they thought they'd done the right thing at the time.

Albert could see now that the lack of support and attention had been detrimental to Korin as a kid. It caused him to have delusional fantasies, only strengthened by his mother and him filling his young son's head with fairy tales. He had never let go of the guilt he felt deep down, that somehow, he had been responsible for Korin's attempt to kill his brother. Then, to top it off, instead of trying to work through things as a family, he and Natalie had made the most grievous mistake of all. They had shipped Korin off to Duluth Asylum.

A sob escaped Albert and he quickly wiped away a tear that fell from his eye. Guilt still haunted him for what they did to Korin in having him committed. That guilt made it a struggle to face Korin, causing him to avoid his son. That's why he never went with Natalie all those years ago to collect Korin from that place.

Albert ran his hand though his thinning hair then gripped tightly and pulled a bit.

"Dammit."

And every time he tried to overcome his guilt by trying to connect with his son, it always failed.

"I'm a failure," he whispered to himself. "Please don't fail this time." He prayed this trip with his sons and Tate would change the family dynamics. Miracles could happen.

Albert shook his head, trying to shift gears. That was all in the past and having this trip with the boys could be the first step in fixing the future. Korin would be turning twenty-three next month and in graduate school. He was going to be the most successful Perrin. He was the one who was out there on his own in the world, while Davis was at home, without a job, draining the family finances and sucking the life out of Albert. He wanted to throw Davis out, but Natalie always protested. They had brought him into this world, she said, and he was their responsibility. Even though at twenty-five, wasn't it time for him to stand on his own?

His goal for this outing was to build a bond with Korin and have Davis to realize his adult responsibilities. Tate was the positive influence that would help him achieve the latter, or at least he hoped.

Albert sighed loudly as he heard Tate start to cajole and then meekly threaten Davis, telling him that if he didn't get up, he wouldn't have any of Albert's famous jerky.

This was not how his life was supposed to be. While he'd never admit it to Natalie, he did agree with her. They were supposed to have the perfect home to house a loving family that grew up in a stable environment. It was supposed to be different than the way he'd grown up, with an angry father and a silent mother. The plan was for his children to leave the nest once they were of age and take off on their own, while he and Natalie could retire, sitting back and reflecting on their life and how lovely it all was.

No, his life did not turn out that way. Now in his fifties, he was still having to work a dangerous and demanding job, all on account of Davis not leaving the house and taking life by the horns, steering it according to his own whims and dreams. Albert was stuck in his job for the next ten to fifteen years, and that scared him. Carrying around the heavy logging equipment was backbreaking. Climbing down mountainsides to buck up felled logs to the crane, which would then drag them up to the top of the hill, was even more painful. His body and spirit were slowly giving out. He had been in the industry for nearly forty years, starting as a young teenager, and stuck doing the same tasks for almost as long. He had been passed over for promotion so many times, those jobs given to the stronger—and now younger—workers. He didn't know how much longer he could do this. Something was going to have to give, and soon.

The first step was to get Davis out on his own, which was sure to be seen as the end of the world. This trip with his boys was probably going to be the last. Once he'd kicked Davis out of the house, there would be no going back. Davis would hold a grudge against him and Natalie, and most likely hate them.

It had been a struggle to come to this decision, but if you have a child who refuses to do anything with his life, wasn't it better to push him out of the nest and force him to fly on his own rather than enabling him to just sit in the nest until the day he died, doing nothing?

Addy heard Mr. Perrin leave the bathroom and head into his room. Tate and Davis were still arguing in Davis's room, Davis saying "It's too early" over and over. There was the sound of dishes clattering in the kitchen, and by the coughing sound in the bathroom, she could tell Korin was in there getting ready.

It was time for her escape.

Quietly she slipped from the bed and covered pillows underneath the comforter, making it look as if she were still laying there, tucked away, sleeping. Dressed in warm underclothes, black snow pants, and her green winter jacket, Addy slipped from Korin's room and padded silently down the hall to the living room. She peeked around the corner; in the kitchen she saw Mrs. Perrin had her back to her. Addy tiptoed over to the front door, grabbed her snow boots, opened the door with barely a sound, and slipped out into the early morning darkness. She was not going to be left behind, without her brother.

The rain was a surprise and she quickly put her boots on. The early morning cold froze the rain. Addy hadn't prepared for this. She ran to the station wagon, her boots slipping on the ice that had formed on the sidewalk and driveway.

She opened the passenger door behind the driver's seat and crawled over the seat into the rear of the car. She breathed a sigh of relief that the car hadn't been locked. Addy hid herself between the back of the seat and a few duffel bags. Finding a blanket, she threw that over herself for extra measure, and warmth. Luckily, Mr. Perrin had asked the boys to pack the car the night before. They would never be able to see her under all of this stuff. The only thing the boys needed to place in the back of the car this morning was the cooler of food, and that would go right near the hatch, far from where she was hidden.

The others should be coming out soon, and then they would be on the road.

Albert had had enough. He and Korin sat at the table in the kitchen drinking coffee and eating toast. They were meant to leave at three a.m., and it was already three-thirty. Davis had yet to come out of his room. Tate had appeared with a defeated look and sat down at the table. The second hand on the clock tick-tick-ticked, each second passing more slowly than the last.

Beyond annoyed, Albert started to tap on his coffee mug and bounce his right leg on the floor.

"Albert," Natalie warned as she continued to scrub the coffeepot in the sink. To her right she had neatly filled four travel mugs with coffee, and one thermos, for refills.

"Come on, Natalie," he spat. "This is ridiculous! I said three a.m. and I meant it."

Korin stifled a giggle.

She continued washing the pot. "So what if you get up there at six or seven, or even eight in the morning? All you are doing today is setting traps. Wouldn't it be better to do that when it's light?"

He snorted. She didn't understand trapping. The plan was to arrive no later than four-thirty and get out in the woods by five, to scout dams on the creek. Beavers were most active at dawn and dusk, so their best chance of finding an active dam was to be out just as the sun was coming up, and then again as the sun was going down in the evening. They would set the traps during the day.

"I have seriously had enough of his bullshit. He's an adult. It's time for him to grow up and be responsible."

And with that, he stormed off to Davis's room, accidentally kicking the table and spilling some of Korin's coffee. As he walked out of the kitchen he heard Natalie say to the boys, "I see where Davis gets his temper from."

Korin didn't want to walk into the bear's den. It would be foolish to follow his father into Davis's room. Instead he hovered just outside the door.

Albert had already demanded that Davis get out of bed in a harsh tone. Surprisingly, there was silence from his brother.

"Responsibility, Davis. You have none of it, and it's time to start. You should be more like your brother, who is totally independent. We rarely have to do anything to help him. He is on his own, supporting himself through college, which is more than you've ever achieved."

Korin struggled to digest what his father was saying. Was he giving Korin a compliment or basically saying how happy he was that he didn't have to take care of Korin? A hollow pit formed in his stomach as he realized his dad probably leaned more to the latter thought.

"That's because that idiot hated it here!" Davis's muffled voice said. He probably had the blankets pulled over his head. "He hated living with all of us because you two were the worst parents ever."

Not wanting to be caught listening, Korin backed down the hall and into his parents' bedroom. On the other side of the wall he heard the mattress creak and there was a thud. Davis finally had pulled his ass out of bed.

"How can you say that?" Albert's voice was sharp. "We gave you everything. Anything you ever asked for, it was yours. You are living here, in *my* house, completely free, not working, and you have the balls to say something like that to my face. You have been incredibly selfish, since the day you were—"

"Yeah, well, whatever," Davis said, cutting off their father.

Footsteps moved toward the hallway. Davis exited his room and went down to the bathroom.

The pit in his stomach grew. Korin felt as though he wanted it to overtake him, swallowing him whole. His father just allowed Davis to just walk away, not even asking for an apology for Davis's cruel words. It was as if his father didn't really care about what Davis thought, he just wanted him to get up so they could leave for the cabin.

He heard a sigh from his father as he walked into the kitchen.

"We'll be leaving in about twenty minutes," he said to Natalie.

The legs of a chair scratched across the kitchen floor as his dad sat down to finish his coffee.

In silence, Korin returned to the kitchen. His father gave him a knowing look, acknowledging that he knew Korin had overheard the entire conversation.

Korin returned the look with a glare.

CHAPTER EIGHTEEN

It was freezing outside. It had snowed during the night, but now the precipitation turned into a freezing rain. The cold temperature froze the rain into slick and shiny frozen puddles on the asphalt.

They ended up not leaving until five a.m. Davis took his time as usual to drag his feet getting ready. He didn't have his bag packed, which was to be packed the night before, and took his time in gathering his clothes. While Korin knew his father seethed inside from being over two hours late in leaving, his father did well to maintain a cool exterior attitude.

"Looks like we'll be facing some icy roads on our drive up," Albert chuckled, each word punctuated with a visible breath.

Korin grunted his agreement as he helped Albert carry a heavy cooler full of sandwich fixings and his mother's homemade chili to the station wagon. They also loaded an empty cooler to store whatever pelts and meat they collected during the trip, along with their hunting rifles. All processing would be done at the hunting cabin. Natalie absolutely refused to allow Albert and Davis to process anything at home. She didn't want to see a creature whole, and then watch as its body was barbarically broken down, layer by layer.

The first time Albert had processed a carcass in her presence was the first time he'd taken Davis out deer hunting. He used to take the deer to a local processor, but thought that since he had the help of his eldest, who was twelve at the time, they could bond over doing it together, at home.

His mother had pulled into the driveway after taking Korin to the dentist to find a makeshift hoist erected, a dead deer hanging by its back legs from the oak tree in the front yard. Blood pooled in a bucket as the deer's slit throat drained out the last remnants of life. The lower half of the deer was skinned. Its muscles glistened, catching rays of sun that peeked through the clouds. Red marbled with white fat and tendons. That was what Korin remembered.

Natalie had hopped out of her beige Datsun, screaming obscenities at his father, then stopped dead as a young Davis stepped out from behind the hanging deer's body. He had a skinning knife in his right hand, and in his left, a piece of flayed skin. He was streaked from head to toe in blood.

Albert started yelling at Davis to drop the skin and go hose himself off behind the house. Korin just stared at the deer from the car. The back of the animal was naked, while the front was still covered in tawny soft fur. The deer's glassy eyes stared at some distant point that was forever out of focus. The bluish tongue hung limp from its mouth.

Korin had vomited all over the seat and floor of his mother's car. He didn't mean to throw up, but that was the first time he had ever seen a deer carcass—the first time he'd ever seen blood, aside from cutting his own finger.

Shaking his head at the memory, he slammed the hatch shut and climbed into the backseat with Tate. His father's station wagon was fifteen years old. Somehow it still ran. It didn't sound too good when his father started it up. The front seat belts were no longer usable, the cloth frayed or dry-rotted, so one day his dad had removed them altogether from the front. Korin was glad Davis always insisted on having the front seat, as he preferred to sit in the back with functioning seat belts.

He settled in and looked at the ceiling, littered with little holes. He and Davis used to try to piss their parents off by poking little holes with their fingers into the foam after it had started drying out with age. Unconsciously, he reached up and shoved a new hole right above his head.

"Korin!" his dad yelled. "Knock that the fuck off! The ceiling is about to fall down as it is, and you're not helping matters."

Up front, Davis snickered.

Though it was just a little over an hour to the cabin, it was going to be a long ride.

The yelling woke Addy up. She had fallen asleep and slept through them getting into the car and starting on the trip. Sweat was dripping down her face, and she realized it was stuffy. The blankets had begun to suffocate her once the car heated up. She didn't know how far away the cabin was, but she hoped they were almost there.

The arguing continued. Davis was making fun of Korin, while Korin was shouting back at him to shut up. Addy's ears hurt. She didn't like the sound of the yelling. It made her sick to her stomach. Fighting and anger were bad. It was like something evil was trying to escape from people when they argued. Too much hate.

She placed her hands over her ears and tried to drown out the noise. Tears began to form in her eyes. Memories of her parents fighting came up. Her daddy telling Mama to calm down, and Mama screaming she was calm and telling Daddy what an idiot he was. Addy didn't like it when Mama attacked Daddy like that. It wasn't fair. If Tate were home, he would come into her bedroom and lie down on the floor next to her little bed. He was too big to crawl into it with her, but he would reach his hand out to her and stroke her hair, and start singing, "I see the moon, the moon sees me." That was a lullaby Daddy would sing to her when she was trying to fall as sleep. It was her favorite song and it always helped her to calm down. She would start to drift off to sleep as Tate sang to her, and when he noticed, he would kiss her on the head and whisper, "I'll keep you forever."

As the bickering continued, she knew she couldn't take much more. She didn't want to reveal that she had stowed away until they were at the cabin; by then she assumed they would be too far away to take her back. But the arguing was placing her on the verge of throwing up, and she didn't want to do that in the back of the Perrins' car.

"Guys, enough," Tate said. After being quiet all this time, he finally spoke up. "I can't believe you still fight like this."

"Shut it, Tate!" She knew that was Davis. "Don't stick your nose where it doesn't belong."

She was mad. Addy sat up and looked angrily at Davis. "Don't you dare tell my brother to shut up!"

The car lurched forward and Addy saw that they were slipping on some ice. Davis flew forward and hit his head on the dashboard. Mr. Perrin spun the steering wheel, trying to get the car righted. Everyone fell to the left, her brother slammed into the door, Korin fell over to his side and hit his head off Tate's shoulder. Addy managed to stay in place, wedged in between the duffel bags.

Davis righted himself, hand to his head, cursing under his breath and saying he was going to kill something. Mr. Perrin slapped him in the shoulder and said, "Knock it off." Then putting the car in park on the empty road, he turned in his seat to look at her. She tried to hunker down and hide behind the seat, but Tate was too quick. He reached over and picked her up, putting her down on the seat between him and Korin.

"Everybody okay?" Albert asked.

She nodded her head.

Albert then looked at her and narrowed his eyes. "What exactly do you think you are doing here, young lady?" he asked.

She looked up at her older brother, tears in her eyes. Her plan had failed, and she would have to be taken home to be left alone. She started to wail and leaned forward into her brother, her words completely incomprehensible.

"Oh my God, this is ridiculous," Davis said. He angrily kicked open his door and got out of the car.

"Davis!" Albert yelled. "Stop acting like an idiot. And don't do that to the car door; you know that the latch is already broken."

Tate pulled her in tight and stroked her hair, telling her it was okay. She didn't want to hear that and turned her head away from him, looking at Korin, who stared out the window at his brother as he paced angrily on the side of the road.

"You were in bed when I whispered goodbye from the doorway, how did you get into the car before us and without us seeing?" Tate asked his sister.

"That was a pillow under the blanket. I went to the car when you were in Davis's room," she said through her tears.

Tate groaned. "I knew I should have woken you instead of listening to Mrs. Perrin telling me to let you sleep."

Tate rubbed his hand on his face and sighed. To Addy, that was a sign that he was frustrated and she feared that now she'd been found, they would have to return to Rachet. She didn't want to be without her brother. She cried harder and tried to talk to Tate, but the words were not coming out right.

"What was that?" Mr. Perrin questioned Addy. She just looked at him, her shoulders heaving.

"She said she doesn't want to stay at home alone," Tate said.

Davis returned to the car without a word and slammed the door shut behind him.

Grimacing, Mr. Perrin asked, "Well, what does she want?"

"She wants to come with us."

Albert sighed. "I don't know. Maybe we should just head back."

"Korin can babysit her," Davis spoke up, a slight edge of humor to his voice. "The real men can hunt and do the repairs to the cabin while he stays indoors and is all domestic."

Addy didn't understand what Davis was saying, but he sounded funny. She giggled. Then looking to Korin, she asked, "Don't you kill things?"

"I don't get my kicks from taking a life," he said, punctuating the response with a tilt of his head in his brother's direction.

Davis turned to his brother in anger, but Mr. Perrin intervened, soothing the conversation by saying, "There's a CB in the cabin. I'll contact the ranger's office and have them call Natalie at home to let her know Addy is with us. That way we don't have to turn around."

He looked at everyone's faces for agreement. All seemed fine with it, except for Korin. Addy knew he wasn't happy she was going to be there, and that he would have to watch her. She didn't know him very well and wasn't excited about him watching her either.

Silence filled the car.

Korin stared out the window, boiling with anger that he was still suppressing, even at the age of twenty-two. He had nothing against Addy and knew she would be no trouble; he just didn't want to watch her. If he'd known he was going to have to babysit on this trip, he would have just stayed at Kelton. Babysitting would be better than helping his family work on the roof, but he was not going to find a single moment of quiet time to work on or think about his thesis.

In the reflection of the window, he could see Addy leaning against her brother, fast asleep. Tate, too, was asleep, snoring softly. Davis was looking straight ahead, and Korin didn't know if he was awake. Not as if he cared much either way.

The silence was momentarily satisfying as they traveled over the small bridge that spanned Bluff Creek. Within the next fifteen to twenty minutes, they would be turning onto Bluff Creek Road and then eventually the driveway to the hunting cabin.

"Davis?" Albert's voice pierced the silence, and Korin's thoughts. "Pour me a bit of coffee, would you? I want a sip before I get out of the car."

Silence.

"Davis?"

Korin felt the agitation seethe from his father's at Davis's immaturity. Albert reached over to the floor to grab the thermos, momentarily ducking his head below the dashboard. Korin sighed. His father was sometimes as immature as his brother. Did he really need to have coffee at this exact moment?

Korin looked ahead and saw a large black bear walking across the road.

"*Dad!*" Korin screamed.

His father slammed on the brakes. The car skidded on a patch of ice, and in an attempt to avoid the bear, Albert turned the steering wheel sharply to the left. The front fender of the car clipped the bear's hind-quarters, spinning the animal and smacking its head off the passenger side. The impact with the bear splashed blood all over Davis's window. The car continued to slide on the patch of ice until it caught the asphalt, catapulting forward.

Screams echoed throughout the car.

Tate reached over to hold on to Addy, who was not secured by a seat belt. Korin braced himself. Davis yelled "Fuck!" over and over again as Albert tried to regain control of the station wagon.

Before them was a mound of dirt that had been pushed to the side when the road was created. Instead of hauling the dirt off to a landfill, the Department of Transportation had just pushed it to the edge of the road, creating a serpentine hill that followed alongside the road for miles. They hit it head-on.

The car shot up the embankment and went airborne, grazing a tree off the driver's side. The passenger side tipped. Everything seemed to move in slow motion for Korin. Through the windshield, he saw nothing but sideways trees and snow-covered ground. Addy's high-pitched scream pierced his ears and the world thundered around him and faded into black.

CHAPTER NINETEEN

Maeve stared at the thin white lines of light that sneaked through her closed blinds. She felt unsettled again. The clock on her nightstand read 12:39 a.m., well after midnight.

Closing her eyes, she willed herself back to sleep. However, there was a soft noise coming from the other side of her dorm room that prevented her from nodding off. A sound that made her think of bread being torn apart. She sat up and squinted her eyes, trying to get them to adjust as she looked past the light filtering through her blinds. She couldn't see anything but her desk and a black mass next to it that she was pretty sure was her chair with a jacket thrown over it. Maybe the sound was coming from the other side of the wall, where the janitor's closet was located.

Throwing off her covers, Maeve got out of bed. Her feet touched the purple shag rug she had put on the floor to cover the cold linoleum. As she walked forward, static on the tendrils of the rug's fibers caught the hem of her long, light blue nightgown as though trying hold her back. She hiked up her nightgown slightly to stop the pulling.

She bumped into her chair as she reached her desk. It was slid under the desk and her jacket wasn't on it. Maeve looked to her right at the black mass and as she did, she clicked on her desk light.

Maeve jumped back with a screech. Korin sat huddled on the floor with his knees up to his chest, his back to her. His hair was shaggier and seemed longer than normal, and it swayed as he bobbed his head.

"Korin?" Maeve whispered, confused. She had watched him drive off to Rachet earlier that morning. How could he be here? And how could he have gotten into her room without her knowing?

He didn't hear her and continued to bob his head. The soft tearing sound was coming from him. He was doing something. Maeve took tentative steps to walk around to face him.

"Korin?" she said again, a little louder. This time his head snapped up and he glared at her. She gasped and took several steps back. While his left eye was covered by a long lock of hair, his right eye gleamed black. Solid black.

Maeve kept walking backwards and soon bumped into her bookshelf, upsetting a few books that were sitting on top of it. They fell to the ground with a thud, but neither Maeve nor Korin broke eye contact. He smacked his lips as he chewed, and that is when Maeve saw that his mouth was smeared with blood. She covered her mouth with her hands as she let out a scream. Korin was eating the flesh off of his right arm.

"Maaaeeeve." The sound of her name sounded like gravel in his mouth. He stood, letting his right arm drop slack. Rivulets of blood streamed down the chewed appendage, dripping onto the shag carpet. He raised his other hand out to her, fingers clawed. His eye burned with a black hellish fire. She couldn't move. She was frozen in place and couldn't get away.

His hand shot forward and he grabbed her by the neck. His fingers dug into her skin and it felt like stabbing ice.

"You don't . . . know me," Korin said, in the same rough voice that didn't sound like his own.

Maeve screamed and sat up in bed. She was freezing, as she'd kicked her blankets to the floor. Even so, her body was covered in sweat.

Wildly she grasped for the switch on her nightstand light. Clicking it on, she looked around the room. No one was here—Korin wasn't here.

She placed her hand on her chest and coaxed herself to slow her breathing.

What a nightmare.

There was a knock at her door and she jumped.

"Who is it?" her voice squeaked. She was afraid of who was on the other side.

"It's Anna, your RA," the muffled voice said from the other side of the door. "Are you okay? I heard screaming."

Maeve got up and made her way to the door, holding on to her neck. She swore she could still feel Korin's icy grip.

Unlocking the door and cracking it open a bit, she saw Anna standing there, concern etched across her face.

"I'm okay, really. Just had an awful nightmare," Maeve said.

"Oh, okay." Anna smiled. "Can you open your door and let me take a peek inside to make sure you're okay."

"To check that I'm alone?" Maeve asked.

Anna shrugged her shoulders. "Protocol."

Maeve stepped back and opened the door wide.

Anna came in and surveyed the room. She looked at the bed and the blankets that lay in a heap on the floor.

"Must have been one hell of a nightmare," Anna said.

Maeve, with her hand still clasped to her neck, swallowed hard and forced a smile.

"You have no idea."

CHAPTER TWENTY

When Korin came to, he and Tate were hanging upside down. Tate's long, meaty arms hung above his head, forearms resting on the ceiling. Korin undid his seat belt, landing on the roof of the car. Pain shot through his head and it took a moment for the stars to clear. Looking forward to the front of the car, he saw no one. Past the seats, through the windshield, the front end was smashed up against a tree trunk. Somehow when they landed, the car had rolled over. Korin couldn't remember.

He sat back and looked at Tate. His friend looked dead. Korin reached over and fumbled with Tate's seat belt, trying to unbuckle it against the weight the belt was holding up against gravity. When he finally managed to unbuckle it, Tate fell to the roof with a crunching thud. As he fell, his shoulder hit Korin on the head, causing Korin to black out again.

Korin woke to a sharp scream. He tried to open his eyes, but pain ripped through his left one. Gingerly, he raised his hand and touched it. It felt like a small apple was pushing through his eyelid. The pain was immeasurable. A crust of dirt or blood coated the skin on the left side of his face.

Through his right eye, he looked around the car. The contents from the back were scattered all over the inside of the roof. The windows were shattered, the dashboard smashed up into the front seat. Rough tree bark protruded in through the windshield. He was completely alone in the car.

He tried to sit up, the sharp scream continuing in his ears. He couldn't hear anything else over the screaming. Oh god, it was making his head hurt.

He surveyed the inside of the car again, looking for Addy to tell her to be quiet, but she wasn't in the car. No one was in the car.

Pushing through the pain, he sat up from where he lay, trying to avoid hitting his head off the backs of the car seats. One of the bags from the back lay partially on top of him, and he struggled to push the weight off. It was so heavy, and he was so angry. Once he was able to heave it off him, he punched it out of frustration. The bag moaned.

It was Tate.

Overcoming his pain, Korin rolled over, lightly prodding Tate. His flesh was cold.

Korin shifted again, feeling dirt, debris, and possibly glass cutting through his jeans and into his legs.

He had to get Tate out of the car. With the roof crunched, the doors would be difficult to open. His best bet would be to pull Tate out of the back window, but he had to clear a path first.

Korin slowly and painfully pushed duffel bags, rifles, and coolers out of the way. Any large pieces of glass that he could see, he threw off to the side. The back window had shattered, and shards of glass were still sticking out of the frame like thin knives.

He grabbed one of the blankets packed in the back of the car to use for protection as he grasped and pulled the pieces of glass out of the frame so he could more easily slide Tate through the opening.

The high-pitched screaming in his ear almost drowned out the growling. Something in his mind yelled for him to back up, which he did, just as a claw swiped through the window and narrowly missed tearing into his chest. He fell back, hitting his head off the back of the seats. Brilliant, white stars invaded his once-again-compromised vision, and he fell to his side, looking up at the bloodied face of a very angry bear.

Its muzzle dripped with blood and its eyes blazed with hate. It had its head leveled at the shattered window, but it was too large to fit through. All the bear could do was angrily swipe a claw at the inhabitants inside.

Korin watched in horror as the last swipe hit Tate's foot. He reached over, grabbing his friend's leg, and then rolled the rest of him to the center of the car. The bear, seeing its prey evade its efforts, bellowed. Tate shifted underneath him, and Korin knew he was not completely unconscious.

The world around him started to shake as the bear withdrew and stood on its hind legs with its front legs on the rear of the car. It started roaring and pushing on the vehicle, causing it to rock back to front. Korin and Tate slid back and forth on the roof in motion with the bear's assault. Then through the back window, Korin saw the bear land on all four feet and start to walk around to the passenger side of the car.

Korin slid himself between the bear and Tate, slowly pushing against his friend's body with his back, toward the driver's side of the car. The bloody muzzle of the bear appeared again, followed by its narrowed eyes. At this range, it could reach the halfway point of the car and would most likely be able to reach Korin's body.

The bear roared one more defiant cry before the attack. Just as the right paw was lowered to shoot through the window opening, above the din of the ringing in his ears, Korin heard a voice yell out.

"Here! Here! Come get me!!"

It was his father.

The bear pulled back, and Korin leaned forward, looking out past the bear. He could barely make out his father against the trees, but the bear saw him clearly. Albert had successfully grabbed the bear's attention. The beast turned and looked at him, roaring its defiance. With one last "Come and get me" to the advancing bear, Albert Perrin turned and ran away.

Korin looked on helplessly as his father disappeared into the forest with the bear hot on his trail. For several moments he stared at the bloodied prints of the bear leading away from the car. The adrenaline once more surged through his body, and he realized he had to get himself and Tate out of the car.

Turning back to Tate, Korin met his eyes. They were finally open, and he was staring at Korin in silence.

"We have to help my dad!" Korin yelled.

"I don't think I can move very far," Tate said weakly. "You go ahead— go after your dad and come back for me later."

"Your sister is out there, too," Korin said, crawling to the back of the car. "You'll have to try to help her, if you can."

Korin watched as Tate's face crumbled in despair.

"I forgot about her," he sobbed. "How could I have forgotten about her?"

Korin had already slid out through the back window and was following the bear's tracks into the woods. His father was his priority. Addy was Tate's.

As Korin ran into the forest he could hear Tate calling Addy's name.

The rain had stopped, but between that and the sun just beginning to peek over the horizon, the snow from the prior night's snowfall started to melt. The bloody tracks from the bear and his father's occasional footprints were becoming harder to track. Korin felt like he had been wandering for hours. When there was a gap between prints, Korin feared he would never be able to pick up the trail again. These woods were endless, and his father and the monstrous creature could be anywhere. Even though the screeching in his ears had subsided to a low ringing, he couldn't hear anything in the forest except for the breeze that swayed the creaking trees.

What was he going to do when he found his father and the bear? What if the bear was attacking his father? What *could* he do? Korin cursed himself for not grabbing one of the .22s out of the car, even though he knew that it wouldn't have much effect on the bear, other than making it more pissed off. He was so confused. He had no idea what to do other than charge forward with determination to find his father.

"Dad!" he yelled out into the stillness. A sharp blinding pain ripped through his face, and he fell to his knees, clutching his forehead to his hand. His left eye seethed and burned, stabbing hot needles into his brain. He had no idea what was wrong with it or what it looked like, but one thing was for sure—it hurt like hell.

Something sounded far off to his right, but he couldn't place the sound. It was something like a scream, but it was sharply cut off. He turned his attention to that area and changed his course to the right. Puffs of his breath rose and briefly clouded the remaining vision out of his right eye. He was moving fast, not running, but walking at a quick pace. He kept straight on the trajectory of where he believed the sound had come from, adrenaline allowing him to ignore the pain in his eye for a bit, until he came to a creek and stopped.

He had no idea where he was.

"Damn idiot!" He cursed himself. His brain was scattered, his thoughts incoherent. He was standing on the bank of what he believed to be Bluff Creek. The creek was about fifteen miles long. He could be at any point along it.

In a panic, he turned right and walked along the bank, his brain becoming more frazzled. He wasn't thinking clearly, his mind jumping from his dad to Tate, from Addy to the bear. He had to find them— save them.

Suddenly he stopped.

"Oh my God," he said, raising his hand to his mouth. "I forgot about Davis." *The last person on earth I want to help*, Korin admitted to himself.

He was continuing his search along the creek bank when he heard a cough behind him that made him jump. He turned around.

Silence and trees.

"Dad?"

No reply. He was completely alone. His imagination was playing tricks on him.

A weariness started to take over, and his body began to sway. Korin ate no breakfast and only drank half of his cup of coffee. His stomach growled with hunger. And anger. His father's stupidity and stubbornness always caused issues. This accident was his and Davis's fault. Maybe he shouldn't even try to find his father.

"Maybe I shouldn't even try to find any of you," Korin yelled and kicked at a fallen branch at his feet. "Maybe I should just go off into the woods and live a life there. As if any of you would care if I disappeared!"

He knew no one was around to hear him, but it felt good to vent. Running away would be better than ever having to deal with his family again. Plus, he wouldn't have to worry about writing his thesis.

An anger boiled in him he had not felt since he was a child. Pursing his lips, he drew in a slow breath to calm himself. He teetered on the edge of falling out of control as the thought of his father, Davis, and Tate succumbing to the elements swarmed through his head. An image of their dead bodies on their backs with blank hollow eyes blindly focused on the sky gave Korin a jolt of excitement. He could live in the cabin and not have to hunt for food for some time given the amount of fresh meat he'd have. And he'd be alone.

But someone would come looking for them.

Korin's hands shook as he pressed them to his chest distract the growing tension under his ribs and growing hunger in his stomach.

Once settled and clear of dark thoughts, he resumed his search for his father.

Amanda Headlee

CHAPTER TWENTY-ONE

Tate sat in intense pain with his back against the passenger-side door. He was not able to go far to search for Addy. Climbing out of the wrecked station wagon had been agonizing enough. He'd had to drag his body across broken glass and other debris, with the pain in his upper right arm so excruciating, he couldn't even move it. He could see that his shirt around his bicep was wet with blood, and he feared a compound fracture. Balancing on his left arm and knees, he made his way across the roof of the car.

Tate Michelson was a very large man. He was not fat, but tall and muscular. He was going to have to squeeze himself through the back window. Luckily for him, Korin had cleared away most of the glass shards. The remaining pieces that would have caught on his clothing he was able to gingerly remove with his fingers, plucking them out of the frame and discarding them behind him. He didn't want the surprise of landing on one because of his own stupidity.

Once the window frame was clear, he slid on his belly out through the window, carefully dragging his right arm. He had to suck in his ribs and force his way through. Pain shot through his chest. He definitely had some broken ribs as well. Not letting it deter him, he continued moving through. The fabric of his Carhartt jacket made tearing sounds as it tore on the small pieces of glass that he'd missed in the window.

Once his upper body was out, Tate rolled to his left side so he could hold on to his right arm, better controlling it the rest of the way. He didn't want his right hand getting cut on any rogue piece of glass.

As he pushed himself out of the window, he rolled to his back and sat up so he could scoot the rest of the way out while keeping his arm stable. Suddenly his right foot caught on something and his leg came down on a piece of glass that he had missed. He gasped as the shard pierced his calf. However, he didn't panic; instead, he slowly lifted his leg straight up. The glass stayed in place as bright red blood flowed freely from the hole punctured in the back of his calf. Tate kept his calm and pain in check as he continued to push his way out the window.

It was Davis's Marlin Model 60 rifle's strap that had caught on Tate's right foot, and it followed him through the rest of the window. He untangled his foot from the strap and grabbed one of the duffel bags near the back window. Opening it one-handed, he found a flannel shirt lying right on top. He pulled it out and managed to tie it around his calf in an attempt to stop the blood flow. He tucked the hand of his useless right arm in between the buttons of his jacket to keep his arm from swinging freely around. He pulled out another flannel shirt from the bag and tried to tie his arm to his body. With only one hand, it was impossible. Keeping his right hand tucked inside his jacket was all he could do for now.

Leaning forward, he grabbed Davis's rifle. It had a magazine attached. Placing the muzzle between his legs, he opened the chamber. A round was loaded. Fucking bastard had a loaded gun sitting in the back of the car with his sister probably lying right next to it! Mr. Perrin's number-one rule was to never have a loaded gun in the car or leave a loaded gun unattended.

Tate allowed the anger to flow through him. He loved Davis like his own brother. His friend had a side to him that he never shared with anyone else. Tate saw it on a few occasions, and he knew goodness existed in him. For some reason, the idiot always had to keep up that greedy, selfish, tough-guy exterior. Tate had spent his life trying to figure out why. What was Davis protecting or trying to keep hidden? He would never understand his friend. It was as if Davis never wanted anyone to get close to him. Like he was trying to keep his true self a secret.

When they were in school, a lot of people had called him an ogre behind his back. Part of that was from a physical appearance aspect, given the grotesque burns on his right arm and hand. The other aspect of the name came from the fact that Davis always got what he wanted— despite what he had to do to get it. If someone had something Davis wanted and they didn't hand it over to him, he'd beat the crap out of that person and take it. He bullied people into giving him exactly what he wanted, when he wanted it.

Sadly, Davis was delusional. He thought he was the most popular kid at school because he had the whole class giving in to his every whim. However, Tate knew the truth. He was Davis's only friend.

And he would always remain his friend. It was his duty to coax the goodness out of Davis.

The school bell rang. Tate and Davis slowly made their way to their high school's front door. They were going to be late but didn't care. No one at this school would care either. The teachers did just enough of their job to get paid. The students only did the bare minimum required of them. If a student failed, the teacher didn't feel that they themselves were responsible for it. The student hadn't tried hard enough. The class bell was more of an idle threat than anything else.

However, some students, like Korin, took it seriously. They would always laugh at him behind his back as he ran like a scared chicken to class at the ring of the tardy bell.

On this day they weren't laughing at Korin, but at a little freshman girl who wasn't paying attention to where she was going and tripped on a raised part of the sidewalk. She went sprawling and the books she was carrying flew out in front of her. Tate burst out laughing upon her impact. The look on her face was the funniest thing he'd seen all day, though he did feel bad that she'd tripped.

Davis started to laugh with him, but then stopped. He looked at her with serious intent. Her blonde hair was splayed all over her back and shoulders and she was sobbing softly. Little trembles wracked her body.

Davis punched Tate in the arm. "Knock it off." He walked over to her and picked up her biology textbook, then chemistry and algebra. Then Tate saw something that he'd never expected Davis to do. His friend knelt and touched her hand. "Are you okay?" he asked.

Tate watched in awe.

The girl looked up at him and panic washed over her face when she recognized who was talking to her. She quickly climbed to her feet.

"I am sorry. I am so, so sorry," she said over and over.

"Shut up and take your books," Davis said, pushing them at her chest. "And stop rushing to class. That tardy bell is worthless anyway."

He turned and walked away from her, shoving his hands into the pockets of his leather jacket.

"Let's go," he said to Tate, and headed for the path that led home.

Apparently he was going to play hooky today. Tate had no problem tagging along. He had just witnessed something he'd never thought he'd see: an act of kindness from Davis Perrin.

After unloading it, Tate placed the butt of the gun on the ground and with his left side, used it as a crutch to help himself get up off the ground. All he could think about was Addy. His baby sister was out there with that bear roaming around and he had to save her.

"Addy . . . *Addy!*" he yelled as loud as his vocal cords would permit, causing his voice to break. Leaning over gently to his right leg, he found that he could support some weight on it. He would be limping, and it hurt like hell. His whole right side hurt like hell. A compound fracture in his arm, broken ribs, and a hole in his calf. What a mess. He prayed that everyone else had fared better.

From what he'd been able to see of Korin's face, the guy had to be hurting, too. His entire left eye was bulging out of his face, and there was a huge gash above it. Blood covered his hairline and streaked down across his eye and face.

Tate prayed his own face wasn't as banged up. He was too afraid to prod around to find out. His arm grossed him out enough.

Addy.

He needed to stop wasting time lamenting over his injuries and go and find his sister. He wasn't making it very far. He limped around to the driver side of the car and collapsed against the door. He was plain out of energy. If he just rested here by the door for a moment, he would regain some strength.

CHAPTER TWENTY-TWO

Davis found Tate slumped against the driver's side door of the car.

He had heard the calls for Addy, which had pulled him out of the dark miasma he'd been in. He'd woken to find himself lying on the ground, staring up at a lit morning sky. Dizziness washed over him as he sat up. He bent his head toward his lap, trying to clear the nausea. Head trauma. He was certain he had some form of head trauma, if not a concussion.

Slowly Davis brought his hands to his head and began to palpate his skull and neck, listening for sounds of crepitus, or whether he felt any pain. Nothing. He tenderly pushed his finger pads against his forehead, around the orbital bones and across his zygomatic arches. Nothing shifted, but there was a dull pain across the left arch and around to the brow.

He breathed a sigh of relief and was thankful of the effort he put into to become an EMT. While he enjoyed using his skills to help others, the time invested was finally going to pay off for him... and to an extent his family. If he was this beat up, surely others were as well.

Davis was certain nothing was broken, but he definitely had some bruising. His father and that fucking car. The passenger-side door's latch had been broken for some time. While it still held shut, if it was hit from the inside with force, it would pop open, and that's just what had happened with Davis. As the car turned over, his body had slammed into the door, popping it open, and he'd slipped out. He didn't remember landing, but taking his injuries into account, it seemed that his right side had absorbed the brunt of the impact, the worst of it a purple bruise blooming on his hip that he found when he'd pulled his pants down to inspect his legs. All in all it could have been worse for him. When he saw Tate and the wreckage of the car, he knew that had he been wearing his seat belt and stayed strapped in the car, he most certainly would have been killed.

He took a closer look at Tate, still leaning against the car. The sleeve of his light brown jacket was stained dark red with blood. He had his hand tucked in his pocket and a flannel shirt wrapped around his lower right leg. Bruises already showed on his face, and Davis worried about head trauma. At Tate's side lay Davis's gun. Tate must have brought it with him as he'd crawled out of the car.

Keeping his eye on the gun, he nudged Tate's left foot with the toe of his boot.

"Hey," he said softly.

Tate's eyes snapped open, and he reached for the gun.

"Whoa, whoa, buddy. It's me," he said, backing away from Tate.

"Davis?" Tate looked at him, confused. He seemed lost, like he'd forgotten where they were. Then his eyes widened as he remembered. "Addy?"

Davis shook his head. With guilt, he admitted, "You are the first I have come across."

"Your dad?"

Davis shook his head.

"God, I hope he is okay. Korin chased after him."

"What do you mean?"

"The bear. It isn't dead. It came back to the car and tried to attack us. Your dad used himself as bait—" He coughed.

Davis leaned forward to put his hand on his friend's shoulder, but Tate pulled away.

"The bear chased him into the woods."

"Oh fuck." Davis let out a long exhalation and turned from Tate to look in the woods. He strained his ears to see if he could catch any sound of yelling. Nothing.

Tate moaned and braced himself against the car, trying to use it as support.

Davis tried to put his hands under Tate's armpits to lift him up.

"Don't touch me," Tate snapped. "This is all your fault."

Davis jumped back and put his hands up defensively. Tate's anger sort of scared him. In all the years that he'd known Tate, he could count on one hand the number of times he'd ever seen him angry. Davis knew that deep down, there was a beast inside of Tate, and when it came to the welfare of his sister, the beast could start to rage. He knew Tate didn't really mean it. It was an accident. Sure, in hindsight, he should have just handed his father the thermos. It wouldn't have killed him to do something for his father for once. Yet there was still an underlying layer of distrust that stirred within him for his father. It made Davis continue to do things just to annoy his father.

Davis knew that Tate's reaction wasn't prompted by just anger or worry over the disappearance of his sister. It was pain.

"Before we do anything, let's take a look at your arm," Davis said calmly, slowly moving to unbutton his friend's bloody jacket. He suppressed his mixed feelings toward his father and focused on Tate.

If the damage wasn't cleaned up, there was a risk of infection, or worse. He didn't want to take any chances, and urged his friend to calm down. Rage still boiled in Tate's eyes, and Davis figured that had he not been so injured, he might have knocked him out, just to control him. "Look," he started slowly.

He watched Tate's face distort into something inhuman.

"Your arm and leg need to be patched up."

Tate's face didn't change.

"Give me twenty minutes. You and I need to be okay before we can try to help anyone else."

This realization overcame Tate. His eyes drifted to the ground in embarrassment. He never acted out like this. The thought of Addy being lost in the woods must have really terrified him.

"What time is it?"

Davis looked at his watch, "It's a little after ten-thirty."

Tate began to suck in his breath and exhale quickly. Davis placed his hand on his friend's cheek and looked him in the eyes and slowed his own breathing to get his friend to stop hyperventilating. It worked.

"We must have wrecked at..." Tate's voice waivered. "At like six?"

Davis didn't reply because he couldn't remember what time they left the house.

"She's been out there alone for like two and a half hours." Tate shifted as though he was going to try to stand up and Davis put his hand on his chest to hold him down. Tate's eyes blazed as he looked at him.

"We fix you first, Tate."

Tate had his arm tucked in his pocket and Davis surmised it must be broken. He didn't know how much longer Tate would be comfortable with his hand only supported in this way. Sensing that Tate had finally calmed down a bit, he turned his attention to the contents of the car that lay scattered about. His dad had some medical supplies stashed away in the vehicle which Davis enhanced with items left over from the ambulance corps, making it more advanced than the typical first-aid kit. With the type of work that he did, Albert Perrin always had to be prepared for the worst.

Now Davis dreaded that the medical supplies were stashed in the car amid pieces of broken glass and piercing metal. His head throbbed at the thought of having to climb back in. He looked through the broken back window and saw the medium-sized blue nylon bag that contained the first-aid kit. He smiled as he thanked whatever deity was listening. The bag was intact and close enough for him to just reach in and grab it.

"Dude," Davis said, coming back around the other side of the car holding the bag triumphantly over his head, "I didn't have to climb into the car!"

Small pearls of sweat dripped down Tate's face as he looked up at Davis.

Davis could tell by Tate's pallor that he was going into shock. He needed help, and soon.

Davis knelt down next to Tate. "Just sit very still and let me do all the work," he instructed. Would Tate make it through the next twenty minutes? He was looking bad. How the hell was he going to access his arm? If he pulled Tate's sleeve down, he risked causing more damage. If he cut the jacket, it would expose Tate to the cold, plus there was a risk that he might cut into the wound.

He raised his hand to rub above his left eye. A sharp searing pain shot through him.

"Your face is pretty fucked up," Tate said groggily. "Nice bruise over your forehead. Injured in the same spot as Korin, but he's a little worse off. I think he lost his left eye." His voice trailed off. The adrenaline surge from the fear over his sister's safety was wearing off.

An uncommon feeling of relief spread through Davis as Tate mentioned Korin's name, followed immediately by horror. His brother may have lost his eye.

Davis looked down at his scarred hand and thought how this accident had given him a chance to get even with his brother—for Korin to know the type of pain he himself had suffered after the fire.

He shook away these disturbing thoughts. Korin was still alive. That's all that mattered.

Looking at the supplies, Davis realized he had to ration them properly, so he'd have enough left over to assist his brother. He didn't know what condition his father and Addy were in, either. Right now he needed to move fast with Tate, decisively using the tools he had, while trying to save back some supplies for the others. Without any pain medication at his disposal, he knew he needed to find a way for Tate to be pumped up with his own body's natural narcotics.

"Dude, fall asleep and I am leaving your ass here. I'll find Addy on my own."

Tate's eyes snapped open, glaring. There it was. The surge was in full swing.

"I am cutting off your sleeve. It's the only way I can get to the wound," Davis explained. "I will find a blanket to wrap you in so that you won't get cold."

Tate was silent, simmering in rage.

Opening his dad's medical bag, Davis found a pair of trauma shears, the perfect tool to cut away the jacket.

"Now I need you to pull your hand from your jacket and hold your forearm tight against your belly. I need to start cutting up your sleeve."

Davis was fairly sure Tate had a compound fracture. He prayed that the amount of blood was worse than the actual damage. He briefly considered whether there might be any damage to the brachial artery, but then rejected it. Had that happened, Tate would have most likely bled out by now.

Davis clutched the trauma shears in his scarred right hand and opened them wide as he moved in toward the cuff of Tate's jacket. A lump formed in his throat as he mentally told his hand, *Keep steady—keep steady*. Any other patient, he would have had the sleeve cut off in no time, despite the difficulties he had in maneuvering the shears at times. Patients were just bodies to him. But Tate was family; a brother. He needed to be more cautious. Plus, being stranded meant there was no room for error, which is why he didn't even attempt to cut using his left non-dominant hand, despite it having more dexterity.

The usual curse went through his head: that he had never taught himself to be ambidextrous. Instead he'd chosen the easier path—laziness, hidden behind his trauma.

If only he could do his life over again. He wouldn't have hidden behind his anger and apathy. It was a thought he'd had several times during his life, but he'd never experienced such a strong desire to be something more until now.

He met Tate's eyes. His friend was handing over the fate of his arm to him. Davis could not let him down.

The first snip easily cut through the cuff. The next snip into the actual jacket material proved to be much more difficult. Davis tried his best to maintain a steady hand, but with each sharp breath that Tate drew, Davis knew time was not on his side. They moved in coordination together, Tate maintaining his hold on his lower forearm as Davis gently continued cutting up the sleeve, the pain hovering over both of their heads, reminding them it was only going to get worse.

The tip of the shears reached the edge of the bloodstain. Beads of perspiration formed on Tate's face despite the cold. Pain twitched on his lips as he lowered his forearm, straightening a path for Davis to cut. Davis made smaller snips with the shears, as he was unsure where the actual damage was located. The last thing he wanted to do was cut into Tate. Even though the whole ordeal felt like hours, it had only been a few minutes. The shears passed through the remainder of Tate's sleeve without any problem.

Now the true test was about to begin. What stood before Davis was something he dreaded seeing. Bile rose in the back of his throat and he fought to keep his stomach contents in place. The white of the bone glistened against pulpy red. Blood seeped from the gaping wound from the humerus that had jaggedly torn through Tate's bicep when the bone snapped in half. His right arm was hanging on by thin strands of muscle and sinew and fat.

Davis, who could normally stand looking at gore, had to force himself to look at the injury. He'd never had to work on a friend or family member before; it was definitely harder, as people always said. Shoving his emotions to the dark place he tended to keep them in order to keep a level head, he leaned his face in closer to the injury. He had to make sure there were no foreign objects embedded in the flesh that might hasten infection. Bits of lint from Tate's jacket clung to the exposed muscle. After putting on a pair of latex gloves from the medical bag, Davis began to lightly pick out the cloth fibers with tweezers he found in a Ziploc bag. He knew they were sterile, as he'd packed them himself.

Tate cringed in pain the moment the tweezers touched his exposed flesh.

Davis turned his head and vomited. He couldn't keep it down any longer. He couldn't meet Tate's eyes when he returned his focus to Tate's arm. Never in his life had he gotten sick over someone's injury. Hell, he'd even been first on the scene to a partial decapitation by chain saw. One of his father's crewmen had hit a knot in a tree and the chain saw had kicked out of the trunk. With the blade still moving—because the stupid operator did not let go of the trigger—he'd made contact with another stupid crewman who happened to be standing too close. The chain saw had cut across the top of his shoulder and halfway through his neck before the operator had released the trigger.

Davis had just been returning from a medical transport with a medic in the rig when the tones dropped, an incoming emergency call. They were only about five miles away. Not that it mattered. The guy was most likely dead in five minutes.

The medic had allowed Davis to do the first assessment, and then he'd followed up with a confirmation before calling it in as essentially a DOA. Police were already en route from the first dispatch, but the coroner had to be dispatched with a second call.

The viscera was something that he had never seen before, enhanced due to the unwieldy spinning blade of the chain saw flinging blood and flesh farther around the area. It was a scene out of a horror movie, and Davis was entranced by it all. He didn't know the guy. The man was just a body, despite his father standing several yards away bawling his eyes out because he'd just lost a member of his team. Davis didn't care for the emotional part. He was more interested in the scientific aspect of the situation. And the devastation.

Yet, here with Tate, it was the opposite. Davis was acting like his father had that day at the job site, his emotions threatening to spill over, while the rational side of him was keeping the tears dammed up, because if he lost it and started crying, Tate would certainly die.

Regaining his composure, he returned his attention to Tate and continued picking out the fibers. Only so much could be done, but every little fiber removed would help. Irrigation would help the most, and he did have a bottle of sterile water in the medical bag. It had expired well over a year ago, which meant it could contain some trace bacteria. And with the cold weather, there was no way to irrigate the wound without soaking Tate's clothing.

He decided against it and prayed he hadn't just made a huge mistake.

There were four large rolls of sterile gauze in the bag, along with two triangle shaped linen cravats to immobilize Tate's arm. Davis lightly dressed the compound fracture, making it tight enough to support the arm. He didn't want to set it. Davis grimaced; he wasn't a doctor or a surgeon with knowledge on how to properly set bones.

Tate helped Davis hold his arm at a ninety-degree angle as Davis secured the arm in a sling, using the cravat. Tate's face was white and covered in a sheen of sweat, catching the rays of the sun peeking through the trees. His lips were starting to turn the same color.

Davis wrapped the second cravat around Tate's girth, under his left arm and over his right elbow, knowing that the gauze should keep his arm from swinging outward.

The wound on Tate's calf was less stomach-churning. Davis removed the bloodied flannel, cut open his jeans, and searched the wound for any more glass shards. As he prodded the flesh with a gloved hand, Tate's calf twitched. He should have been calling out in pain, but the injury to his arm had wiped the energy from him. All Tate could do was feel and accept the pain. Any reaction to it was an involuntary reflex of muscles and nerves.

The second roll of gauze was used on Tate's leg.

Davis felt the cold after his own adrenaline rush had subsided. The warmth of a fire was needed. It would most likely only reach thirty-five degrees Fahrenheit today. Tate would die without the warmth, especially since he was on the verge of shock.

Their packed clothing would do well to start a fire, and there were plenty of branches nearby. Hopefully it would last long enough to keep them warm until Davis could figure out what to do next.

In his dad's medical kit he was surprised to find a lighter. Davis went back to the car and pulled out his own backpack and duffel bag. Tate had already pulled out his dad's earlier. Korin and Tate's bags were nowhere to be found. They had been the last bags placed in the rear of the car and had probably been ejected during the crash.

Tate was in a deep slumber near the fire, which Davis had built into a nice blaze. He slept soundly and his breathing was rhythmic.

Davis crawled over the serpentine embankment that stretched as far as the eye could see and made his way up the road. He saw a patch of blood and pieces of metal and glass from the car. That damn bear should have known better than to stand in the middle of the road.

A clear path was carved through the edge of the forest. The flying, turning car had torn off the tops of the little saplings that grew near the road. When it landed the car had scarred the ground as it slid to the base of a mighty oak tree that blocked the car from continuing any further. The forest floor was littered with metal, glass, branches, and the occasional object that had fallen out of the car.

He walked down the mound and back toward Tate and the fire, which needed to be stoked. Along the way, he found no prints or trace of which direction Addy, his brother, or his father could have headed. The morning sun took care of whatever snow remained and if there were any tracks on forest floor, they were indistinguishable to him. The debris of leaves and dead ferns from the Autumn covered what could have been mud made by the melting snow and rain. Davis only had a vague idea of the direction Korin might have taken, based on Tate's memory, which his friend admitted was pretty fuzzy.

It was as if Davis's family had slipped from the car and disappeared out of existence.

CHAPTER TWENTY-THREE

Addy had never seen a bear in person before, and it scared her that the car had hit it. The blood on the windows scared her. Tate tried to hold on to her, but the car was like a roller coaster. Burying her face into his body, she had kept her eyes shut tight until the ride was over.

Addy had felt no pain except for when she'd landed on the upside-down roof. Her face had hit first, causing pain to shoot all through her head. She touched the top of her lip where it felt wet. On her fingertips was blood. There was blood running down her face and dripping onto her jacket. Tate had once helped her with a bloody nose that she got after running face-first into a closed glass door. He'd laid her on her back and put a towel on her nose. She didn't have a towel now, but she lay back on the roof of the car, putting her scarf to her nose. More pain shot through her face and head as she touched her nose. She opened her eyes once the pain had subsided, looked up, and screamed.

Tate was hanging from his seat, suspended by his seat belt, not moving. He was dead. Then she saw Korin hanging next to her brother. He was dead, too, and his face was bloody. She cried for her dad, but then she remembered he couldn't help her because he was dead as well.

Fearing that Tate's and Korin's ghosts would come for her, she carefully climbed out of Davis's window. More tears fell from her face when bits of glass cut into the flesh of her hands. As she climbed through the shattered window, her snow pants tore through to her knee and a glass shard drew blood. It stung.

Once outside of the car, she ran into the dark woods. Away from her dead brother and Korin. Tears blurred her vision and she didn't see the tree branch on the ground. She tripped and rolled across the forest floor, hitting her head on a rock. Her jacket became wet from the ground and her scarf fell away from her face. She lay there staring up into the trees, crying, hurting, and sad. And then everything faded to black for Addy.

When she woke, it was lighter out and the woods were not as dark. Addy's body ached and pain throbbed in her head. She wiped away what she thought was hair on her face, only to pull her hand away to find her fingers covered with blood.

"Tate. Daddy," she said, her small voice trembling. Sobs and the cold wracked her body. She didn't want to be here, injured in the woods. She wanted to be home. With Tate. A wail escaped her lips and echoed off the trees. Addy did not think she would ever stop crying.

"Get up and stop crying. It's annoying," a voice said.

Addy screamed and sat up, scared because for a moment she thought it was a ghost, until she realized it was a living, breathing Korin that stood in front of her.

There was an ugly gash above his left eye, and the eye itself was closed. It puffed out of his face like a chameleon's. Korin held his left side with his right arm. He was alive. Maybe Tate was alive too!

"Where's Tate?" she asked.

Korin looked around and muttered, "somewhere, maybe he's still alive".

"You don't know?"

"I got turned around in the woods. He was barely alive when I left him," he snapped at her. "Just get up and be quiet."

Tears streamed down her face, mixing with the blood that dripped from her now. She sniffled, trying to subdue another wail.

"Sorry. My head hurts," he said, more softly this time. "Please get up."

Addy looked him in the eye and stood.

Korin bent down and looked at her face. He untied the scarf around her neck, found an unbloodied part, and put that up to her nose. She winced in pain, and he lessened the pressure. Then he grabbed her hand and put it up to the scarf. She knew he meant for her to hold it in place.

He stood, turned, and started walking.

"Are we going home?" she asked, her voice muffled by the scarf.

He ignored her and kept his pace.

Biting her lip against the pain that she felt on her face, hands, and knee, and burying the thoughts of her brother, she followed Korin deeper into the forest.

A shiver woke Davis. He sat up with a gasp. He had passed out. He'd been having a violent nightmare of his father being eaten alive by the bear. The fire had burned out and the full effect of the winter bit hard into his bones. He needed to get the fire relit. However, Tate needed attention first.

Davis crawled over to Tate and lightly touched his uninjured shoulder. Although his blue eyes were open, glassy and cold, there was no response. Davis felt his heart pound.

"Oh, Tate," he said with sadness as he raised his hand to his friend's face. He couldn't look at Tate's open, dead eyes.

"What?" Tate asked.

Davis jumped, his heart leaping into his throat. "I thought you were dead!"

"Oh," Tate said. "I was just thinking about Addy and must have dozed off."

Davis said nothing in reply. He didn't know how to address the fact that Addy was still missing. Along with his father and Korin.

"How is your arm?" he asked.

"It hurts," Tate said.

"Let me look at it."

Tate slowly pulled off the layers of clothing to expose his bandaged arm. The linens were soaked through with blood. Luckily, it had all frozen and most likely clotted. Davis didn't want to remove any of the existing bandages for fear of pulling apart the clots.

From the medical kit, he pulled another roll of sterile gauze. He undid one of the cravats and wrapped the fresh gauze over the soiled bandage. Even though Davis was trying to touch Tate very gently, the slightest pressure made his friend wince in pain. He didn't need to ask how he was doing.

"Okay, man, you are all set," Davis said, helping Tate to a seated position.

Earlier, he had found a bowl in the car. He'd scooped snow into it and set it near the fire. When the fire had gone out, the melted water had started to freeze. Luckily it was only partially frozen, so that meant the fire had only been out for an hour or so. However, that had Daivis worried. It was supposed to get warmer throughout the day. The water in the bowl starting to freeze meant it was getting colder. Looking to the sky, the color deflated him. It was hazy and overcast, the sun completely covered. He prayed that didn't mean rain or snow was on its way.

From his pocket, he pulled out a tattered bag of granola. Handing the bag along with the partially frozen water to Tate, he said, "I need to get this fire going to keep you warm while I go out to search."

"No," Tate said.

"What? Why?"

"Because you are in no shape to walk around these woods alone. And I am in no shape to sit here any longer," Tate replied, without any emotion behind his voice. "We need to get to the cabin and call for help on the CB. We're not doing anyone any good by staying here. I have faith we'll find Addy along the way."

Davis said nothing in reply as he once more looked up through the tree canopy to the sky. In his bones he could feel that bad weather was advancing. He was annoyed with Tate for making the suggestion, but knew that he was right. They needed to be safe themselves first in order to be able to truly help.

Davis estimated that the car had flown and then slid about fifty yards from the embankment. It was pure luck that there hadn't been any large trees closer to the road that would have stopped the car sooner. They might have all died if the car had slammed full force into a tree.

He looked at his watch. The face was shattered, but it still worked. Nearly noon.

Davis walked around the crash site and collected all the duffel bags that he could find, which was unfortunately just his and his father's plus his backpack. The other bags were still missing, probably fell out of the car somewhere when they wrecked, and he wasn't about to go wandering around to look for them. Dumping out the contents of the bags, he found that he and his father packed the same. As they were both well suited for the cold, and because they were just trapping not actually hunting game like deer, their bags only contained what was minimally needed for this trip: a thermal base layer set, underwear, wool socks, a pair of thicker canvas-like pants they'd wear while trapping, a pair of jeans, and a couple of t-shirts and sweatshirts.

Despite the gravity of the situation, Davis found himself chuckling at the fact that he and his father think exactly alike when it comes to packing for a trip. If only he knew where Korin and Tate's bags were, they surely would have clothing much better suited for colder weather. Tate lived by the boy scout code to always be prepared. And Korin, well, he was a baby.

He took one of the now-empty duffel bags and re-packed it with the food from the cooler. He left the eggs and milk, but took the Tupperware of his mother's chili, and the tin of his mother's chocolate chip cookies. He looked at the cheese but thought otherwise; he hated the stuff. But thinking of Tate, he ended up grabbing the orange-colored slices, adding them into the duffel bag. In his backpack, he would put a loaf of bread, crackers, and his father's beef jerky. He also found the thermos that his father had been reaching for right before they'd wrecked. It was full. He opened it and smelled the coffee. He was so thirsty. He took a sip and found it lukewarm. Putting the cap back on, he put it into his backpack.

There was a pop of wood at the fire. One of the damp branches he'd found and thrown on the fire was starting to burn. Out of the car, he cut off material from the seat cushions then collected the thinner clothes, like t-shirts and underwear, to burn. Most of the kindling and wood that he found was damp or quite wet. As the fire burned with the items from the car, he set the driest wood next to the fire to help further dry it out. While the fire started to work itself into a blaze, Davis added most of the warmer clothing that he found into the duffle bag with the food. In his own pact, he put in a base layer set and sweatshirt. There were a couple of blankets in the car. One went into his pack and covered Tate with the other two. The food he placed at the top of his backpack.

When he looked at Tate, he saw that his friend was asleep again. He was in no condition to move, and Davis had no idea how far away from the cabin they really were. He thought he remembered someone in the car saying they were almost there, right before the crash, but he didn't know for sure. He should have a better idea of this, since he went to the cabin several times a year, but his brain was a fog at the moment when it came to spatial reasoning.

He knew if he found the creek and followed the bank to the right, it would lead him to the dirt road to the cabin. He could cross the old wooden bridge and then follow the road right to the cabin. All he had to do was head north and he'd run into the creek.

While going back to the main road and following that to Bluff Creek Road was the surest way to not get lost, he knew there would be less of a chance of running into his family. If he stuck to the woods, he had a better chance of finding a trace of someone.

And hopefully they would still be alive.

He had to go now. He couldn't wait for Tate to wake up. Davis felt guilty, but he couldn't wait for Tate to wake. Besides, there's no way he could physically move Tate given both of their injuries. He knew he shouldn't leave his friend, but he also knew he couldn't waste any more time in getting to the cabin where he could call for help. Besides, he had more than just Tate who needed rescuing.

"I'm going to go out and look for everyone and leave you here. If someone drives by on the main road, they'll see the wreck and find you," Davis said, hoping that Tate heard him, even though he looked to be asleep. "You stay here in case that happens."

He placed the duffle bag full of food and warm clothes next to Tate and the melting bowl of water next to the fire to keep it in its liquid form. Davis left his own gun with his friend and pulled his dad's rifle out of the back of the car. He found a box of ammunition and loaded a clip.

"I'm heading out and going to the cabin. I'll be back for you as soon as I get the distress call out with the CB there. I'll try to look for Addy along the way."

Davis hefted the weight of his pack onto his back and shouldered his father's rifle. He took one last look at Tate. What he just did for his friend, was all that he could have done.

"I'll see you soon, buddy," Davis whispered and walked away.

CHAPTER TWENTY-FOUR

The sun poked through the crack in the curtains, catching Natalie across the face. She had had a fitful night of sleep.

She had gone back to bed after the men left. A nightmare had left her in a panic, but she couldn't remember any of the details. As a mother and wife, she worried for her family when they went out on their own. When her husband or kids were out of her sight, they were out of her control and she couldn't keep them all safe. She was a chronic worrier.

The clock on the nightstand read 8:10 a.m. The little girl sleeping down the hall usually woke around nine. Natalie always wanted to make sure Addy had enough to eat, so she knew she needed to get up and out of bed so that she could start on a healthy breakfast for Addy.

Natalie had just finished beating up the pancake batter and placing slices of bacon in the oven for herself, since Addy didn't eat meat, when the phone rang. She turned the burner under the skillet down to on medium-low before lifting the phone receiver and saying "Hello."

"Where's Tate 'n Ad?"

Natalie cringed at the sound of the slurred voice at the other end of the line.

She looked at the cat-shaped clock on the wall, which read 8:37. Phoebe Michelson was clearly struggling with a hangover, calling the Perrin residence looking for her kids. Apparently she had once again forgotten what her children were doing.

"Tate is out hunting with Albert and the boys for the next few days, and Addy is still asleep," Natalie said.

" 'Kay. Send 'em over whenever. I'll be here all day."

"Fine," Natalie said, slamming the receiver down a little harder than planned. Her blood boiled. That woman really couldn't care less about her children. Phoebe clearly didn't listen to her when she reminded her that Tate was away.

The woman was a train-wreck and had been her whole life. At least that is what Albert said. They grew up together, though he kept his distance from her. He said she was crazy with anger issues. Phoebe never had friends growing up and Natalie was quite sure she never had a serious relationship until she met John Michelson.

That man would have given her the world. He nearly gave up his dream career as a geologist for her to live in Rachet, since that was her hometown and she refused to leave.

Phoebe treated him terribly, despite the sacrifices John was willing to make.

When Natalie and Albert were early on in their relationship, they had seen Phoebe and John at Quiggly's bar. Drunk, Phoebe stood at the bar, one moment giving him an earful about something that had set her anger off and the next she was kissing him and seductively begging him to take her home.

A year later, John had enough and broke up with her. But the news of her unplanned pregnancy sealed John's fate and the man strove to be a good father—despite becoming a philanderer in the end.

Natalie was appalled to have learned when John Michelson would be away during the week at the Duluth Center for Geologic studies, he was living with a woman down there. In *her* apartment. Albert told Natalie to mind her business. If he and the Michelson kids were happy, that's all that mattered. She could never get a good read on Tate's happiness, but Addy was over the moon for her father.

His death was tragic and particularly distressing for Addy. Luckily, from what Natalie knew, the child was spared the details of his demise. She didn't think Addy would handle it well knowing that her father died during a boating accident while out on vacation with another woman who wasn't her mother. The poor child always believed he wasn't around because of work. While Natalie knew he dearly loved his children, his wife created for him a toxic environment and he took every opportunity he could to not be there. A shame he left the kids there.

Natalie was never comfortable sending Addy back home—alone—after Phoebe had been out all night, drinking. She resolved she would take her usual good old time sending the little girl home. First, Addy was going to have a nice meal.

With years of experience, Natalie expertly poured the pancake batter in the heated skillet. The batter formed little bubbles on the surface, popping with little puffs of hot air. Once the bubbles around the edges of the batter popped and left an indentation, it was time to flip the pancake and cook the other side. Once both sides were golden brown, she slid the spatula under the fluffy cake and flipped it onto a plate, then continued making another "pannycake." She smiled at the memory of what Korin used to call his favorite breakfast.

"Mommy, I want some pannycakes," he would say, his brown eyes just peeking over the edge of the table. He was towheaded then. She had hoped he would take after Davis with his pale blue eyes and blond hair. She had wanted twins and was sorely disappointed when it turned out Davis was alone in her womb. The idea of look-alike children was a dream that would never come true.

Albert had never wanted more than one kid, so she'd put away her dreams of a second child. Yet, deep down, she'd always imagined herself balancing two little tykes on her hips as she kept house. But since Albert didn't want that, they had stopped trying consciously for another baby.

Until one night after spending a tiring day minding Davis and scrubbing the floors, Albert had come home drunk. She'd already put Davis to bed, so she unleashed a fury of whispers at her husband as he walked into the house, well after eleven p.m., tracking dirt on her freshly cleaned floor. He apologized to her. Right then and there on the kitchen floor.

A few weeks later, her period didn't show up. A few more weeks after that, during a visit to a doctor in Grand Portage, she learned she was pregnant. She was thrilled, but hid her excitement from her husband. At dinner that night, when she told Albert that he was going to have another child and Davis was going to have a younger brother or sister, Albert broke down in tears. Davis started crying because Albert was crying, or so Natalie assumed.

Natalie finished whipping up two short stacks of pancakes—one for her and one for Addy. She listened for movement in the back of the house but heard nothing. It was after nine. The little girl was usually awake by now. Natalie removed the crisp bacon from the oven and allowed it to cool as she headed down the hallway toward Korin's room, where Addy was sleeping. Quietly, so as not to startle the girl, she opened the door and peeked into the room.

Addy still slept. Natalie went over to the bed and placed her hand on the small lump under the comforter, giving it a gentle shake. Her hand oddly depressed into the soft mound.

"Addy?" Natalie asked. No movement came from under the comforter. Natalie grabbed the fabric and pulled it back, revealing two pillows laying in the place where a little girl should have been.

She backed into the hall and saw the bathroom door open and the light off. Addy wasn't there either. Natalie searched each bedroom, calling for the little girl. Each time she called Addy's name, her voice became a little more frantic.

The Perrin house was a single story, with a basement. Natalie searched every square inch. There was no sign of Addy.

Grabbing her coat and leaving the breakfast to grow cold in the kitchen, Natalie dashed out of the house, running down the road as fast as her feet could carry her on the icy road toward the Michelson residence.

Natalie banged on the peeling red door, frantically yelling for Phoebe to answer.

Phoebe Michelson's flushed and puffy face appeared in the crack of the open door. Upon recognizing Natalie, Phoebe opened the door. Before she could ask Natalie where Addy was, Natalie pounced first.

"Did Addy come home?"

"What?" Phoebe said, annoyed.

"Is Addy here?" Natalie asked. "She isn't in my house."

Phoebe's face turned even redder and she slurred, "Would I've called you like thirty minutes ago 'bout sending her home if she was here?"

Natalie's mouth opened and closed, unable to form the words that she wanted to say. She had no idea where Addy was.

"Where. Is. She?" Phoebe said, punctuating each word, and putting a hand to her head as if to soothe her hangover headache.

"I don't know," Natalie said.

"You are a fucking awful mother," Phoebe seethed. "You better find her."

And with that, Phoebe slammed the door in Natalie's face.

The engine in Natalie's car sputtered to life as she twisted the key in the engine. The tires slipped on the icy macadam as she slid out of the driveway and down the road toward the police station.

Her gloved index fingers tapped against the steering wheel, a nervous habit of hers that she relied upon to keep her mind from going into a full-blown panic. Her attacks were debilitating, often leaving her curled up and gasping for breath. Something she always hid from her family. When she would feel one starting, she would quell it in her throat until she could get to the bathroom. Then, turning on the exhaust fan, she'd lay on the floor, curled up in a ball, and remain motionless, her eyes fixed upon the base of the toilet. She'd hold her breath while her fingers unconsciously pinched the underside of her arms where they crossed over her chest. With each pinch, she would breathe, and that was how she kept going until the attack was over.

Drumming her fingers was a way to distract herself from having a panic attack. It kept her mind occupied on a song that their rhythm tapped out. The rhythm kept her from curling up in the driver's seat and crashing off the road.

Large puffy snowflakes started to fall from the sky, snapping Natalie out of her trance. She watched them cascade from large gray clouds. A warning of the oncoming storm. Anyone who lived this far north knew the threats. The big puffy flakes would form into smaller ones and pummel the earth, accompanied by howling sharp winds that cut to the bone if you were caught outside and unaware.

She needed help finding Addy fast. She silently prayed that the girl was not outside.

Natalie rapped with her knuckles at the window that separated the lobby from the inner offices at the police station. She couldn't see anyone milling about. She knocked again.

"Hello? Hello?" she yelled.

A door in the far back corner of the dark office opened and some-one walked out. She recognized Deputy George Connor, dressed in a button-up light blue denim shirt and dark denim jeans. A toothpick was tucked into the corner of his lips below a salt-and-pepper mustache.

He unlocked the window and slid it open.

"Yer causing quite a ruckus out here," Connor said. "What in hell is going on?"

"George! Please, please," Natalie began breathlessly, "you've got to help me. My daughter—er—I mean, my friend's daughter, she's missing.

She was spending the night at my house with her brother, and when I went in to wake her for breakfast, she wasn't there. I couldn't find her anywhere in the house." A sob escaped her lips as she felt herself crumpling.

"Now, Natalie, calm down. I'm sure the little tyke is around somewhere."

"No, you don't understand. She's nowhere in my house, and she never went back to her own home."

"Okay," he said reassuringly, pulling out a notepad and a pen. "What's her name?"

"Addy. Addy Michelson."

"John Michelson's little girl?"

"Yes." Natalie started to sob again.

"Natalie, you gotta calm down."

She backed off on the crying a bit, but her tears were still streaming.

"Now, tell me what happened from when you last saw her until you noticed she was missing. Oh, and does Phoebe know?"

"She knows, and doesn't care," Natalie snapped, her tears replaced with anger.

Connor just nodded. Natalie knew he'd had one too many run-ins with Phoebe Michelson. Usually it was around midnight when he picked her up down at Quiggly's bar, drunk as a skunk. Quiggly would always give the police station a ring for him to pick her up and take her home. The last thing the town needed was a habitual drunk driver. Rachet may be desolate, but Phoebe could still kill people. She'd always had a problem with drink, but it had gotten much worse after John died, leaving her alone to fend for herself and the kids.

"Addy fell asleep on our couch last night and we moved her to Korin's room before everyone else went to bed. Both Addy and Tate spent the night because the men were leaving to go to Albert's father's hunting cabin for a couple of days, for beaver trapping. Tate brought Addy along last night because . . ."

Her voice trailed off. She didn't need to say any more; everyone in Rachet knew.

The deputy nodded again for her to go on.

"The boys left around five this morning, and I went back to bed. Then a little after eight I got up and started breakfast. It was a little after nine o'clock when I realized I didn't hear her moving about, so I went to wake Addy—we'd moved her to Korin's room once the guys were up, so she wouldn't be disturbed—and she wasn't there. The bed wasn't warm, and her boots and jacket are gone. I searched the house high and low, but she isn't there. And like I said, she never went back to Phoebe's."

"Could she have gone with the boys hunting?"

"Absolutely not! She's too young. Tate never would've taken her.

Besides, someone would have said something to me about it if they had."

Connor paused for a moment and rubbed his mustache.

"What if she snuck into the car and they didn't know about it?"

Natalie opened her mouth to say something, then quickly closed it. Addy wasn't mischievous like that. But she also refused to be separated from her brother. Because of the big age difference between the two, Natalie believed that Addy looked at Tate as a father figure, now that her dad was no longer there. George could be right.

"Can you radio the cabin to check?" she asked him.

"Of course," he said, turning and heading to the radio room.

Natalie stood by the window, waiting. After ten minutes, she was tired of standing, so she sat on a chair in the lobby. After what felt like ages, but was only another ten minutes or so, Deputy Connor walked out the door from the main office, cup of coffee in hand, and sat down on the empty chair next to Natalie. He handed her the drink. She noticed it had cream already in it, and just the aroma emanating from the cup gave her a jolt of energy.

She looked at him for an update.

"Well," he said, rubbing his hand through his thinning gray hair, "I couldn't get in touch with them through the CB, so I called the ranger office in Covill, and they are sending someone out to the cabin to check. Give them a few hours."

"A few hours? But I need to know where she is right now."

"Natalie, the ranger has to go out to the cabin. It could take some time, especially if the roads are still a bit icy up that way," he said, trying to get her to calm down. Her hands were shaking so badly that hot coffee was splashing out of the cup and onto her bare hand. In her terror, she didn't notice.

He gingerly removed the cup from her hand.

"But what am I supposed to do in the meantime?" she asked, tears welling up in her eyes.

"Go home and wait. I will call you as soon as I hear from the rangers. Besides, if she just stepped out for a walk this morning, she could be back at your house by now."

Natalie jumped up with a start. "Thank you, George!" She gave him a hug and dashed toward the door, in hopes that Addy would be sitting on her porch when she returned. "I'll speak with you soon."

Natalie left the police station and quickly headed home. It was only a fifteen-minute drive, but it felt like an eternity. She silently prayed that Addy would be sitting on her doorstep, waiting for her to return.

That silly girl. *Why on earth would she just disappear like that and not tell me?* She would give her a stern (but gentle) talking-to. Natalie knew she couldn't punish the girl. Addy wasn't hers. She'd just have to take her back to Phoebe's and let her handle the discipline. There most likely wouldn't be any.

Natalie made a right off Main Street and headed up the mountain lane. Their house sat halfway up the climb in a secluded area. They were close enough so that they could walk into town if needed, but far enough to be away from people—even though there were fewer than three hundred souls in the area.

She passed the Michelson home. The lights were all off. Natalie thought for a moment about stopping to see if Addy had returned there, but she was pretty sure the little girl would not have. She was afraid of her mother and never wanted to be home without her big brother.

I'm more of a mother to that little girl than Phoebe will ever be, she thought. Phoebe didn't even care that Addy was missing.

And with that thought she pushed the gas pedal down and floored it past Phoebe's house.

Tate was the one who took care of everything. He had managed quite well in the time since John had died. She knew Tate would never leave home. He couldn't abandon his sister. And he probably couldn't abandon their mom, either, despite the fact she never acted like a true mother.

Albert had been able to get Tate a job with his logging crew, and he was due to start next month. Tate had spent the last nine years since graduating from high school working at the only gas station in Rachet. He managed the little shop, pumping gas and washing windshields, helping folks to change out their wiper blades, things like that. He was not a mechanic, but he did what he could to make his employer proud. They were sad to hear that he'd be moving on to a different job, but he had provided them the courtesy of a month's notice, so they could hire a replacement and he could spend some time training them.

If only Davis were that ambitious. She sighed. Her eldest was still not working, despite graduating at the same time as Tate. The only thing he did besides watch TV was volunteer occasionally with the local ambulance service, whenever he felt like it, which was once a week—if she were lucky. Because of his lack of commitment, they would never offer him a paid position.

She worried about what would happen to him after she and Albert passed. At least he'd have his brother to lean on. Albert had been saying for a while now that it was time for Davis to go and find his own place to live, to take care of himself.

Natalie didn't agree with him. He was her baby—her firstborn. She'd care for him until her dying day. Though she wouldn't mind if he'd go out and get a job to help with the finances. As a grown man, he ate a lot of food.

CHAPTER TWENTY-FIVE

When Natalie pulled into the driveway she noticed the yellow VW beetle sitting there, and someone sitting on her porch. Her heart was in her throat. For a moment she hoped it was Addy. Then the person stood up and Natalie could see she was quite tall, with dark hair.

She hopped out of the car excited that whoever was on the porch may have news of Addy. While she struggled to run on account of her limp, Natalie moved as quickly as she could from the car and up the steps to the porch. As the stranger walked toward her Natalie asked excitedly, "Is Addy here?"

The woman looked at her, perplexed. "I'm sorry, I'm not sure I understand what you're asking."

Natalie waved a hand, dismissing her. "Who are you?" she snapped as she opened her front door.

"Mrs. Perrin?" the girl asked.

Natalie looked at her out of the corner of her eye, giving a slight nod.

"I'm Maeve Alders. Korin's girlfriend."

Natalie's attitude changed, her worry over Addy momentarily forgotten.

"Oh Maeve, it's nice to meet you. I have heard so much about you."

She'd actually heard nothing about her but her name. Korin rarely brought up his girlfriend.

"Umm, won't you come in?"

Maeve followed her into the house.

"Apologies if I seem a little out of sorts. Davis's friend's sister spent the night here because her mother was . . . umm . . . out of town. When I woke up, she was gone."

"I'm sorry to hear that. And I apologize for arriving here unannounced," said Maeve. "I just had this awful feeling . . . I had a terrible dream about Korin, and I was worried about him." She paused for a moment. "You have a lot going on here. I can go." Maeve began to turn around.

"Oh no, you don't need to leave," Natalie said from the doorway. "There's nothing I can do right now. I've searched everywhere, and the police are looking into it now. It's best that I stay here in case she shows up."

She gave a fake smile, trying to tamp down her nerves. George was looking into it. There really was nothing she could do right now. She needed to be near the phone in case he called.

"Tell me about this dream."

"Last night I woke up after a horrible nightmare about Korin," Maeve said. "I can't shake this feeling that something is wrong. I figured I would drive up to check on him."

"He isn't here," Natalie said, as she stared at this strange girl. *She had driven hours to be here because of a dream?*

"I know he's out hunting with his family. I had nothing to do today, so I thought I'd just come up and check with you—maybe see where he grew up." Maeve shook her head then looked down at her feet. "I'm sorry. I just can't shake this awful sick feeling I have, that something happened to him."

Ah, there it was. Korin was gone a day and this girl missed him already. She must be in absolute love with him. Natalie felt excited for her son and the relationship he had with this sweet woman.

"Come on," she said to Maeve as she walked into the house.

Maeve followed her in, a bit hesitant.

Natalie set her purse on the table by the door and walked to the kitchen. Breakfast still sat next to the stove.

"Are you hungry?" Natalie asked Maeve. "I could heat this up? I know it is closer to lunch than breakfast, but it's all going to waste just sitting here." She motioned for Maeve to sit at the table in the small kitchen.

"That would be lovely, thank you." Maeve pulled out one of the chairs, sat down, and placed her purse on the floor next to her feet.

"Did Korin leave you our address? Just curious as to how you found our house."

"Oh, umm . . . not quite," the girl stammered. "He never told me his address, but I have a friend in the registrar's office. She snuck into the office this morning and got the information for me."

Natalie turned, a look of shock across her face. "It's that easy to obtain someone's personal information?"

The girl looked at the table, sheepish. "Yeah, I know it's not right, but you have to understand, I never get feelings like this. Something is terribly wrong."

Natalie waved her hand in front of her face. "They're fine. This is just one of their usual trips. Albert and the guys usually go to the cabin a few times a year. Nothing could go wrong."

She went about heating up the pancakes and bacon, making a fresh pot of hot tea. She filled Maeve's plate, setting it in front of her.

The way the girl dug right in, Natalie surmised she hadn't stopped to eat anything along the way.

Maeve broke the silence. "Again, Mrs. Perrin—"

"Call me Natalie."

"Okay. I'm sorry, Natalie, for showing up unannounced. Korin has no idea I was coming. I just—" She paused, taking a sip of her tea to calm the lump in her throat.

Natalie didn't wait for her to finish. "Please, give me the details of your dream. It obviously has you upset."

Maeve shook her head. "That's the thing—as the day goes on, I'm finding that I can't really remember the details. I'm just left with the feeling that something terrible has happened to him. Also, for the past week or so, he's been a little . . . off. I can't really put my finger on it, but I feel like there's something wrong, and it may have something to do with his brother."

Natalie brushed her off. "The only problem they may have is some sibling rivalry, but nothing more. They are all out at the cabin, hunting and trapping, and they'll be returning in two days." She cleared her throat and changed the subject. "Now this situation I have on my hands—that's something to worry about. I am waiting on word from the police station that they've found her."

"Oh, I didn't ask. When did she go missing?"

Natalie could tell Maeve was a little unnerved to change the focus to Addy, but she didn't care. This was clearly more important than Maeve's dream, which probably stemmed from her fear that Korin was going to dump her or something.

"This morning. As I said, she was spending the night here. When I went to wake her up, she was gone. Out of the house. Vanished."

Natalie's shoulders began to shake as her intense fear for Addy returned. She dabbed at her face with a napkin in an effort to suppress her emotions.

"The police seem to think she might have snuck away in the car with the boys when they left this morning." She sighed and looked up at the ceiling. "I pray they are right."

Both women sat there in silence for a few moments. Maeve had just started to reach for her bacon when Natalie broke out into hysterics. She put her head on the table on top of her crossed arms and sobbed.

Maeve paused with her hand hovering over her bacon and stared at her.

Natalie wiped her face with her hands, clearing her tears. "I'm so sorry," she said.

"It's okay," Maeve replied.

"No, it isn't," Natalie said, and tears began to stream down her face again. "I'm a terrible mother." The hysterical sobbing started again. Maeve stood and moved her chair closer to Natalie. In a tentative motion, she reached out her hand and patted Natalie on the shoulder.

"I'm sure that's not true."

"It is! I just wanted us all to have the perfect life," Natalie wailed, and started to unleash a torrent of reasons as to why she was a terrible mother, starting with when Korin pushed Davis into the fire.

Maeve listened somberly as Natalie recounted all of the terrible things the brothers had done to each other. She was disturbed as she began to understand that Korin was not as quiet and well-mannered as he'd made himself out to be. Also, Davis didn't seem to be as bad as Korin had described, either; he sounded more misguided and lost than anything else.

Although she felt uncomfortable as she listened to a different side of the story, Maeve sat back and took it all in. Clearly Natalie was fine with unloading all of her self-doubt upon meeting her for the first time. It was people like this that she wanted to help, who gave her the courage to get through grad school. Natalie definitely had a lot of problems. Maeve found herself starting to diagnose the woman. She believed Natalie was someone who held in all her thoughts, and never spoke a word of her true feelings to anyone. And from the hint Natalie gave about losing her parents as a kid then having to be raised by her mostly absent aunt, she definitely experienced a level of trauma at a young age.

"And I tell you what," Natalie continued, "most people believed Davis to be this evil little demon. Even their grandmother thought so. How could people believe that of my baby?" Natalie looked outraged.

"Why do you think their grandmother thought that?" Maeve asked, leaning in to what Natalie was saying, trying to coax more out of the woman to understand better the family dynamics. She was starting to get a rush off Natalie's emotional breakdown. The future psychologist in her was eager to see where this was going.

Natalie paused and shook her head. "I shouldn't say. I did something terrible."

"I'm sorry," Maeve said. "I don't quite understand."

Natalie cleared her throat.

"After their grandmother, Glory, died, we were cleaning out her house. We brought a lot of her stuff to our house because Albert couldn't part with the memories. There were boxes that sat in the basement for years. One day I'd had enough of the clutter down there, so I started going through the boxes."

She paused to take a sip of her tea. Maeve sat patiently and waited for her to continue.

"In one of the boxes of books, I found Glory's diary. I should have honored her privacy and thrown it away, but I was just so curious." Natalie's body began to shake as she started to cry.

Maeve, breaking the protocol she'd been taught in school, reached out a reassuring hand and placed it on Natalie's.

"Go on," she urged Natalie.

"Oh, what I read in there was just awful." Natalie paused again.

Maeve kept hold of Natalie's hand, hoping it would maintain a connection and help Natalie to finish the story. The clock over the stove ticked away the seconds.

"Albert's father used to hit Glory. What Glory recorded in her diary was horrifying, and so detailed." Natalie pulled her hand away from Maeve and waved it in front of her face. "She was always fixated on her husband's eyes when he attacked her. She said his eyes would go so dark that she felt like she was looking into the pits of hell. It was pure hate."

"What would make him hurt her like that?" Maeve asked, appalled.

"She wouldn't be doing anything to provoke him, just cleaning, or reading, or watching TV. She said it was like something other than her Thomas would come into the room and just attack her out of the blue. She never understood it, but was happy when the day finally came that he died. Her love for him had died the first time he hit her."

Natalie reached for her tea again and took a sip. "I feel terrible that we never knew. How could we not have suspected anything?"

"Those who are abused are very good at hiding what is being done to them," Maeve said. "They are afraid that if they reveal what is happening, the abuse will become worse. They have a hard time seeing how they could escape. Glory may also have been afraid of what would happen to the family if she admitted to what was happening."

Natalie looked down at the table and took some deep breaths. "Would the abused take it out on someone else?"

Maeve shifted in her seat. This was territory she was not comfortable entering, especially with a woman she'd just met. She reluctantly replied, "Sometimes. Why would you ask that?"

"Because I feel like she treated Davis horribly."

Maeve straightened in her chair and stared at Natalie. The stories that she'd heard from Korin about his brother and what his mother had just told her started to piece the jigsaw puzzle of Davis together. "How so?"

"I remember the first time I handed Davis to her when he was a newborn. He was sleeping. She took him in her arms and just smiled at him. Then he woke up and looked at her. Her whole demeanor changed, and she thrust him back into my arms, saying that he had his grandfather's eyes.

"From that day on, she rarely interacted with him when she visited us. We did try to send him to stay the weekend with her sometimes. Albert and I thought it would be good for her to spend some time with him, since it had been several years since Thomas had died. We were ignorant about how she really felt about Davis."

"I'm not fully following," Maeve said.

"She hated Davis. In her diary, she admitted to hating him. She wrote about how his eyes were just like Thomas's—how it brought her right back to her husband's abuse." Natalie started to cry again. "When we sent Davis over to her, she would ignore him or push him out of the way whenever he tried to follow her around."

"All of this was in the diary?" Maeve asked, disgusted.

Natalie nodded. "He never said anything to us, but he would throw a fit every time we tried to take him over there." Her hand covered her mouth and she leaned over, sobbing. "We . . . we sent him—we sent him to her, and he was being treated like that."

Maeve sat back in her chair, even though she wanted to hug the woman. She needed to learn how to draw a line between her and her clients in order to be a good therapist.

"What did your husband say when you told him about the diary?" Maeve asked.

Natalie sat up, her crying ceased. She looked at Maeve, face streaked with tears and eyes red, and said in an even tone, "I never told him."

"You never told him?" Maeve said, her voice rising a little higher than it should have.

"It would crush him to know that his parents were not nice people," Natalie replied, emotionless.

"What about Korin? Did Glory ever do anything to Korin?"

"She finished the last page of her diary a few months before he was born. I never found another diary in her belongings. I thought she loved Korin, too, but now I'm not sure how she felt about him," Natalie said. "There was never any reference to him. Even on the day we told her we were expecting again, there was nothing written about the news. So I don't really know…"

Maeve, noting that Natalie was becoming distant, tried to change trajectory. "What happened to the diary?"

"I burned it." Natalie buried her face in her hands and sobbed. "I'm a horrible mother. We subjected Davis to Glory's cruelty, and then Korin . . .oh god, Korin . . ."

Maeve reached out and placed her hand on Natalie's shoulder. Her heart pounded as she waited to hear what had happened to Korin.

"We had him committed after he attacked Davis. I don't know what happened to him there, but I don't think I brought the same child home." Natalie started to wail again. "I failed them! I failed both of my sons!"

Maeve, shocked to hear about Korin being committed, withdrew her hand from Natalie and just stared at the crying woman. Korin had never mentioned anything to her about being in an asylum. She had so many questions for him, and for Natalie, especially why she believed she hadn't brought the same boy home again.

The phone rang and gave both women a start.

Natalie jumped up and dashed over to pick up the receiver.

"Hello?" she said anxiously.

There was a pause. Maeve could hear someone talking on the other end but could not make out what was being said.

"I see," Natalie said.

Maeve looked back to her plate but had lost her appetite.

Natalie hung up the receiver with a little force.

"That was the deputy. He hasn't heard back from the ranger station yet. He's going to swing by and give me an update after he's handled a few things. He wouldn't tell me anything over the phone. Said he be here in about an hour."

"What does that mean—handling a few things?" Maeve asked.

Natalie shivered. "I'm sure we'll find out when he gets here. More tea?"

Clearly the conversation they'd been having had ended.

Maeve was disturbed about what Natalie had told her, but she didn't want to make things worse by pushing her right now. She'd try to pick up on their conversation about Korin being committed to the asylum once they had found Addy and things had calmed down.

Maeve's stomach felt queasy, and once again something in her mind gave her a nudge of warning.

CHAPTER TWENTY-SIX

He thought of nothing but saving the children. Without a moment's regard for his own safety, Albert Perrin ran out of the tree line, screaming at the bear that had its head stuck through the passenger side of the upside-down station wagon.

"You bastard!" he yelled. "Come on—come and get me. Hey . . . *hey!* Come and get me!"

He hopped up and down, waving his arms above his head. He had so much adrenaline coursing through his body at this moment. Despite being thrown from the car and landing several feet away from the wreckage, he felt all right—even though he knew he must have some injuries. There was a rattle in his chest when he inhaled. Yet it wasn't the health of his body that he was thinking about, but the children. And of the three who were still stuck in the car's wreckage with a bear out for revenge. At least one of the kids had gotten away. He'd seen Davis slam against the car door, which gave way under his weight. He was thrown from the vehicle.

Albert had to pull his thoughts away from his eldest and focus on the children in front of him. The ones who were about to be eaten.

"Hey!" he made another attempt to get the bear's attention by yelling. "Hey! Come on!" He ended the call with a sharp whistle, and that was what finally worked. The bear backed away from the car and pulled its head out of the window. In the rising morning sun, Albert saw the blood dripping off its face as it stared him down.. Then it started to run toward him.

Albert paused for a moment with a silent prayer that the blood didn't belong to any of the kids before he turned to take off into the woods.

The rattle in his chest increased as his exhalations accelerated. A sharp pain started to jab him on his left side. It threw his balance off a little, but he still managed to weave through the trees. For a moment he slowed to see if in fact the creature was following him. He turned his head to look behind him and saw that the beast right behind him, crashing through the brush.

"Bad idea," Albert muttered through his chugging breath. He wasn't

163

entirely sure if he was referring to momentarily slowing down to look behind him or calling to the creature in the first place. In any event, it didn't matter. He'd succeeded in getting the bear away from the kids. Yet he couldn't understand why the bear came looking for the kids and was now chasing him. Most bears want to be left alone by humans. *Maybe getting hit by the car scrambled its brains… or it has rabies,* Albert surmised.

But what was he going to do now? He couldn't outrun this predator. It would soon catch up to him. The only reason he was still ahead of it at this point was because he was smaller and nimbler around the trees. Had they been in an open area, the bear would have caught him in no time.

He felt his feet starting to slow, and that's when Albert realized that he'd run straight to Bluff Creek. He was quite close to the creek bed—not a place he wanted to be, as it was too open. He didn't know what to do, but his instincts led him to turn to the right. He was completely unaware of his surroundings, yet something inside of him told him where to go. He was heading toward a rocky outcrop along the opposite side of the creek. Up ahead there was an area where the water was only calf-deep.

Hitting the water at full speed slowed Albert down even more, and he lifted his legs high out of the water to take quick, big steps. The water was freezing.

The bear must have paused for a moment because Albert hit the other side of the creek before the bear had even launched itself into the water. However, it was not as slow as Albert in the water, and he realized he shouldn't have stopped to look behind, as the bear was nearly upon him again.

He sprinted toward the rocky outcrop, and seeing a small path blazed between the rocks, he followed it. The bear's breath was hot and ragged behind him, and Albert knew the animal was as tired as he was. However, it wasn't about to give up.

The small path led to what looked like a small cave. Without a moment's hesitation, Albert shoved himself in, feetfirst.

The cold rock weighed down on Albert Perrin as he wedged himself into a small crevasse. It wasn't a cave after all, but a large crack between two boulders. Nonetheless, the small gap in the rocks made for a small shelter away from the sharp claws and teeth of the bear.

The bear stood outside of the rocks, bellowing its desire for revenge.

How long could this beast seek his blood? Albert knew he had to escape and get back to the kids. His throat tightened. He didn't even know if any of them were still alive. He had failed them by not keeping them safe. Davis, Korin, and Tate—they could all be dead. And Addy, little sweet Addy. A sob choked in his throat. He may have killed his own kids along with two children who were not his own. The sweetest kids he had ever met. He desperately needed Tate around because he helped bring a balance to Davis. Davis may act like an arrogant, spoiled guy, but deep down, Albert knew his son was lonely and depressed. He didn't know why.

Often, he and Natalie would try to discuss what could possibly be wrong with Davis. Why he always had to be the needy one, the one who was in constant need of attention. They could never come to an agreement. She always believed it was because he'd never been as smart as Korin. He was seeking the same kind of approval that Korin received.

Albert didn't quite agree with that. He felt that as parents, they treated the boys equally, each in their own unique way. They always knew that Korin was independent—the one who would solve the world's problems. With Davis, they'd honestly thought he was destined to be in professional sports. Albert would scoff at Davis's desire to be a surgeon. The kid had no ambition or drive to do that. Besides, with his hand . . . No, Davis should have focused on sports and his physical therapy exercises, working to get dexterity back in his hand. Physical therapy could have solved his issues in commanding a hockey stick. He could have been the celebrity of the family.

Albert realized that there was something missing in Davis that others seemed to have. Natalie would laugh and say it was gumption, but Albert wasn't so sure. There was something more, something deeper that was missing in his eldest son.

A blast of hot, rotten-smelling air hit him in the face as the bear tried to pull itself into the crevasse after Albert. It was determined to have its revenge, and a meal. It bellowed at the trapped man, and seething hatred boiled inside Albert as he stared down his pursuer. He yelled back at the bear, hoping that the scream would scare it, but the bear didn't even flinch. Bear mouths disgusted him. He despised how their lips were so large and flappy. They could wiggle them around like an extra finger. It was gross. This, combined with the drool that was starting to drip from its lower lip and the continual putrid breath that emanated each time the beast exhaled, made it one of the most disgusting creatures in North America. He'd always hated bears since he was a kid. Now, being face-to-face with one, he wished the whole species had become extinct during the Ice Age.

The crevasse was narrow enough that the bear could not slip its massive shoulders through the opening, the only thing keeping Albert from immediate doom. However, he did have another problem. His cold-weather hunting clothes were all in the car. All he had on at the moment was a pair of jeans and a heavy flannel shirt—both of which were quite damp from his run through the woods and creek. Lying in the cold, dark crevasse was not allowing him to get warm or dry. Hypothermia would eventually take hold.

The bear continued trying to jam itself further into the crevasse, to no avail. Then suddenly it stopped making noise. It closed its ugly mouth and looked at him. Its big brown eyes bore into Albert's own blue ones. The ears on its head twitched, and as if something from behind had frightened it. As quickly as the beast had chased Albert, it now pulled its head out of the crevasse's entrance.

Albert lay still, listening to the noises outside of the small cave. He could mostly hear some shuffling and growling. Whatever was out there, Albert believed it had been enough to spook the bear. A moment later, he heard the bear take off, hopefully back into the woods.

After a few more minutes, Albert pulled himself toward the opening, wincing in pain from moving for the first time since hiding in the crevasse. Looking at his watch, the face was cracked, and the hands stopped a little after seven thirty. It must have happened when he climbed into the crevasse. Overwhelmed with exhaustion, he had no concept of how long he had been chased or trapped between the rocks. And with the adrenaline surge gone, Albert was now certain he had broken a few ribs. Being cautious to not make noise lest he attract the bear or whatever else was out there, he surveyed the area from the mouth of the crevasse.

It was a place he once knew well—a small open area within the forest a few miles from the cabin. He could easily make it back to the car, help the kids, and get them all to the cabin to radio for help from the old CB radio that his father had restored from old parts. He hadn't realized how close to the cabin they actually were. No wonder it had all felt so familiar when he'd entered the small grove.

His father used to take him and his brother hiking in these woods. They would spend hours traipsing around, exploring. This was the spot where they would often stop to eat a late packed lunch before looping back to the cabin. He and his brother would play, using this outcrop that contained the crevasse as a medieval castle. He was a knight while he always made his brother be a dragon. He silently laughed at the memory and fondly thanked his subconscious for saving his life in directing him where to go. There was trail nearby that closely followed the creek back to the old sawmill. From there, it was just a little over two miles down the worn logging road to the cabin.

Now he just had to get out safely and silently make his way back to the kids.

Albert groaned loudly as he pulled himself the rest of the way out of the crevasse. He stopped and looked around, fearful that the noise would alert the bear to his escape. Fortunately the beast was nowhere in sight, nor was there any sound of it—or anything else, for that matter. Holding his right side, for the pain in his ribs roared like fire, he slowly made his way down the small rocky hill.

Suddenly there was a shuffling sound behind him. Before he could turn around, he was cracked in the back of his head and a weight pushed him forward. He landed facedown on the ground with the weight sitting on his back. A warmth flowed from the back of his head and around the tops of his ears. The world tipped.

His left arm was crushed under his body from where he'd been holding his ribs. He felt his extremities twitch and he wanted to get up, but he could no longer move. He couldn't see anything past the ground and his blood. He moaned, and then he started to scream.

There was a sharp hot pain in his right shoulder and then he felt his right arm snap. The pain was so brilliant that he couldn't feel the vicious tug that detached his arm from his body. His screaming stopped as he could no longer exhale.

As he laid there unable to move or see, with his right shoulder drilling pain into his body, he felt claws begin to tear into his back.

Albert's world became black, wet, and warm. The pain and his terror subsided. He could no longer feel anything. Absolute silence took him over and all became nothingness. It was then that he accepted his fate of being eaten alive by a bear.

Amanda Headlee

CHAPTER TWENTY-SEVEN

Ranger Tom Boyd woke sharply from his nap to the crackle of the CB radio that sat on his desk. As he flinched awake, his feet slipped from his desk and fell to the floor, jolting him upright. Deputy Connor from Rachet was calling out his name.

"Dammit, Boyd—answer me!" Connor's voice was trailed by a hiss.

Boyd smirked. Connor sounded like a snake, which he was—as well as a weasel. Boyd grumbled as he reached for the handset, remembering the last game of poker he'd played up at Connor's cabin with some of his hunting pals. Connor had nearly wiped Boyd's bank account clean for the month. Boyd knew that somehow the old sneak was cheating. There was no other way he could have won so many hands in a row.

"Whaddya want?" Boyd snapped over the CB. He had stopped socializing with Connor after that game, so he knew the call was strictly business.

"Glad you finally woke up from your nap, Ranger." Deputy Connor mockingly drew out the word "ranger," which made Boyd furious. Connor was always rubbing it in his face that he outranked him.

"Get on with it," Boyd barked. He threw the handset on the desk, the old wooden desk chair creaking as he leaned back in it and crossed his arms across his chest.

"We may have a stowaway with a hunting party heading up your way. A little girl, six years old. Name's Addy Michelson. I need you to go up to the old Perrin cabin and check to see if she's there with the family. Party of four, including her adult brother Tate."

Boyd was being ordered. "You are out of your jurisdiction," Boyd said, picking up the handset again.

"Seriously, Boyd, a little girl is missing. We just need to check that she is with the family before we send out a search party. You are a sick asshole for—"

Boyd held down the response button to cancel out whatever Connor was saying. He couldn't deal with this jerk any longer.

"I'll let you know if I see her."

And without waiting for a response, he turned off the radio. The nerve of Connor, sounding so condescending and demanding. After he finished his morning paperwork, he'd of course go check at the cabin to see if she was there. He wasn't a heartless asshole. He had a very strong and tender heart.

This was the thick of trapping season, and Boyd was used to getting calls nonstop at the Covill Ranger Station. Most of them were from old ladies or crotchety old hunters who had no right to be traipsing through the forest at their age. "Someone is illegally walking on my property wearing orange . . . Someone shot my deer . . . Someone drank my coffee at camp." All ludicrous calls.

He never got any interesting ones anymore—about poachers, or someone falling and breaking their leg somewhere in the woods. This call about the girl could be interesting, if she were in fact missing. But most likely she was just sitting somewhere drinking hot cocoa with an old hunter. A hunter who was probably her father and took her along because for damn sure he was going to teach his kid to hunt—even if she was a girl. Her woeful mother had probably gone to the Rachet police station, crying that her dainty and delicate baby girl shouldn't be hunting; she should be home playing with dolls and having tea parties. He wouldn't be so lucky to have an actual missing persons call.

His old Ford pickup bounced along the logging road that led up to the Perrins' hunting cabin. This was where Arthur Perrin was born and grew up and eventually died. He had willed the house to his son Thomas, who used it as a retreat during the hunting season. He in turn had willed it to his son Albert, who used the place for the same purpose. It annoyed Boyd that such a nice place was slowly rotting away because it was only used from October through March, whenever the weather and hunting season permitted.

Boyd himself wouldn't mind having a small one-room dwelling like the Perrins' cabin for himself. Situated far out in the forest, totally secluded. That's why he'd taken the job as a park ranger. To be in the forest each day. Sadly, on most days, he was stuck in the office, filling out paperwork.

That's why this assignment excited him. He got to go out. And he was going to take his own sweet time, that's for sure. He knew the girl was probably there, so there was no need to rush.

About thirty minutes after leaving the station, while on the road that connects Grand Portage to Rachet, Boyd noticed some heavy skid marks on the road that were quite fresh. He slowed and looked at the marks. There were tracks that went up the embankment, and broken tree branches everywhere. Bits of metal were strewn about. Boyd gripped the steering wheel tightly; he had a sinking feeling. Picking up the CB, he radioed the station.

"Ranger Boyd on site of an accident along sixty-one. Copy."

Silence.

"I said, Ranger Boyd on site of an accident along Route 61, heading to Rachet. Does anyone copy?"

Silence.

Damn it. He looked at his watch.

Junior Deputy O'Malley wouldn't be in for another twenty minutes. No one was at the station. Cursing again, Boyd pulled his truck off to the side of the road, threw on his flashers, and exited the truck. He climbed the embankment and let out a low whistle when he saw what lay on the other side.

A station wagon was lying on its roof, its contents strewn everywhere.

"Oh my God!" he yelped when he spied someone lying against a tree, looking quite bloodied. Boyd hurried down the embankment to the body. *Please be alive, please be alive*, he whispered.

"Hey," he said softly as he reached out to feel the man's neck. His face was smashed up and covered in blood. His right arm looked to be destroyed, and was tied to his body. There was little chance this guy was still alive. As his fingers touched skin, the eyes of the man flashed open and he snarled, lashing out with his good arm. The attack was too slow and Boyd was able to step back in time. He held his hands up to the man.

"Whoa, easy there. I'm Ranger Boyd."

He took a step back and knelt in front of the man—outside of striking range.

Fear left Tate's eyes. With as much energy as he could muster, he whispered to Boyd, "Please—help me."

Boyd nodded his head and moved closer. "Is anyone else here?"

Tate's eyes grew glassy. He hadn't seen Davis in what felt like hours, but he'd been in and out of consciousness. He didn't know where anyone was.

"Addy," he whispered, and started to cry.

"Addy!" Boyd exclaimed. This must be the girl's brother.

"It's okay, Tate," he said, reaching out to put a hand on the man's good shoulder. "I know who you are. Is your sister here?"

With tears streaming down his face mixing with dirt and blood, Tate shook his head.

"I haven't seen her since the crash."

"Okay, then, let's find her," Boyd said, trying to add some enthusiasm to his voice. "Wait here for one second."

He walked away from Tate and surveyed the area. There was no evidence of anyone else present. He tried to recall what Connor had said about the number of people on the trip. Boyd thought he'd heard four, meaning with Addy, that would make five total. However, with no one else in sight at the moment, he had to get the one person he'd found somewhere safe.

"Okay, Tate, I'm going to help you up and we are going to climb over that embankment and get into my truck," Boyd explained. "Then I am going to drop you off at the hospital and come back here with a search party."

Tate started to bawl. "Noooo!" he cried. "You need to find Addy first. She has to be safe!"

Boyd paused for a moment. There was no way he was getting this big guy out of the forest by himself. He easily had fifty pounds on Boyd, all muscle. This guy was ready to put his sister's life ahead of his own, which meant he would fight Boyd every second. Boyd looked down at Tate's legs and grimaced. Tate was going to have to help walk out, on the one good leg he had. There had to be some way he could get Tate to safety and then look for Addy with minimal time lost. Darkness would be here before they knew it, and he worried that the little girl wouldn't survive the dropping temperature. He knew for certain if he didn't get Tate out of the cold, the boy would die tonight.

"Tate, how about we go to the Perrin cabin? I'll drop you off there and you can rest in the warmth. I'm sure there is a CB radio there; if you could use it to call for extra help I can go out and waste no time starting the search myself. I'll tell you what to do to manage that."

Tate wouldn't look up at Boyd as he spoke.

"I'll go out and search for Addy in the meantime."

Tate glared up at him.

"You are in no condition to walk, let alone search these forests. Come on, we need more people to come with medical supplies and search parties. You can keep up the communication with the station." Boyd knelt next to Tate again. "It isn't just Addy that we have to look for, right?"

Boyd watched as guilt swept across Tate's face. He'd been so focused on his sister that he had completely disregarded his friends.

"Let's go," Tate said sullenly.

Boyd reached down to help support Tate's left arm and helped him to his feet. There was a sharp hiss from Tate as he put weight on his torn left leg. Boyd immediately threw Tate's left arm over his shoulders.

"Use me as a crutch," Boyd instructed.

Tate put his weight on Boyd, who almost went down with the amount of weight that now leaned heavily on his shoulders.

"Davis was with me at one point," Tate muttered.

"Oh yea, how long ago was that?"

"I can't remember. Maybe an hour ago, maybe ten minutes ago."

Boyd asked nothing further. The guy's head was scrambled from the accident and probably from the pain, leaving him with no concept of time. Tate was Boyd's priority now, then the little girl. When the search and rescue team arrived, he'd help them find Davis and the others.

The embankment back over to the road was not as steep as it was from the forest. They made it up the slope with minimal trouble, then slid down the other side.

Getting Tate into Boyd's beat-up Ford proved to be the most difficult part, as the guy was a tower. It was a struggle to get him folded up and contained in the truck's cabin without causing too much pain.

Once they were in, Boyd took off at a sharp speed down the road and toward the cabin.

When they arrived they were both disappointed to see that no one else had made it there yet, even though they hadn't really expected anything else. Boyd got Tate out of the truck and into the cabin, laying him down on a dusty bed next to the CB radio. Boyd turned the radio toward Tate and gave him two frequencies to try: one for his station, and one for Connor's.

"Just tell them we need a search-and-rescue party, medical, food, and warm clothes and blankets." He handed Tate the microphone, adding, "You are on my station's frequency, but you can bounce between the two. You never know if and when you will catch someone at either."

Boyd turned and went over to the fireplace. There were a few cobwebs and a fine layer of dust on the mantel. He knew Albert Perrin would have been here a few weeks ago, giving the place a scrub before returning for trapping season, but that didn't prevent new dust from accumulating.

There was a pile of firewood and kindling stacked up neatly against the wall. He used that to build a roaring fire for Tate. As he set it up, in the background he could hear Tate on the radio, calling for help.

Flames leapt up the chimney following the curling smoke. The musty cabin was soon filled with the scent of burning wood. Once satisfied, Boyd returned to Tate and knelt next to the bed.

"I am sorry that I have no food or water, but at least you won't freeze to death." He laughed, but it was the wrong kind of joke when the guy's sister was lost in the woods with night soon coming.

Tate said nothing, just gave Boyd a hard stare.

"Well, keep trying at that," he said pointing to the mic. Standing, he grabbed his hat off the top of the CB radio, turned, and left the cabin. As he left, he looked back at Tate.

"I'm going to try to go up the old sawmill road first."

Tate said nothing, turning back to the CB microphone.

Boyd cleared his throat and pushed the door open, leaving Tate alone.

Tate shifted on the bed, trying to get comfortable, but every little move made him wince, either sending a shooting pain from his broken arm or his torn leg. He was a mess.

He prayed that Addy was okay and uninjured. The tears stung his face as they seeped from his eyes. He had lost her. He'd lost the only person that meant something in his life. She was the reason he kept going, and he had failed her. Now he wasn't even able to go out and help look for her. At least he could do his damnedest to bring in a search party.

Clicking the mic, he called out in a deep voice, "Emergency, emergency. Please send search party and emergency medical personnel to the old Perrin cabin off Bluff Creek Road. There was a car accident and all parties are lost and injured in the woods." He depressed the mic and listened. He heard nothing. Once again, he called out over the CB radio for help. After listening again, with no response, he switched channels. Over and over he called for help. His voice was cracking and fatigue was threatening to overtake him again, but the thought of his sister being out there, alone, drove him on. He wasn't going to rest—or die—until she was safe.

After what seemed like hours of calling for help and switching frequencies, a voice finally cracked over the radio. "This is Deputy Connor at Rachet Police."

Once outside the Perrin cabin, Boyd took a quick look around for any evidence of someone being there recently, but there was none. Even with the snow that started to fall a little while ago, no footprints marred the pristine ground.

"Hallo!" He called out into the woods, hoping someone was within earshot. No answer. All was silent and still. He knew the trail that the hunters in the Perrin family typically traveled was the old sawmill road that led toward the main road, then looped up to the base of Mount Brisbane, at the foot of which sat an abandoned sawmill. The old road was the easiest way to get deeper into the forest without having to trek through the dense trees.

Boyd walked back to his truck, locked the axles on his front wheels, and climbed in the cabin. He put the truck into four-wheel drive, as he had no idea how bad the road was. No one maintained the road, and the unexpected snow continued to fall. He hoped to get up to the sawmill and back before the snow began to really pile up and he lost sight of the road altogether.

He turned onto the road and navigated crossing the creek back over the rickety wooden bridge that was about three hundred yards away from the cabin. He had not been out here in years and was surprised at the deterioration of the wooden structure. Didn't seem like Albert really took care of it. He'd been too focused on Tate to notice how much the bridge had decayed when he first drove over it. Heading back over now, he held his breath, wondering if it would fall apart with him on top of it.

Boyd made it over safely, although pretty rattled by the creaking of the boards. When he reached the point where the old worn path led to the abandoned sawmill, he made a right. The road hadn't been tended to for about fifteen years, ever since the mill had burned down. Hunters were the only ones who used the road now, driving up to the old mill property to park. All that was left of the mill was a wide expansive field. The burned timbers had decayed and any pieces of metal had been picked clean by either the sawmill company or looters. The company had handed the property over to the state for game lands.

Boyd had always had the feeling there was something suspicious behind that transaction. No one just "gives" up a tract of land. Local legend had it that the area was cursed by the spirits of the natives who had been forced away from their homes. Supposedly that is why the mill burned down. He, on the other hand, was pretty sure it had been arson. He never believed in all of that hocus-pocus mumbo-jumbo.

The old path wasn't too hard to navigate since the winter season's hunters had kept it clear. A few divots caught him off guard here and there, threatening to pull the wheel right out of his hands. After a few minutes of driving, he had to stop. There was a tree down in the middle of the road. He sat looking at the tree, trying to figure out how to get around it, when he noticed a large black mound about sixty feet away from the fallen tree. It was large and fuzzy. Because it didn't move when his truck approached and stopped, he knew it was dead.

Even though he was far away, he knew in his heart that it was the old sow black bear that roamed these woods, giving birth to many lineages in the area. He would have to break the hearts of the bio students who were studying the forest's ecology, telling them that their beloved bear was dead. Everyone knew she'd been close to the end of her long life. He needed to make sure it was her, and that she was, in fact, dead. If not, then she must be gravely injured, because bears didn't typically just lay there when a truck comes upon them. The best option was to put her out of her misery.

He pulled a shotgun down from the window rack behind his head. He checked that it was loaded and pulled two more shells to put in his pocket. Then he left the safety of his truck and advanced toward the bear, silently praying she was dead.

Something felt off as Boyd's feet touched the ground. The forest was eerily silent. While in his bones he felt a snowstorm was coming, there would still be winter birds chirping away. There was nothing but a slight wind, which carried a faint pungent odor. The bear smelled terrible. Of blood and mud and musk. He held his shotgun in a ready position, just in case.

With each step forward the overpowering smell of death surrounded him. He slowly began to let his guard down. The bear was making no movement. For a while all he heard was the sound of his feet softly crunching in the new-fallen snow. But when he was within a few feet of the bear, something started crying. Was it the bear? No. No animal cried like that.

It was the cry of a child—one who was lost, or in pain. Addy. He couldn't believe it.

"Addy?" he called out.

No response.

"Addy?"

As he advanced, he saw a small blonde head on the other side of the bear carcass. There she was. And then the reality set in. The child was crying next to the body of a dead bear. Where was everyone else—and why was she alone here?

"Addy! We've been looking for you. Are you okay? Where is everyone else?" he said.

Panic rose in his chest as he started to worry that he had a real situation on his hands. She was alone, which meant there were three others still missing.

As he walked over, he leaned his shotgun against the body of the bear and bent down to talk to her. She looked up at him with her green eyes, big and brimming with tears. Her mouth opened as if she was going to scream, and then Boyd's vision went black. He felt pain crack at the back of his head and reverberate through his body as he slipped into unconsciousness.

Amanda Headlee

CHAPTER TWENTY-EIGHT

Under the soft light of the rising sun, Korin found an imprint of his father's shoe in the soft banks of the creek. It looked like he had crossed. Korin looked across the waters, and the world tilted a bit. He needed to sit. Exhaustion finally took hold of him and he started to take account of what his ailments were.

As he gently touched and prodded his body, his stomach rumbled. He had never felt this hungry before. His watch indicated it was a little after seven. Another growl emanated from his stomach. As he rubbed his abdomen in an attempt to quell the hunger, pain shot through the right side of his ribs. He was sure there were some broken. And his eye. Korin reached up and touched it. It bulged far out from its socket. Touching it felt like a thousand hot knives stabbing into his skull. He winced, then leaned over to look into the water to see his reflection. The eye was partially open and he could make out the iris. Closing his right eye, the world went dark. He had no vision out of his left eye.

A growl emanated from the other side of the creek, distracting him from his injuries. *The bear,* he thought. If the bear was there, then maybe his father was close by.

Korin carefully hopped across the stones to keep the sound of his approach down, and also to prevent himself from falling into an icy bath, or further jarring his ribs.

This whole situation was his father and Davis's fault. Especially his father's, as he could have corrected Davis for being disrespectful to him in the car. But no, dear old Dad had to be a child and try to show Davis by reaching for the thermos—disregarding the task he had at hand, which was driving!

This made it easy for Korin to sit in the tree line and watch as the bear his father had hit cornered Albert Perrin among some large boulders. A gleeful smile was etched across Korin's face as he heard the growls from the bear, and the smile only grew when his father screamed back.

Korin reflected back on all of the times he'd been pushed aside for Davis. How many times had he been ignored? How many times had he sat alone in his room with no one ever coming to check on him?

How many times was he left to his own devices to figure out how to navigate life?

Korin had never truly had a father, just a man who provided him with shelter and food growing up. All of Albert's attention had been given to Davis, to try to make him a success in life. No one had ever wanted him. His parents had tried to get rid of him by locking him away at the asylum. When that didn't work out and Korin returned home, he was just a body that existed in the household, without a role. His family had never cared about him.

And now, his father's lack of care had nearly cost Korin his life.

He put his trembling hands on his lap to calm the rage beginning to boil again. His father had almost killed him. And now, Korin wanted nothing more than to see the bear maul his father to death. Tearing his father apart piece by piece, splattering blood all over the boulders and drawing in the scavengers.

He laughed loudly, then covered his mouth to silence it. But it was too late. The bear had heard him. The beast pulled its head out from between the rocks and looked in Korin's direction. Their eyes met and a sharp and hot angry surge coursed through body. He wanted to unleash it on the bear.

Korin stepped out from the tree line. He maintained eye contact with the bear, staring it down. *I will kill you. I will consume you.* He repeated this over and over again in his head.. The beast was walking toward him, teeth bared and saliva dripping. It was frenzied, as the side of its head was quite bloody. Korin didn't know if it was its own blood, or his father's. He wanted the bear's blood. It was strong. The strongest he ever would have consumed. And he was quite hungry.

Keeping his eyes on the bear, he reached down and picked up a large rock at his feet. The bear charged him and then pulled off when it was twenty yards away.

Korin snickered—it was a bluff. *He* wasn't bluffing, however. He was going to destroy the creature and steal every ounce of strength it had. The truth behind what he was going to do must have finally reflected in his eyes, as the bear took a step away from him. Then another. And another. He saw its fear. He could smell its musky odor getting stronger with the adrenaline that was coursing through its body. It looked to the tree line to its right, took one last look at Korin, and turned, taking off into the woods.

"Fuck," Korin growled. He sat down on the edge of the hill, placing the rock at his feet. He was starving.

There was a loud groan from the rocks behind him, and not knowing if it was the bear returning, he moved over into the brush to camouflage himself. If it was the bear, he would take it by surprise.

But he was the one taken by surprise when he saw his father awkwardly crawling out from the rocks. There must have been a crack there that he'd hidden in. Korin seethed, infuriated to see his father still alive. The man had tried to get rid of Korin: first, by shipping him off to an asylum, and now, by trying to kill him in a car accident. His father had no right to be alive.

As his father leaned against the rocks to pull his battered body out of the outcrop, Korin came around the far side, hiding himself among the conifers. As he got closer, he could hear Albert's labored breathing. Korin could smell his blood. Albert's skin was pale and clammy. Korin figured he wasn't long for this world. And Korin was so hungry. He ran up behind his father with the rock held high in his hands and brought it down hard on his father's head.

Albert Perrin fell forward. His hands twitched and blood pooled around his head.

Korin leaned in to smell it—deep, earthy, and wild. He started to salivate. A groan came from his father—he wasn't dead yet. Then the screaming started, and the blood continued to pool. Korin was excited, too hungry to wait for his father to expire.

He pulled the hunting knife out of his boot and sliced open the cloth, then the flesh at his father's right shoulder. He felt a carnal urge for the delicate meat on Albert's face but suppressed the feeling and focused on the fleshy back. The shoulder blade was in the way, preventing Korin from getting the meat underneath it. He picked up the bloody rock again and brought it down heavily upon the shoulder blade. There was a loud crack of bone. He brought the rock down once more to ensure the bone was fully separated, then with his knife, he cut through his father's muscle.

In frustration, Korin stood, placed his foot against his father's shoulder, and yanked hard, tearing the flesh and the shoulder blade from his father's body, revealing the flesh underneath. Blood gushed from the severed veins and artery. The ground became a shiny crimson red.

The screaming stopped.

Satisfied, he stepped back, holding some flesh, but before he could enjoy his meal, he saw that his father was still breathing. Enraged, he jumped on his father's back and stabbed him.

The noise that his father made caused Korin's head explode. Pain was shooting like an electrified wire between his temples. He couldn't wait for his father to die. The man was a damn fighter and would find some way to survive—like a cockroach.

Korin raised the hunting knife up high and brought it down over and over again into his father's upper back. Bright red blood shot from his father's mouth and in the blood that pooled in the stab wounds, there were little bubbles that formed and popped. Albert Perrin's last exhalation was long and agonizing.

When it finally stopped, Korin flipped his father's body over and proceeded to cut open his chest. He wanted his father's heart. Wickedly he smiled.

His heart is all I ever wanted.

He dug and cut his way through the cavity until he found what he was looking for. Pulling a red-and-white bandanna from his pocket, he wrapped up the heart.

Then he looked at his father's face. His eyes were intact. With his knife, he cut the delicate flesh from around the left eye socket. He placed this chunk of meat in the bandanna and wrapped it up before placing it into his coat pocket.

Then he shoved his fingers into the eye socket and grasped the soft orb. Tugging, it popped out of his father's head. With another tug, he separated the eye from the optic nerve. Korin looked at his father's eye with his own remaining eye. It was brown, like his own. He had his father's eyes.

"An eye for an eye," he whispered as he put the eye into his mouth and bit down. It burst in his mouth with a meaty, pork-like flavor. He slowly chewed, savoring the soft texture mixed with a light, delicate crunch.

As Korin chewed, he looked at his father's body. It looked too much like he'd been killed by a human, when actually, it was a bear that started it. He flipped the body back over on its stomach, exposing the mutilated back, which Korin felt looked more like an animal attack.

He put his hand up to his mouth and giggled. People will think the bear killed him.

He took a little more meat from the shoulder, and with his pockets full of his father's heart and flesh, he swallowed the last bit of the eye and walked back into the forest.

CHAPTER TWENTY-NINE

The rough bark of the tree caught some of Davis's hair as he leaned his head back against it to rest. He was exhausted, and he had a throbbing headache. He needed a moment to reset, as disorientation threatened.

He pulled out his knife and placed it on the ground, the tip pointing in the direction he needed to travel to get to the creek. He feared that after a break, he wouldn't remember which direction to take. The bark continued to bite into the back of his head and jacket as he slid down, sitting on a large root above the snow.

Davis leaned forward and placed his head in his hands, closing his eyes and listening to the forest. The wind was light and there were little snaps and cracks all around him. Just the normal sounds of a winter forest. No sounds of human life could be heard aside from his own breathing.

He could live out here forever. Maybe that is what he should do: convince his father to let him live in the cabin. He could live off the land and do whatever he wanted. Deep down, however, he knew he couldn't do it. He didn't want to be alone.

A soft sound in front of him, different from any of the other forest sounds, brought Davis back to reality. He lifted his head. Several yards ahead stood a doe, sniffing and chewing at whatever she could find that was edible on the frozen forest floor. There'd been a time in his life when he would've been eager to kill her—to cut her open and examine how she was put together because he was curious about biology. To taste and smell her, experience her existence—her life. Yet now as he looked at her, knowing that his family members were injured and lost, he felt nothing but emptiness. He had screwed up badly in life. Instead of trying to fix his wrongs, he had dug himself into a deeper hole.

Davis put his face in his hands and sobbed quietly, so as not to alert the deer. He'd really fucked up. He'd pushed everyone away from him. And instead of apologizing, he had demanded everyone's attention, making their lives miserable if they didn't comply. It was as if there was something within him that wasn't him—something that made him do these awful things while the real Davis was tucked away in a box within his mind. He had lost control of himself, and it had cost him dearly.

And out of everyone that he had hurt, he knew he most regretted destroying his relationship with his father, something that could never be salvaged.

Blood was the warmest at the moment of death. There was a different smell to it when it was that fresh. It smelled wild and gamy, full of adrenaline, because death was usually a surprise. The hormonal surge was one last attempt to fight or take flight. A futile attempt.

When a corpse bled at the time of death, the blood was at its richest color, as it was the essence of life draining away, taking with it all the vital nutrients and oxygen needed to keep a creature alive.

Davis liked this kind of blood the best. Blood that was spilled at the moment of death. It was warm and rich and gave him something new. A relic of strength from the life he'd just taken. For it was his to take—to study, to understand, to absorb.

The first blood he'd ever tasted was from a deer, one that he had perfectly killed. Within seconds of it collapsing, Davis was on top of it, examining the bullet hole that bore through his chest cavity. Blood oozed from the buck's wound all over his hands. In the thick, glistening liquid, he saw something. Something that he wanted. Something that he craved, which the deer itself owned . . . or had owned.

His father had taught him to never let anything go to waste. Something carnal within Davis told him that there was something he needed within that deer's blood. He continued to watch it run over his hands as he probed his fingers into the bullet hole and stretched the skin, trying to get to visibility of the muscle beneath.

Curiously, he smelled the warm blood, and upon the first whiff, a craving roared in his stomach. Without consciously thinking about what he was doing, he lifted his hands to his face and started to lick the blood off his fingers. A musky, iron taste covered his tongue. He swallowed.

A trigger tripped in his mind that signaled to him that he needed this meat, and tore through the skin and into the flesh. Something ferine from within his mind overtook his scientific curiosity. Chunks of muscle that detached—pulled apart by his hands—were popped into his mouth.

The buck was bleeding out, but he wasn't dead yet. Immobile, all he could do was look to the sky, eyes so large that the whites were showing.

And Davis craved for every bit of flesh. He felt nourished. The strength of the deer was transferring to him as he tried to consume the buck. He ignored the popping and gurgling noise coming from the animal's mouth as he tried to grab one last breath.

Rough hands ripped Davis away from his prey. There was a hard slap across his right cheek. A deep husky voice was screaming at him, words that Davis struggled to comprehend. He was in a trance. For a moment he didn't know if he were still a boy or if he had become the deer, since he had ingested her life. Being shaken by the shoulders drew him out of the fog, whereupon he realized that he was, in fact, still a boy.

He fixed his eyes on his father, who was shaking him, hard, but the words that angrily spewed from Albert Perrin's mouth fell on deaf ears. A small smirk on Davis's lips only enraged his father more. There was nothing his father could say or do that would make Davis feel bad in this moment. This moment was his. Finally, for the first time in his life, he felt that he was whole.

However, this event changed the relationship he had with his father. Where at one time his father was always there for him, after this, Albert Perrin regarded Davis as something different, something darker, something not his own. He dealt very carefully with Davis, backing down from fights or walking away completely. When they would go hunting together after that event, it wasn't as father and son, but more like two strangers in the woods together. With every kill, Davis knew his father watched him, so his ritual had to remain a secret. He would save some raw meat for later to eat away from the watchful eyes of his father, although the saved meat never compared to his first kill.

A couple of years after this event, when he and his father took his brother out hunting for the first time, Davis was no longer satisfied by secretly eating the fresh flesh of his kills. He was done being controlled by his father. In an act of defiance and hunger with the kill that day, he showed his father and brother that he was a strong warrior. No one could control or overpower him. As he gutted the deer, he reached up into its rib cage and with his knife cut out its heart. This was how he was going to gain strength and determination, by taking it from the deer. As he raised the heart to his lips, he saw his brother advancing on him with a sick look on his face. Good, thought Davis. Korin is not strong enough to take on this level of strength.

He bit down into the sinewy muscle, then held out the heart toward his brother, just to make him feel even worse. His father just watched him from behind his brother, his face red and angry. Albert pushed Korin aside and stormed up to Davis. His father's eyes met his own with a glare and he smacked the bloody organ out of Davis's hands. There was a look on his father's face that said if he even tried reaching for that heart, Davis would be beyond sorry.

Davis left the rest of the heart on the corpse, stood up, and walked away. He was satisfied and whole again.

Anger rose up in him again, as it always did, remembering the look on his father's face that day. From that point on, Davis had lost whatever remaining trust he'd had in his father. This episode was the final nail in the coffin, forever damning his and his father's relationship. It spawned a multitude of emotions, the biggest of which was jealousy, a beast that took over his body and made him do things that he didn't want to do.

His parents always saw Korin as the successful one. The one who would take care of them when they were older. They needed him.

They never needed Davis. As a kid, Davis saw to it that he always showed *he* needed *them*, making it his mission to remind them of it every chance he got. It worked out well for him for many years. Until the beast of jealousy infected Korin too.

The difference between Davis and Korin was that Davis believed he could control his inner monster, while Korin never could. His younger brother allowed his jealousy to quietly rage on in a sinister and stealthy way. Korin's lack of control over his jealousy haunted Davis every day of his life.

The pain was agonizing.

Although his parents rushed him to the hospital, the pain was unbearable, to the point where he wished Korin had pushed him completely into the fire and just burned him to death.

In the backseat of the car, his mother—for some stupid reason—held his arm up high and above his head while keeping the bags of frozen peas wrapped around it. His father was in the driver's seat, swearing up a storm. Yelling at Davis that he needed to get along with his brother. That what happened tonight was all his fault. That Davis had antagonized Korin.

With the mention of Korin's name, his mother started screaming,

"We left him at home! We left him home alone! Turn the car around."

"He'll be fine. We have to get Davis to the hospital."

"But my baby. My baby is home alone, and at night." The tears started flowing and she started wailing, right in Davis's ear.

He couldn't believe it. Here he was, sitting with a burned arm, caused by his brother, and his mother was blubbering that they had left the little jerk home alone.

"*Enough!*" his father yelled at her.

Then, looking in the rearview mirror, directly at Davis, he said, "If anything happens to your brother, it is all your fault."

All my fault, Davis thought. Everything is always my fault.

His jealousy monster would make him pushy about some things. It liked to get its way, which caused Davis to at times be in the wrong place at the wrong time.

Like with Granma. The old bat had hated him from day one. His earliest memory of her was when she would stare him in the eyes, breathing cigarette smoke in his face, saying "You have ugly eyes." He eventually learned that he had his grandfather's eyes. For that, his grandmother always punished him, by ignoring him, telling him he was ugly, or by locking him up for a few hours in the guest room when he visited, so that she didn't have to deal with him for the entire length of his stay.

He hated her. And he hated how she treated his brother completely differently than him. Again, his brother was the golden child, and Korin received her constant adoration. Yet, with all that, all he'd ever wanted was for her to love him. He tried too hard one night. And it killed her.

During the last time Davis and Korin were ever at their grandmother's house, Davis had convinced her to go upstairs to get her alone with him. When they got to the top of the stairs, he tried in some way to connect with her.

"Can you tell me again about Grandpa?" he asked her as they walked into her bedroom.

"Why the hell do you want to hear about him?"

"I'm just interested, that's all. I want to know more about him, and you."

She ignored him and rummaged through her purse that was sitting on her dresser. In the reflection of the mirror, he saw a deep frown on her face. It was her look of hatred. This wasn't working the way he had wanted it to. He just wanted to talk to her. Just the two of them. No Korin.

"Granma—" he started.

"Here, you little shithead." She shoved five dollars in his hand. "Ungrateful little brat."

The words stung. He didn't need her money. The story about needing new blades for his ice skates was just an excuse to get her upstairs.

She turned and walked out of her room toward the stairs.

"Granma, wait!" he yelled, running out of the bedroom and grabbing her arm.

She turned quickly with a hand raised to hit him. Taking a step backwards to brace herself for the impact across his face, her foot touched nothing but air. Davis froze, not quite grasping what was happening. And he let go of her arm.

She missed the stairs entirely and landed at the foot of them, her neck bent off to the side.

Davis stood at the top of the stairs, clutching the five-dollar bill, unsure of what to do next.

Korin came racing into the room, and it was his high-pitched screaming that snapped Davis out of his trance. His brother looked up at him with accusing eyes.

Davis's heart hardened. There was no way this blame was going to be put on him. He was just trying to talk to her. He wouldn't let Korin see his weakness.

"Wh-what happened?" Korin asked.

Davis hated his brother more than ever in that moment, and he put up a wall around himself, to not let his brother see any emotion.

"Her greedy butt tripped on something and she fell," he said. The words felt raw in his throat. "Karma's a bitch. She should have thought twice about giving me only five dollars."

Korin looked down at the body of his grandmother, curled up next to her, and sobbed.

That's when Davis remembered he should call for help. There was a number that he needed to call for emergency services. The three digits popped into his head.

"Guess I will go call nine-one-one while you lie there like a slobbering idiot," Davis said.

He turned and walked back into their grandmother's bedroom, toward the phone that sat on her nightstand. Tears started streaming down his face.

CHAPTER THIRTY

After he killed his father, Korin walked away from the site, crossed the creek, and tried to find his way back to the car. On the way, he chewed on the heart that had once been housed within his father's chest. The blood was still warm and had a sharp iron taste, but it tasted like normal human blood. Nothing interesting or exciting about it.

However, he was hungry, and as he chewed away with dull teeth at the heart, he could feel something within him growing warm. It was comforting, and he wanted more. He didn't know how long he'd be out in the woods, and knew he needed to ration the chunks of arm flesh that he had still wrapped up in the bandanna. There was no way he could return to his father's body. The way he had it laid out, he'd tried to make it look like the bear had taken vengeance on him. Any more flesh taken from his father's body would probably start to look suspicious.

Besides, he did kind of want to leave the body there for the bear, too, should it come back. His father had tried to kill it, after all.

Korin's teeth were too dull to tear through the cartilage of the valves, so he dropped those pieces on the forest floor. It wasn't worth breaking his teeth on them. He salvaged a few final bites that were not too tough and wrapped them back up in the bandanna with the other pieces of his father's flesh, putting them away in his jacket pocket.

As he was trying to retrace his steps, he passed a fallen tree and caught the faint sound of crying. He listened closely for it and knew it was Addy.

She was alive.

After walking for a few moments, he found her sitting at the base of a tree, sobbing.

"Get up and stop crying. It's annoying," he snapped at her.

She screamed and jumped up. Her porcelain face was streaked with tears and blood. She had quite a bad bloody nose, as blood covered most of her lower face and was all over the front of her jacket. She must have wiped at her face and then her eye at one point, because there was a streak of blood leading up to her right eye.

"Where's Tate."

Korin didn't want to tell her that he left Tate behind at the car.

"Somewhere, maybe he's still alive."

"You don't know?"

"I got turned around in the woods. He was barely alive when I left him. Just get up and be quiet." As he spoke, he felt a hot, dark sensation crept up his spine as she continued to question him.

He stepped toward her.

When he got closer to her, he saw that the blood was all caked hard on her face. The darkness subsided and he felt a weight form in his stomach. It was worry.

He told her again to get up, more gently this time, and then pulled at her scarf and held it up to her nose, releasing the pressure when she winced. He didn't want to hurt her, so he grabbed her hand and gently put it up to her face. Once she was holding her scarf to her nose, he stood and started to walk, hoping she would follow.

"Are we going home?" she asked.

He didn't want to answer her. He didn't want to go home.

They walked on a little bit in silence. Until he heard Addy start to breathe heavy.

He looked at her.

"We're lost." She sniffled and dropped her scarf. "And I want Tate!" Her wail made Korin wince.

"Addy, be quiet. That bear could be somewhere around here still."

He honestly wasn't quite sure where it had stalked off to, and he had no intention of running into it.

Addy put her hand over her mouth, and her body shook with sobs.

"I don't mean the bear is right here at this moment," Korin said softly.

She lowered her hand, bloody snot trailing out of her nose and sticking to her palm. She wiped it off on her jeans.

Korin gagged. After getting over his initial revulsion, he used his jacket sleeve to wipe the caked blood, tears, and snot off her face. She wasn't perfectly clean, but he did manage to wipe off a good portion of the mess. He gingerly touched the middle of her nose where he could see some bruising. She flinched. There was probably a fracture.

He had to get her to the cabin where she'd be out of the elements. Korin didn't like how the late morning sky had become overcast. So much for a nice, mild day as predicted by the local weatherman. He was also getting colder by the minute, which meant the temperature was dropping. Tate would be absolutely crushed if he found out something had happened to Addy. Especially if she were under Korin's watch.

He wasn't even sure if Tate was alive. The last thing he needed was to take Addy back to the car to find her brother dead. The safest place for her now was out of this environment and into some real shelter.

Korin took her hand and started leading her in what he believed was the right direction for the cabin.

Addy crawled over to Korin and curled up by his side. He had fallen asleep against a tree when they sat down to rest. He agreed with Addy that they would sit for a bit. While this delayed in getting her to the cabin, it gave him time to think and figure out where they were. Korin wouldn't admit it, but he was lost.

The feeling of her small form leaning on him woke him woke up immediately. "What are you doing?" he snapped.

"I'm cold," she said.

He groaned and tried to push her away, but being so tiny, she found a way to snuggle closer to him. He stood, which made Addy fell over. She was getting too comfortable with him, and it bothered him. He wasn't her brother. He wasn't anyone's brother.

The sky was a dark gray slate when they started walking again. It was too early in the afternoon to be this dark. A storm was brewing.

Korin touched his bulging eye. The searing pain had gone away, and he thought that the swelling may have gone down. He smiled. Eating his father's eye may have been just what was needed to heal his own eye.

"Where are we going?" Addy asked, her voice piercing his thoughts.

"This way," he muttered, not even turning to look at her.

"Okay" was her only reply, and she ran to catch up with him. She reached up and grabbed his hand. Hers was ice cold. He stopped and looked at her. She had no gloves or hat, but at least her clothes were warm enough.

Korin reached into his jacket pocket, the one without the meat, and pulled out his own gloves and knit cap. It was one his mom had knitted for him years ago. She actually had done a good job with it, and he wore it often. It was warm.

Kneeling down, he grabbed Addy's arms and put his gloves on her. Then he pulled his cap over her head. He pulled it down a little too far and covered her face.

She giggled, and he grinned for a quick second.

When she pushed the cap up over her eyes to look at him, his usual annoyed demeanor returned. "They are too big for you, but at least you'll be warm." And with that he turned and continued walking.

He could hear her walking behind him. She hummed a little tune that he'd never heard before. In any other situation, that would have annoyed the hell out of him. But out here, in the desolate forest with all the snow, he was comforted. He struggled to understand this feeling, because he'd never felt comforted by anyone.

A howling scream echoed through the trees, halting Korin in his tracks. It terrified Addy, and she ran to Korin, wrapping her arms around his legs. He reached down and put a hand on her head. A dark smile crossed his face as he reached down to untangle her, took her hand, and continued walking.

That scream was all too familiar. It was one he heard often in his dreams. The recurring dream of the flesh burning off his brother's arm.

Davis had found their father's body.

Korin laughed silently to himself so as not to alarm or confuse Addy. He won't lie to himself—he's a little surprised by the emotion behind the scream. Davis must have loved their father after all. Here, all this time Korin had thought Davis was just using him.

Good. The asshole was probably kneeling next to their father's body right now, crying his stupid eyes out.

Addy started making a squeaking noise, and Korin realized she was crying and trying to muffle it.

"What's wrong?" he asked her.

"I'm scared," she whispered. "There are monsters in the woods."

"There are no monsters here."

"Please, Korin." She pulled down on his hand to get him to come closer to her. "Please don't let them eat me."

He laughed. Addy had a crazy imagination. He assumed it was because she lived in such a broken household. Korin didn't know her well, but felt a slight bit of pity for her. If it wasn't for Tate, no one would want her, either. Tate was most likely dead by now. She would be alone. He didn't want that for her. He didn't want her to feel like him, alone and abandoned.

Korin resolved that he would take care of her, take her on as a younger sibling. He'd be the oldest, just as he'd always wanted. Then if he and Maeve ever got married, they could adopt her as their own.

A family, he thought. He could have a real family. A family in which he was wanted.

Korin reached down and started to pick her up, letting out a sharp gasp as the pain in his chest shot up and down his body.

She pushed him away. "You're hurt," she said.

"No, I'm not."

"Let's see. Lift your shirt," she commanded, as authoritatively as a six-year-old could.

He obliged and shivered when his skin met the freezing air.

"Eww," she said, wrinkling her nose. "You're deformed."

Sure enough, when he looked down he saw that there was something terrible going on. His ribs were indented and gaunt. The skin on his chest was turning a sick shade of gray. He must be more injured than he had thought.

"Your eye looks really gross too. It's running."

Korin reached up and touched the liquid seeping from his eye. It had a thick viscosity to it. Definitely not tears. Closing his right eye, he was still enveloped in darkness.

They really needed to get to the cabin.

As if Addy was thinking the same thing, she grabbed his hand and started walking ahead of him, thinking she was leading him in the right direction.

He smiled and was happy that she was now his family. He was glad that he had found her alone in the woods.

It seemed like hours since they had heard the scream. Korin knew he was woozy, and it was messing up his sense of direction. They should have reached the creek by now—or at least the road.

"We didn't cross a creek, did we?" he asked. Forgetting for a moment that Addy was with him, he jumped when her little voice said "No."

Unfortunately, that question broke a dam inside of Addy. As Korin continued trekking on, trying to figure out exactly where they were, she started asking questions. Lots of questions.

"Korin, what's that sound?"

"Korin, I'm cold."

"My feet hurt."

"Did you hear that?"

"Korin, is something coming to eat us?"

He'd finally had enough when she asked "Are we there yet?"

He spun around, full of pure anger. He felt it burn from his stomach, up his throat, and into his face.

Addy looked in terror at him as he felt his face contort.

"Will you shut up?" he growled at her.

She buried the lower part of her face in the neck of her jacket and nodded "Yes."

He calmed down and his face returned to normal.

"Good, let's go."

After more walking, Korin stopped. Something didn't sound right. He turned around and saw that Addy was gone.

"Addy!" he bellowed, and started walking back the way they'd just come. Grumbling the whole way, he was struggling to decide whether he was going to slap her or pick her up and carry her once he found her. Stupid little brat, wandering off in these woods. She had no clue where she was.

After walking for a few minutes, he happened upon her standing at the base of a birch tree, peeling off its bark. He watched as she started to raise it to her mouth.

"What are you doing?" he snapped at her.

She jumped with a scream.

"I'm hungry," she said, and began to cry again.

He stood there glaring at her.

Addy shuffled backwards to a tree, trying to hide behind it.

Korin looked up. Tiny snowflakes began fall, light and random. They melted as soon as they hit the ground.

"Great," he said in disbelief, "just what I needed now."

Addy shivered as she pressed closer to him. She then let out a big yawn. He wanted to continue on and try to right himself directionally, but Addy was tired. He needed to let her rest, get warm, and eat to regain her strength. These small snowflakes be a sign of something worse coming. He pulled out a lighter from his hip pocket, one he carried despite never even trying to smoke a cigarette in his life. It had been a gift from Tate on his eighteenth birthday. Even though it was his special day, Davis had managed to upstage him. The lighter had a naked lady etched on it. A joke from Tate, now that he was "legal." Davis had glared at him across the table as Korin flushed with embarrassment and their mother chastised Tate for giving him such a disrespectful gift.

"You won't use it," Davis said, leaning toward Korin with his hand stretched out. "Give it here." Korin had refused and immediately pocketed the lighter. Davis started to insult Korin and they argued back and forth. Their mother hid behind Tate with a sad look on her face while their father just got up and left the table to go to the basement. Davis was relentless and Korin gave up, left the table, and hid in his room for the rest of the night. Neither parent tried to stop Davis, letting him have his way in ruining Korin's birthday. He'd heard them out there all calmly talking, enjoying his birthday evening without him.

That night Korin had pulled the lighter out of his pocket and run his finger over the engraving of the woman. He'd flipped the lid open and struck the wheel, igniting the flame. What would happen if he just dropped this on his bedding and set the whole house on fire?

"Korin?" Addy said meekly from behind the tree.

Korin's eye focused on her and he remembered he had to feed her. She was hungry.

With Addy still hiding behind the tree, watching his every move, he found a few semi-dry branches. They would take a while to burn and the flame wouldn't be big, but it would be something.

Once he got the fire started, he sat down. Addy peeked out from behind the tree to look at him. With a flick of his hand, he motioned for her to come over. She stepped toward him tentatively, trying not to stir his anger. She sat next to him in silence for several minutes, her eyes fixed on the fire.

"Korin?" Addy asked, leaning up against his left arm.

He'd been unaware of how close she was and pulled away.

She wasn't fazed. "I'm hungry."

"I don't know what you want me to do about that. I don't have any food on me; we have to go find some." He still held back from fully admitting that he wasn't quite sure what direction the car was in, or else he would have taken her back there to where there was food in the cooler.

And then he realized he did have food. There was some meat wrapped up in his bandanna.

"Wait a minute, I think I've got something here for you."

He pulled the bloodied bandanna out of his pocket, unwrapped it, and held it to her face.

She instantly gagged. "It's meat!" she said, tears in her eyes.

"You're hungry, aren't you?" he barked at her.

"But meat. It's evil."

"You are messed up in your little head," he said, starting to wrap up the bandanna. "Fine, if you don't want it, I'm going to eat it all later."

He watched her look around the forest and then he heard the soft grumble of her stomach.

"Korin," she said softly.

"What?"

"I'll eat it if you cook it."

"Glad you came to your senses." He unwrapped the pieces of flesh and stuck them on the end of a thin stick, holding it over the fire. He chuckled as he realized what he was cooking.

"What's so funny?" she asked as she sniffed the air and smiled.

195

"Oh, nothing really," he said, as a smile spread across his face. "This just sort of reminds me of when my dad took us camping once and we roasted hot dogs over the fire."

CHAPTER THIRTY-ONE

"Hello? Hello!" Deputy Connor shouted into the CB mic. He had just heard Tate Michelson calling for help. They were at the hunting cabin and something had happened to them, but Connor hadn't quite caught the details. He thought he'd heard something about an accident. But was the girl with him?

"Tate . . . Tate!" Connor tried to raise Addy's brother again through the CB, but there was still no response. "Damn!" he shouted throwing the mic down on the desk.

He wheeled his chair over to the receptionist's desk and picked up the phone, dialing Sheriff Middleton. It was the sheriff's day off, but this was an emergency.

"Hallo?" a gruff voice snapped on the other side of the phone.

Connor swallowed, knowing he'd be pissing off Middleton, but something had to be done.

"Sheriff, it's Connor. We have a situation here. We need to get up to the Perrin cabin. I think there's been an accident and we may have folks up there who are injured or lost." Connor wasn't certain about the lost part, but he wanted all resources sent in case they needed to do a search and rescue. Time was not on their side with the impending snowstorm.

"What do we know so far?" the sheriff asked in a sharp tone, the gruffness fading.

"First we have Addy Michelson, age six, who's been missing since early morning," said Connor. "I sent Ranger Boyd from the Covill Ranger Station to see if she was with the Perrins, who were going to their old hunting cabin for the weekend. I hadn't heard back from him, but I just got a call on the CB from Tate Michelson, her brother, saying something about needing help and there being an accident. I can't raise him again, so I have no idea what's going on."

Middleton took a moment before responding. "You know that ain't our jurisdiction?"

"I'm wanting to do this off the books here, and just get a group with some sniffer dogs to go and take a look."

Connor could envision the big sheriff leaning back in his rickety chair.

"Ol' Kenny's got some tracking bloodhounds, and I think he's home," Middleton said.

Connor took that as approval, muttered his thanks, and quickly hung up the phone. He'd swing by Kenny's on the way to Natalie Perrin's. He realized he should update Phoebe Michelson, too—she was Addy's mother, after all—but she was probably passed out drunk, not even thinking about Addy's well-being.

On his way out, he made a quick call to Natalie, letting her know he was on his way, offering no additional details. He then called on Mary Prudence to ask her to reach out to some townsfolk, letting them know he needed some people to come and help look around the area for Addy Michelson. That old town gossip would probably have the whole town waiting outside of the station in twenty minutes.

He needed to hurry.

Connor pounded with a fist on the Perrins' front door. Natalie whipped the door open with a look of terror and concern. Her eyes were red from crying. There was a young woman sitting at the table in the kitchen, anxiously looking at the deputy.

"Ladies." Connor said, taking off his hat.

Natalie stepped back, allowing him to enter the room.

"Did you find her?" Natalie asked anxiously.

"No, ma'am, not yet. And there is a new situation that just came up."

He looked down and slid the brim of his hat back and forth between his fingers. This was the part of the job he hated the most—giving bad news. He coughed, clearing his throat.

"Right after I called you, a call came in via the CB from Tate."

"What? What did he say?" Natalie said, grabbing Connor's arm.

He put a reassuring hand over hers. "He said that help was needed at the cabin, and from what I think I heard, there's been an accident."

"You *think* you heard?" Natalie spat.

"There was some static in the transmission, but yes, that's what it sounded like."

"Are my boys okay?" Natalie asked, becoming instantly frantic.

This time, the girl that was sitting at the table came around behind Natalie and guided her to the sofa. Connor followed.

"Look, I don't know anything for certain, but I'm organizing a couple of search parties—one to stay here and look for the girl, the other to go up to the cabin in case we need to do a search-and-rescue up there. We'll have medical on hand, too."

The girl was sitting next to Natalie, holding her hand.

"Maeve, get your things. We are going, too," Natalie said, detaching herself from Maeve's grip and standing up.

"Natalie, I don't think that's such a good idea," said Connor. "We . . . umm . . . we don't know what we will find, and it may be too much for you women to handle." He said the words as quickly as possible.

Both women were staring him down, Natalie's face flushed in anger. At least the younger one didn't look like she was ready to slit his throat. Natalie stood real close to Connor, and instinctively he wanted to take a step back; he knew he needed to hold his composure. He was the man here, after all. But, by god, this woman was terrifying.

"You listen here, you little misogynistic prick. Don't you ever tell me what you think I can or cannot handle."

Connor swallowed hard and lowered his eyes. He had stepped in it, bad.

"Umm, okay. Let's go," he said, adding, "I'll drive."

Natalie went to the closet to get their jackets.

"Natalie," Connor said, and she spun to look at him. He could see daggers in her eyes, poised and ready to be thrown. "Kenny said he needs something of Addy's for his sniffer dogs. Do you have anything?"

She nodded. "I have a shirt that she spilled chocolate milk on the last time she was here. Luckily, I haven't washed it yet. I'll go get it."

As soon as Natalie left the room, Connor turned to Maeve. "I never introduced myself. I'm Deputy Connor with the Rachet Police Department."

"Hmm, and I thought you were a baker," she said sarcastically. She didn't like him much. "I'm Maeve Alders, Korin's girlfriend."

Connor couldn't help himself. "Korin? Korin Perrin has a girlfriend?"

Now the girl looked ready to slit his throat.

Amanda Headlee

CHAPTER THIRTY-TWO

The gray clouds that had been gathering in the sky were finally starting to let loose. Davis held his hand out, allowing the small snowflakes to touch down, melting on contact. He knew he was right about the storm and this was just the beginning.

In the distance Davis could hear the swishing sound of water. He was close to the creek. As he neared the water his mind drifted back to his friend that he'd left behind. He was tormented by guilt, but there was no way that Tate could have survived this trek. His injuries were quite extensive. Davis wondered if he might have some internal damage. Leaving Tate at the scene of the accident was the quickest way for him to be found and taken to safety.

Davis recalled the blood and bits of the car left on the macadam. Somehow, as hard as the bear had been hit, the damn thing had not only managed to survive, but then chase his father into the woods. Davis hoped that his father had gotten away. He tightened his hands around the rifle. Despite the lack of a father-son bond between the two of them, he was going to murder that bear. There was a rage flowing through him that he had only felt once before, and that was when Korin had pushed him into the fire. He knew his brother had done it as a form of revenge, believing Davis had killed their grandmother.

Davis carried the physical scars and Korin, the mental ones, from their attacks on each other.

He continued on alongside the creek. The waters were rushing, but they were still low enough that he could walk across. He saw a rocky outcrop ahead, and wondered if it was the place where his father and uncle used to play when they were kids. He remembered his father telling him stories about a bunch of big rocks a few miles away from the cabin. They used to pretend it was a castle. It even had a cave they would use for a dungeon.

Davis stepped down onto the bank of the creek. There were some larger stones in this area he could probably hop across to get to the other side. It would be the best way to stay dry. With the rifle held in both of his hands, he jumped to the first rock. It was a little slippery, but the surface was wide enough that he didn't have anything to worry about. He hopped to the second. Then the third. When he landed on this one, he teetered a bit, but with a flailing of his arms he regained his balance.

A small sweat had broken out on his forehead. The water looked much deeper here. He jumped to the next rock. Instead of jumping to the next one, he took a large step forward with his right foot. While the tip of his boot made contact with the edge, the gap was bigger than he'd expected. As soon as he shifted his weight to try to bring his other foot over, his boot lost hold on the rock and he fell into the icy water. The gun fell out of his hands as his body hit the water and sank to the bottom.

He got up quickly. The water was above his knees here. He walked through the rushing current and made it to the other side, climbing up onto the bank.

His relief was short-lived, as he had a dire situation on his hands. His boots and pants were soaked, along with his socks, and the thermal underwear he wore underneath. He'd fell forward, and grabbed onto the rock, in an attempt to save his entire body from going under, but up to his waist did go in. Spinning around, he realized there was no way he was going back in the creek to retrieve the rifle.

"Arrgh!" he yelled in frustration. He couldn't walk through the woods this way. He would freeze to death.

Davis took off the pack and unzipped it. The second pair of thermal underwear that he had at the top of the pack was dry, as was another flannel shirt. The other pairs of jeans and socks were soaked, along with all the food he'd brought. The jerky was the only thing salvageable. The crackers and bread had disintegrated, as he had poorly closed their bags from when he took a snack break. He had left the remaining packaged food with Tate.

Davis took off his jacket and shirt and put on a base layer top and sweatshirt. The bottom of his jacket was wet, but he would have to suffer with that. His core would get too cold without it. Then he took off his soaking wet jeans, thermal long underwear, socks, and boots. He pulled on the dry base layer bottoms. They were not at all thick and warm like the ones he just took off. Unfortunately this was all he had to cover his legs. He had no other footwear but the wet boots, so he shoved his bare feet into them. Putting them back on made his toes ache from the cold.

He couldn't go on like this. He couldn't go back to the car, because that meant crossing the creek again. His only option was to stay put, make a fire, and attempt to dry out his clothes.

Davis looked around the forest. Everything near him was covered in a light layer of snow. The temperature was plummeting, causing the snowflakes to become bigger and stick to the cold ground. He wasn't going to be able to make a fire with any of this. He looked ahead, at the outcrop of rocks that sat in the middle of the trees. Maybe he could find the cave his father had spoken of; there might be some dry kindling in there.

He looked at his watch. It was after three. He maybe had three more hours of light. If these were the rocks that his father used to play at, they were a good distance away from the cabin. He might be stuck out here for the night, and this may be the best area to stay. Picking up his pack and soggy clothes, he hurried toward the rocks.

The rocks were more like boulders up close, haphazardly strewn on the forest floor. It was like a giant had picked up some pebbles and tossed them around. While he was literally at the base of a large hill, called Mount Brisbane by the locals, he couldn't see any other boulder-like rocks nearby. This had to be the place his father had described.

Davis walked up to the rocks and followed a path that wove between them. Suddenly he saw something large and dark laying across the path. He dove into the brush on his left, watching the dark mass for a couple of minutes. It didn't stir or move. He couldn't hear it making any sound either. He figured that if it had been alive at some point, it wasn't anymore.

Davis bravely stepped out of the brush and walked closer to the mass. As he drew nearer, he realized it was a human body. He began to feel like there was something familiar about the clothing.

He stood over the body. The back was torn up with many puncture wounds, and the right arm was missing. The hair on the head was indistinguishable, as the back of the skull had been smashed in. Brain matter peeked through the shattered hole in the skill. Some animal had killed and started eating this man. His mind continued to block the acknowledgment of the familiar clothing.

"Oh, I hope you are dead," he said, kneeling down next to the body. A wave of dizziness swept over him. Davis grabbed the man's left shoulder and tried to roll him over so that he could get a look at the face. He was heavy. With a couple of pushes, the corpse ungracefully rolled over with a wet smack as the back met the ground.

The first thing Davis noticed was the gaping hole in the man's chest where the ribs had been ripped open and the insides torn out.

Then Davis saw the man's face.

All the blood in his face drained away and his head spun. He locked eyes on the face again and let out a bloodcurdling scream that echoed far off among the trees.

Davis sat there staring at the man's face. He knew his body should be shivering by now, but the shock of seeing his dead father lying in front of him, mutilated, had sent adrenaline coursing through his body. Right now, Davis felt nothing.

The bear had caught up with his father and gotten its revenge. Davis knew this was an attack of spite and vengeance as, for the most part, the body was whole. But the bear had made sure to tear open his father's chest and eat his insides.

Davis couldn't bring himself to look at what specific organs were eaten. He couldn't stand the sight or the smell. The body reeked of putrid food and waste. And death.

All the anger and resentment that he'd felt for his father unraveled, dissipated, the past forgotten. Davis wept over the body, regretting all the time lost because he had allowed his anger toward his father to keep them apart.

"I'm so sorry, Dad." The words scratched at his throat. Words that he truly meant, but also struggled to say. His father never trusted him, and he had never trusted his father. That was wrong. There should have been apologies and trust from both.

Snow had started falling harder. Davis's mind was telling him to seek shelter. His heart was telling him to stay put. But the brain asked what good was he to his father sitting here. The answer was none. If he stayed, he too would soon be dead. Especially if the bear was still around.

"Shit!" Davis exclaimed, jumping to his feet.

The icy wind weaving through the trees had hit his unprotected legs, causing them to feel like they were being burned by a cold fire—if that were possible.

"Shit, shit, shit."

He spun around looking at the woods that surrounded him. The bear was still alive and probably roaming around. It was going to come after him next. And he no longer had a weapon, aside from a long and wide Bowie knife his father had gotten him for his eighteenth birthday.

Birthday milestones usually meant gifts of some kind of weaponry in the Perrin household.

The thought of his father brought tears to his eyes. He gasped and clutched his chest as grief flooded through him.

This was his father.

He thought he'd hated the man. He didn't.

As grief tore through his body, he realized that he'd wanted nothing more than acceptance from his father. Deep down he had truly loved him. Subconsciously he had been trying to get that acceptance all along by doing little things for him, like packing the medical kit for his car, and wanting to stay home to take care of him and his mother in their old age. Though hidden behind a rough guise, Davis just wanted his father to want him.

It was all his fault. All of it—and especially this. If he'd only passed his father the thermos . . .

Another icy blast of wind cut through the trees and raked against Davis's thinly clad legs, bringing him back to the dire situation he was in. He couldn't stay here with his father's body. He had to get out of here. He needed to get himself to safety and call for help. A search party to rescue Tate and find Addy and Korin, then recover his father.

He reached for the Bowie knife's sheath that was attached to the belt on his pants, only to remember he didn't have on his jeans. They lay in a soggy pile behind him.

Davis looked down at his father's body, fully clothed. The jeans were frozen around the calf area, and the front was soaked with blood. Yet, they were less wet than his own. And his father's shoe size was the same as his and were dry. In order to survive the trek to the cabin, he was going to need his father's clothes. He had to take the jeans and boots. It was Davis's only chance to survive and get help.

With a long inhale, Davis held his breath and leaned forward to unbuckle his father's pants. He tried not to look directly at the gaping hole in Albert's chest, nor did he breathe for fear of smelling the mutilated insides. He gagged as his scientific mind tried to coax him to look at what the inside of a real human chest cavity looked like. This was his father, he focused on the belt.

The blood on the jeans was only partly frozen. Davis's hands were soon stained red, but he didn't care.

After he got the buckle and button undone and the zipper unzipped, he rolled his father back on his stomach. Davis couldn't handle looking at his father's face anymore, especially now that he was robbing his corpse of his clothing.

"He won't be angry. I'm his son. I'm going to die," he whispered over and over again to himself as he slid his father's pants down. Then he bent up one leg to access the boot's laces. He untied them and took them off. He repeated the same process with the other boot. Then, with some tugging, he successfully pulled off the pants. The legs hit the ground with a sickening thud. Like a wet sack of potatoes being dropped. Davis kept moving to subdue the wave of nausea that swept over him.

He quickly got dressed, ignoring the blood that was all over the pants. He put on the boots, lacing them up tight. He then slipped the Bowie knife sheath onto the belt and fastened the belt, cinching it tight, his father's waist being much bigger. As he stood there adjusting the belt, he couldn't help but stare at the back of the corpse. The wounds weren't right for it to have been an animal attack. The back of his father's head was cracked open. And the lacerations to his back were too clean, even where the area where the shoulder blade looked to be removed. He leaned forward, swallowing his fear, and probed the puncture wounds on the back. All the wounds were thin and deep. Worst of it all, there were no bite marks.

Davis swiftly turned his head to the right and vomited. This attack was too clean for an animal. There was no way an animal could have done this without causing more destruction to the body or leaving behind bite marks. No, it was something much more sinister.

He flipped his father back over and looked at the face. The chest wound was too precise. Davis was not about to look inside the wound to see what organs were missing. Moving his focus to his father's face, the only damage aside from a few small scratches was that the skin was torn around the left eye. And the entire eye was missing. Ironically, it was the same eye that Tate mentioned Korin had injured in the accident.

CHAPTER THIRTY-THREE

Korin sat with his back to a tree, facing Addy, his head drooped forward and his right arm protectively across his chest. Snow was beginning to stick to the ground.

Korin looked up at Addy, her cap was dusted with larger snowflakes. "Let's get going."

She got up wordlessly and they continued their trek to the cabin. They had crossed the creek above the rocky outcrop. Not wanting Addy to get wet, he had her crawl up on his back. Pain seared in his chest as he hefted the extra weight and waded across the ice-cold water. He set her down after walking out of the creek and they crossed over the trail that ran parallel with the creek. Suspecting that Addy might ask about following it, he cut her off and told her that they needed to find the road on the other side of the trail.

She started fretting about his legs getting cold after walking through the water. He just ignored her. He had his bearings again after hearing Davis's scream and finding the creek. It was still a bit of a hike to the old sawmill, through the woods. Once they reached the road, it was a little over a mile south to where the road intersected with the cabin's long dirt driveway. Korin hoped they would get there by dark, but he was slowing down from the pain in his ribs and Addy was not a fast walker. She was struggling to keep up with him. Unfortunately, he didn't have the strength to carry her.

His stomach growled. He was starving. The remaining meat he had left he'd fed to her. She devoured every bit and was satisfied. He enjoyed watching her eat it. He shared a bond with her now that he didn't share with anyone else on the planet.

His mind went back to wishing she was his sister as opposed to having Davis as his brother. This kid paid more attention to him than his brother ever had. And she never made him feel worthless. She was an angel. Not something evil, like his brother.

A wave of heat flashed across Korin's face and he felt something start to burn within his chest. For the first time in many years, thoughts began to resurface again in his mind—that Davis was a monster. The intensity of the heat in his chest strengthened as the feeling of hate started to seep through his veins. His brother, the one who always demanded attention. His brother, the one who got everything he ever wanted. His brother, the one who had killed the only person who every truly loved Korin—killed her because she hadn't loved Davis at all.

Tremors began to vibrate under his skin and his breathing increased. He hated his brother. Hated him with every ounce of his being. He was a cancer that had been allowed to live and thrive freely while Korin had had to be shackled to responsibility.

"I wish they were here." A light voice interrupted his thoughts.

"Who?" he snapped. Addy had broken his trance. He felt like he'd just fallen from the sky. His head was woozy and his chest ached.

"Tate and Davis."

He stopped walking and she bumped into the back of his legs. Korin looked up. The bare tree limbs looked like claws reaching up to the sky. Or claws reaching down to crush them.

Hearing his brother's name out of her mouth sent a wave of anger through him that didn't just emanate from his chest but his entire core. Davis's name sounded so vile coming from her. It's like she was tainted by speaking his brother's name. The periphery of his vision darkened as if he were looking through a tunnel. He exhaled and his breath formed a billowy cloud.

Addy looked up at Korin, wondering what he was doing. His shoulders shot back and there was a popping sound. Addy took several steps back and away from him. She pulled the brim of his cap over her eyes so she couldn't see him anymore. She couldn't grasp what she was seeing. It looked like Korin growing taller. But that couldn't happen. That was impossible.

There were more popping noises and she pulled the cap down further over her face and put her hands over her ears. She started humming "I see the moon and the moon sees me" loudly to herself to drown out the noise. Her humming changed into singing, and as she was about to start the song all over again, the cap was pulled off her head and her arms were grabbed.

She opened her eyes and Korin had his face almost right up against hers.

"What are you doing?" he asked. There was no emotion to his voice.

"Singing," she whispered.

"That's not what I meant," he said, taking a step back. He looked normal again. The right height for him. He was glaring at her.

"Humming?" she said, not sure if it was a statement or a question.

Korin brought his face down to hers again and tightened his hold on her arms. Tight enough that it was starting to hurt.

"Don't you ever mention his name to me again."

"Who? Tate or Da—*ouch!*" she yelled, and started to cry as he clamped his hands tighter around her arms. "You're hurting me." She tried to pull away.

He let go of her, pushing her back hard enough that she fell on her backside. Her arm flew up and she hit herself in the nose. Her vision went bright white as the pain registered in her brain from the contact with her broken nose. She had no idea what she'd done to suddenly make him so mad.

The cap lay in the snow next to her. Her hair was wild from the static of having it pulled off. She felt her nose running and attempted to wipe it away. It was bleeding. She said nothing. She just pulled the cap back on, stood, and held her gloved hand to her nose. She didn't want to make Korin any angrier.

He turned and continued through the woods in the direction that she hoped would lead to the cabin. Korin was going to get her there, despite her ever-growing fear of him, so she continued following him.

Korin stood over the bloodied bear that had finally succumbed to its wounds, dying near the abandoned logging road. He kicked its bashed-up muzzle and thought, Finally. His stomach grumbled loudly with hunger, but not for the bear.

"There, you can eat that," Addy said brightly.

Korin whirled around. After he had gotten angry with her for saying

Davis's name, they had continued walking alongside the creek in silence. Eventually, they happened upon the road that led to the old sawmill site. He had noticed something massive lying next to the road. Unsure of what it was, Korin had instructed Addy to hide behind a large oak tree and not to follow him.

"I told you to wait back at that big tree."

Ignoring him, she said, "Why don't you eat that? I heard your stomach growl. You're hungry."

"Because it isn't meat."

"It's a bear."

"It's bad," he seethed, his anger growing from hunger and the annoying little girl. He had given her all the good meat that he had. His stomach growled again, and for a moment, his mind drifted, thinking differently of her. *No*, he shook his head. *No, not Addy.*

Off in the distance there was the rumble of a truck. Korin stood in fear, realizing that the truck was driving on the logging road in their direction. *Someone is looking for us.*

He grabbed Addy and carried her to the other side of the bear carcass. They hunkered down behind it.

"Stay down," he snapped, raising himself a little above the carcass to watch for the oncoming truck.

"I don't wanna be here. It's dead!" Tears started to fall.

"I said stay down and keep quiet," he snarled, and out of fear, she complied.

The truck stopped about fifty yards away on account of a tree lying in the middle of the road. Korin peeked around the carcass and saw a ranger get out of his truck and walk in their direction.

Korin whispered to himself, "Now *that's* meat."

Addy, hearing him, asked loudly, "What is it? A deer?"

"Shhh." He lowered himself down and looked her in the eyes. She wrinkled her nose and made a disgusted face.

"What?" he asked.

"Your eyes are turning black," she said in a worried tone, mimicking Natalie's motherly voice. "You really are getting sick. We have to get you to a doctor."

He gave her a look that basically said *Do what I say or else.*

"Look," he said to Addy, "I don't have time to explain, but I need you to stay hidden and cry loudly as soon as I disappear into the brush." He pointed to the undergrowth right behind them.

"Why?"

"Stop asking and just cry."

"Why?"

He grabbed her shoulder, digging his fingers tightly into her tiny muscles. The black in his eyes had consumed his usual eye color. "Just do it, or else something really bad is going to happen to you."

Addy was terrified. The cries that came out of her were real as Korin silently slipped into the brush.

She put her hands to her eyes, not wanting to see Korin's scary face anymore. Harder sobs tore from her because she just wanted her brother here. He would have kept her safe.

"Addy?" She heard a soft voice call her name. She took her hands away from her eyes and saw a man standing on the other side of the dead bear.

"Addy! We've been looking for you. Are you okay? Where is everyone else?"

The hurried words spilled from the park ranger as he started to walk around the bear to pick her up. But before she could utter the words *Please help me*, Korin appeared behind the man with a thick, heavy branch in his hands. Korin lifted the branch up high and brought it crashing down on the man's head. Again. And again. And again. Bits of blood, bone, and brain matter splattered everywhere, some of it landing on Addy's jacket.

Addy looked at Korin's face, her breath ragged. His face became hollower and his eyes shone with the darkest black. Sharp teeth began to protrude over his lips. He was wholly focused on the body of the dead man in front of him.

Addy didn't utter a sound as she watched Korin flip the man onto his back and with his bare hands, tear open the man's chest. The snapping of ribs pulled Addy out of her trance, and she got up and ran down the road.

"Tate! Tate, where are you? *Tate!*" she screamed, running away from the horror.

There was a sharp pain in her right hand, and she was lifted from the ground by her arm. She saw a gray hand with long black claws holding on to her. She was turned, still dangling from her right arm, to meet the hateful one-eyed gaze of Korin.

Or what used to be Korin. His face was no longer human.

She let loose a high-pitched scream.

The creature tightened his grip on her wrist and there was a snap of bone. Addy screamed in agonizing pain.

The creature lifted his left hand to show her what he was holding. She could not see what it was through her tears, but it was coming toward her face. Instinctively she closed her mouth just as the raw human heart smashed against her lips. Blood seeped from the organ, and Addy, not quite getting her mouth completely tight, could taste warm iron with her tongue.

"Eat it," the creature rasped.

She tried to kick him; her pain intensified as she swung from her arm.

The creature dropped her to the ground, lowering himself to her eye level.

"Are you hungry?" the creature asked, but the voice was softer, and sounded just like Korin.

"Go away!" she yelled, flailing out a leg and kicking the creature in the face.

He pulled back for a second, shaking his head, but then looked right back at her face, his eye burning into her.

She turned away from the grotesque face and putrid breath.

He grabbed her face, one of his claws cutting into her skin at the jawline.

"Are. You. Hungry?" Bits of spit landed on Addy's face as the creature yelled at her. She opened her mouth, but no sound come out.

"Because I am," he roared.

"Please, Korin, no," Addy cowered. "I am not meat!"

CHAPTER THIRTY-FOUR

Tate lay on the old dusty bed in agonizing pain. It felt like hours since Deputy Boyd had left and Tate had contacted Deputy Connor. He knew Connor was sending help and a search party. But how long would it take everyone to get here?

He looked at the fire as he tried to figure out the timing, but the constant pain jolting up his arm and legs would interrupt every thought. Best to just lie here and not think about things, he thought as he stared at the fire that was still burning strong. Boyd had built up a good one. It did cast some light, but because it was getting darker out, most of the interior was hidden in shadow.

Tate felt like he was in a cocoon, thankful for the fire. It would last some time before it needed to be fed, and hopefully by then the others would have arrived. As he stared at the fire, the room started to tilt. Tate felt a headache coming on. He closed his eyes, trying to wish the vertigo and headache away. In an effort to stop the pain, he thought about Davis coming through the door, carrying his little sister on his back. They both would come in smiling and Davis would say, "See, man, I took care of her for you."

Davis and Korin were truly good people at heart, and good friends. Hopefully one of them had found Addy and was taking care of her. Tate was sure that's what was happening, and this was what danced through his head as he began to drift off into unconsciousness.

As he drifted deeper, he heard the front door open and footsteps coming closer. He was too tired to open his eyes, but felt a small smile pull at the corner of his lips. They were here.

It was a weight on his chest that pulled Tate out of the darkness. When he began to stir, the weight lifted, and he felt something drop into his lap. His head lolled on the pillow and he forced himself out of slumber.

Something was going on. Someone was here with him. Addy?

His eyes shot open and he stared at the ceiling. Whoever was here wasn't near him. He rolled his head to look around the room and saw someone large hunkered down by the fire. Tate groaned and leaned up on his good arm.

"Hello?" Tate said through parched lips.

The person next to the fire didn't move.

Tate looked to see what was on his lap. He reached out to touch it. It was small and wet with a thick, rubbery texture. He couldn't see it clearly and picked it up. There was a surprising weight to it, and when he brought it closer to his face, he could see it was a heart.

Tate screamed and threw the organ to the foot of the bed, stirring up dust where it landed.

The shape that had been near the fire had moved so silently that Tate hadn't noticed it had come closer to him. It stood in the shadows of the room and Tate still couldn't make out what it was. Tate could hear a wheezing and cracking breath. Then the shape stepped closer to him and the light of the fire illuminated it.

Korin stood there, naked, with blood smeared across his mouth and down his neck and chest. The skin on his body was gray, and black fur had started growing down his arms and legs. Each hand and foot was elongated and tipped with black claws.

Tate recoiled as he looked at Korin's emaciated face with a single eye blacker than the night. Where the other eye should have been was a hollow socket. Through the smeared blood, Korin's lips parted and sharp teeth were revealed. Tate couldn't tell if it was a smile or a snarl. Thick antlers, like those of an elk, protruded from Korin's head and nearly scraped the ceiling.

"K-K-Korin?" Adrenaline surged in his body. He was terrified.

Without feeling any pain, Tate pushed himself further away.

Korin just stood there breathing heavily and staring at Tate. He made no movement.

"Korin, did you find Addy?" Tate asked. It was the only thing that popped into his head. Something he hoped would connect with his friend.

There was a soft chuckle from Korin.

Anger started replacing Tate's fear. His sister. *Where was his sister?*

"Korin," Tate said more strongly, with the last bit of energy he had. "Where is Addy?"

Korin said nothing, just pointed toward the foot of the bed.

A wave of intense nausea swept over Tate as he collapsed on the bed, moaning. Tate could see Korin still standing there, pointing. Pointing toward the heart that lay at the foot of the bed, a smile plastered across his face.

"You fucking asshole," Tate yelled through his tears. "It should have been you who was pushed into the fire and burned! Not Davis."

The smile disappeared from Korin's face and he wavered, looking confused and hurt by Tate's words.

"You are a fucking monster!" Tate yelled.

He felt himself being lifted off the bed and slammed to the floor, landing on his already shattered arm. The heart flipped off the bed and landed right in front of his face. He screamed out as pain tore through his body, and he rolled forward over the heart. Trying to protect what he believed to be the only remaining part of his sister.

Blood started pooling around him as he felt his damaged right arm pulled backwards. Then there was a sick snap as his tendons, muscles, and skin let loose. He heard a crunching sound as his arm was eaten.

Tate lay there in agonizing pain, crying, the right side of his face to the floor, petrified of the monster that was standing over him. He was looking toward the foot of the bed when he saw Addy step out of the shadows. She knelt on the ground and extended her hand toward him. Her eyes were covered by a large black cap, but he knew she was looking at him. She had come to take him with her. Light sparkled around the periphery of his vision. She looked so angelic. Again he was filled with regret that he hadn't been able to protect her.

He reached his remaining hand toward her, but they were too far apart. His arm was slammed to the ground by a dark hand and a heavy weight sat on his back. The heart that he was trying to protect was crushed under his chest.

"Take me away," he pleaded to his angel sister, with blood flecking the floor in front of his face. Tate felt an intense but brief pain between his shoulder blades. He looked at Addy. Her hand was still outstretched to him. Darkness fell around her and she disappeared.

Outside of the cabin, Davis stopped in his tracks at a scream that came from inside. A scream that was suddenly cut short.

He took a few steps back. Could it be Korin? Tate was back at the car. His father . . . dead. It couldn't have been Addy, for the scream was a man's. It definitely had to be Korin.

Davis's face flushed and he could feel heat rising within himself. It was fueled by anger and hate. The scream was one of agony, so his brother must be injured. *Good.* Davis hoped that his brother was horribly wounded. And now he was going to end him for killing their father.

He unsheathed the hunting knife.

"I'm sorry, Dad," Davis whispered as he neared the front door and grabbed the knob. With a deep breath he charged in with what he hoped was an element of surprise on his side, but stopped short when he saw what was in front of him.

The face was Tate's, but the rest of the body was not. At least it didn't look like Tate. His whole right side was missing—arm, leg, everything. All that remained was the bloody pulp of his left side and his head, which was pointed toward the door, glassy eyes staring Davis down.

"No, no, no, no," Davis said as he lowered the knife and took several steps closer to his friend, but a deep growling coming from inside the cabin made him stop advancing.

He and Tate were not alone.

From the other side of Tate's remains, something stepped out of the shadows and into the firelight. It was massive. Tall, with antlers on its head nearly scraping the ceiling. The face looked like a mangy deer with long yellowed fangs. One single eye stared straight at Davis. The other eye, missing.

The creature took a step forward, stepping on Tate's remains in the process. Over the low rumble of a growl was the sickening wet snap of bone. Davis took a step backwards to the door, raising his knife and not letting the beast out of his sight. It continued to slowly advance toward him, terribly skeletal with a bloated belly. And it smelled of rotting carrion.

Movement off to the right of the creature caught Davis's eye. Addy. She stood next to the decimated body of Tate. A heaviness pressed down on Davis as he looked at her. She stared back at him with a blank look in her eyes.

A low growl made them both look to the source. Davis took a step closer to Addy. He had to get her out of here. The creature growled again.

"Are you sure?" Her bright and cheery voice seemed to echo in the dark cabin. Another growl. She ran toward Davis and he pointed the tip of his knife at the monster in an attempt to guard her. Addy ran past him and out the front door. He was about to make a quick move to turn and bolt the same way.

The beast, as if sensing that Davis was about to attempt an escape, snarled and shot forward, arms and claws outstretched. Davis took one look at the arms coming at him and he turned and ran, keeping a tight grip on the knife. He leapt off the front porch and pounded the ground toward the woods. There was a crashing, scraping sound behind him along with a bloodcurdling howl.

He chanced a glance behind him and saw the beast was stuck in the doorway, caught by its antlers. It had one clawed hand on the antlers, trying to wedge them through. He stopped. Addy was in plain sight running down the cabin's driveway in the direction of the main road, her footprints leaving a trail in the freshly fallen snow. However, the monster's focus wasn't on her. The single eye of the beast burned as it glared at Davis, and he knew that the glare was his brother's.

The woods were moderately familiar to him, but in his panic, Davis had lost his way. He had no idea where he was.

He found himself surrounded by low-growing conifers, a small patch of trees that formed a pine tree glen amid the other deciduous trees. He had never seen this area before. Davis sat down on a log to take a breather and tried to think what direction he'd taken from the cabin. It was fruitless. He ran off in the opposite direction of Addy praying that he would be the one followed. Hoping to be the decoy. But now he was lost and had no idea where the creature was. He prayed Addy was still safe, still alive.

Oddly enough, the creature didn't seem like it was going to harm her when they were in the cabin. In fact, it seemed to communicate with her by the way she replied to its growls. And she stood so still, seemingly calm next to Tate's body.

Davis pulled his arms in tight around himself and fell forward in a silent scream. What the hell had happened to Korin? That . . . that *thing* had to be him. The look in the monster's eye was all too familiar. It was the same look he'd seen in his brother's eyes as he lay upon the carpet screaming, his burned arm being held in the air. A look of hatred and jealousy.

There was no logical explanation for what had happened to Korin. None. A man didn't turn into a beast. It was not fathomable. And yet, here he was, sitting in the crosshairs of this beast. He knew he was being hunted.

"Rational—be rational!" he said to himself, slapping both sides of his head. "A man doesn't just turn into a monster. It's impossible."

Yet somehow Davis knew it might be possible. All those stories that Korin had been obsessed with as a child, the fairy tales and folk-lore—they were cautionary tales, lessons on how to be a good and ethical person. If you are a human who commits immoral atrocities, as punishment, you will be changed into a creature. The form may have been different, but the story line was the same. If you did something bad, you became a beast.

Korin had killed their father. He had killed Tate. He had once tried to kill Davis. All the hatred that Korin held in his heart had changed him into a monster.

Davis had to stop him. But how the hell was he going to do that? He only had a knife on him. It was a large knife with a broad steel blade, but still, just a knife.

The snow fell harder and began to pile up. He surmised about three to four inches fell since he found his father's body. The cloudy sky grew darker as the sun set behind them. He couldn't sit out in the open like this all night.

Davis saw that his footprints were already starting to fill in. He was going to need a fire for warmth. Even though Korin was out there, Davis had to keep his cool. Now wasn't a time to panic, as then he would die for sure out here.

He began to walk toward the copse. He had no idea what kind of coni-fer they were, but they stood tall and had very low and dense sweeping branches. A place he could hide. He went as deep as he could among the trees and chose one of the largest. It looked like a giant green cone sitting on top of the snow. Other trees were tightly packed around.

This will do, Davis thought.

Pushing back the low sweeping branches, he found clear and dry ground underneath. No snow. And there were plenty of broken branches around. Maybe he could start a fire underneath the tree. Potentially deadly, should he set the tree on fire, but if he cleared the area well enough, he should be okay.

Pulling the knife out of the sheath again, Davis rubbed his hand over the leather-wrapped handle. He could feel the lump underneath it. A piece of flint. His father always wrapped flint in the handle of his hunting knives.

"You never know when you'll need a fire," his father had always said when Davis would watch him prepare his knives for a trip. Albert would get a long thin strap of leather and a solid stick of flint. He'd hold the flint against the handle of the steel blade and wrap it tightly with the leather strap, securing the flint in place. Davis's father was a true survivalist.

A heavy lump formed in his throat and he choked back tears. It took Albert's death to make Davis wish he could change the past and have a relationship with his father.

He shook his head to get rid of the thoughts. He had to stay strong.

With his hands, he swept the fallen pine needles and dead branches into a pile, clearing a large area of dirt near the trunk of the tree, next to a crook in the base where the roots rose up right before plunging into the ground. Then he broke off all the branches above the crook to give his head and fire some clearance. He placed some of the boughs that had living needles in the crook for a soft place to lie down, which would provide some separation between him and the ground. Finally, he gathered up all the dried bits that he'd swept away, placing them into a pile.

Unraveling the leather strap and taking the piece of flint with fingers that were losing dexterity due to the cold, Davis struck the piece of flint against the sharp blade of the knife. After several tries, some sparks caught hold of the dried tinder and began a tiny blaze. He then fed the fire larger broken-up branches. The fire was tiny, but was giving off some heat, which Davis desperately needed.

He then turned to the trunk of the tree. Taking his knife, he began to cut hard into the trunk, making the tree bleed sap. Davis wasn't sure if it was safe to eat sap from a tree, but he was at the point of being too hungry to care. He licked the wound of the tree. The sap was thick and sticky and cool. Heavy with the scent of pine. The taste was woody with a hint of sweetness. It wasn't much, In fact, there was very little sap that came from the tree. But just having something in his mouth brought some satisfaction. It didn't quell the hunger, but it provided some relief.

He turned and sat down on his bed of fresh boughs. He had found a heavy branch that seemed to have recently snapped off one of the neighboring trees. It was thick and long, but strong because it had not started to dry out yet. He picked up the thinner end of the branch, which was still quite stout. Then, with the leather strap, he tied the Bowie knife to the end of the branch, creating a rudimentary spear. He was ready to defend himself, should Korin find him—if he could get his antlers unstuck, that is.

Davis laughed, then clamped his hands over his mouth. He had to remain as quiet as possible. He needed to make it through the night.

By god, was he thirsty. It would take forever to melt snow on this tiny fire, and he knew from his father that eating snow wouldn't help with hydration.

He settled back down into the boughs, gripping his spear, and stared at the fire. He was prepared to cover the blaze with snow the moment he heard anything unusual. Davis gripped the spear tighter in his hands and double-checked the leather wrapping that held the knife to the branch.

It was time for the hunter to become the hunted.

CHAPTER THIRTY-FIVE

"Hey. *Hey!*" He felt his shoulder being shaken and the voice of his father yelling in his ear.

Davis's eyes shot open and he sat up. Looking around, he saw that he was still alone under the tree. Shivering, he called out in a loud whisper, "Dad?" No response.

The fire was out.

"Fuck," he said as he fumbled for the piece of flint. He had fallen asleep. He never fell asleep out in the woods when he was hunting. His hands were numb and his feet were . . . He looked down. His feet were covered in snow and he couldn't feel them. Davis pulled his legs back and nothing happened. It had snowed heavily, and during his sleep, he'd slid down the tree to lie down flat. His feet had been stretched out past the protection of the tree.

In a panic, he started to dig at the snow. It was heavy and dense. His fingers were freezing, but he kept digging and pulling, and eventually he freed his feet. His left foot came out bootless. Digging further, he was able to recover the boot, but like its mate, it was soaked. He needed to relight the fire and get things dried out.

Luckily the tree had protected the rest of him from all the snow. Peeking out through the branches, he could see the snow had fallen almost to knee height, and it was continuing to fall. Davis knew he couldn't stay here the rest of the night, but right now, he couldn't leave.

He scraped more dried needles and small branches over into a pile and relit the fire with the flint and steel. Again, it was small, but gave off some warmth. He put his feet close to the flames, along with his boots.

The forest was eerily silent. Wet snow could be heard falling and landing on the existing blanket that covered the forest. Every so often, he'd hear a soft thud, which would make him jump. He realized it was branches giving way to the heavy snow, which landed in a heap on the ground. Other than that, everything was silent. So silent that he heard the sound of heavy breathing. It wasn't super close, but it was nearby, and growing closer.

He scooped the snow over the fire. It could be a deer, but that wasn't likely.

Davis knew he needed the element of surprise. The fire sizzled as it went out and he quickly fanned at the little black tendril of smoke that started to make its way up the canopy, breaking up the smoke so it wouldn't be seen.

Davis reached for his rudimentary spear and readied it in front of him. He slid his feet underneath and struggled into a crouched position. He wasn't going to be caught lying down. Pain shot up his legs and he winced. His feet were starting to thaw out. He had no dexterity in them, but he could still manage to get up. Unfortunately, he had no boots on, and didn't want to be caught while trying to put them on.

He sat on his haunches for what seemed like an eternity. The breathing sounded like it was coming from all directions and he couldn't pinpoint it. Adrenaline was surging through him and he could feel his heart beating heavily in his chest and in his temples. He tried to slow down his breathing to calm himself. There was a good chance Korin wouldn't find him.

A strange call warbled, like that of a whippoorwill but deeper, darker, and haunting. Drawn out.

Davis's body tensed. He had never heard a sound like that before.

"What the hell?" he whispered, shivering from a mixture of cold and fear.

He heard it again, closer this time. Davis fell into a state of shock, but he remained in his crouched position, ready to fight or flee.

He heard a low growl. A growl of satisfaction.

Davis had been found.

The tree sheltering Davis burst apart, branches and needles and snow raining down on him.

He stood up tall against the trunk, ignoring the debris. His spear was raised up high in front of him. Targeted at what stood just ten feet away.

Every rib on the creature was visible. Its face was skeletal, and its lone gleaming eye seemed to have sunk even further into its skull. It was much thinner than it had been when Davis had first seen it several hours ago, but it was the same creature. The same beast that had torn Tate apart and consumed half his body—that had killed his father and maybe even went after Addy, eating her as well. A monster.

His brother.

"Korin!" Davis shouted.

The beast took a step back in confusion. As if it wasn't sure what to do about this little animal that stood in front of it.

"Why?" Davis cried out, his voice cracking.

The beast's eye softened as it looked down at Davis. It gave a sad groan.

Could it be remorse?

It took a step back.

Now was his chance.

Davis pushed off his haunches and jumped through the gap that the monster had created when it had ripped the tree branches apart. Ignoring the screaming pain in his feet, Davis did his best to run in the snow. An ear-splitting screech sounded behind him, but he didn't look back. Ahead of him was the darkness of the forest, which was becoming less visible through the falling snow. He caught sight of a fallen tree. If he could just get behind that, he could use it as a barrier to separate himself from the creature, who was gaining ground behind Davis, breathing heavily.

The bark was rough and icy as Davis launched himself over it, surprised at his dexterity, given his frozen appendages. He wasn't going down without a fight. He quickly pivoted on his feet to turn and face the advancing monster, spear raised over the top of the fallen tree, ready to attack.

But there was nothing there.

Davis, still in an attack position, scanned the forest, looking at the trees and trying to discern whether there was anything unnatural standing among them. There was nothing. He was alone.

Yet if there was one thing that could be said about Korin, it would be that he's tenacious. Davis knew his brother was still out there, and close by.

He took a step back from the tree trunk and, keeping the spear raised, turned to head in the direction he'd initially been running. He was so turned around, he had no clue where he was. He prayed he wasn't heading deeper in.

Movement from the falling snow played tricks on him. Making him believe he was seeing Korin coming at him from the side.

Davis turned sharply to his right, the tip of his rudimentary spear cracking hard against a tree trunk. The sound was amplified by the snow, giving away his location. He cringed and weaved around a few trees, hoping to put a distance between himself and the tree he hit. Though his footprints were not filling up fast enough, giving away his location.

He backed himself up against a large standing tree trunk, hoping that it provided him some visual cover.

"Do something," he whispered to himself, the puff of breath momentarily blinding him as it floated past his eyes.

The creature stepped out from behind a tree in front of Davis. It was down on its hands and knees, and the exposed spinal bones seemed to bristle with anticipation.

Davis had nowhere to run. Before he could draw in a deep breath, the beast advanced.

Davis pushed off the tree as the creature advanced on him, mouth agape, revealing a row of sharp fangs and teeth. Its arms shot forward to grab Davis, and Davis's spear found its way into the monster's mouth, plunging upward into its brain.

Not soon enough. Claws shot forward and slashed at Davis's stomach. Despite the blazing pain, Davis followed through with the spear. The beast fell to its side, thrashing about as its brain bled through its skull. Davis leaned back against the tree and reached down to his stomach to feel how deep the wound was. It couldn't be that bad, he thought, as he felt nothing but a warm burn.

Then his fingers touched the edge of his shirt where it was torn clean through. It was wet and soft. He let his gaze drop and watched as his intestines uncoiled from his abdomen.

Blood from both brothers soaked the snow, painting the area red.

Korin's remaining eye stared at Davis, but gone was the look of hate and anger, replaced with confusion and sorrow.

"I'm so sorry . . . for everything," Davis gasped as he slid down the tree and sat next to his brother, who spasmed, and then went still.

CHAPTER THIRTY-SIX

Addy ran away with her back to the cabin, her feet slipping in the snow and clutching something in her uninjured hand. She didn't look back.

Tate had abandoned her. Korin had abandoned her. She was all alone and lost.

"Korin, please," she cried out. "Where are you?"

A shiver shook her body and a freezing wind blew her hair. She had left Korin's knit cap back at the cabin. She had put it on Tate's head to keep him warm, since he couldn't come with her. She had smoothed back his hair as she'd slid the cap on and kissed his cheek good-bye. Tate was a good brother.

Addy tried to follow the road but had lost it in the falling snow. She'd started to wander off, back into the forest. She didn't want to be here. She wanted to be somewhere warm. With food.

At the thought of nourishment, her stomach growled.

She didn't know where she could go. She was too afraid to go back to the cabin. She didn't want to see her brother, because he really wasn't there anymore. And Korin. She didn't know where he was. He had left her behind by the dead bear.

She struggled to remember the sequence of events.

Korin had disappeared and then there was a monster. She was mad at Korin because he had told her there were no monsters in the woods. However, after her initial fright, the monster had fed her and taken her to the cabin. It was like the meal Korin had fed her earlier. She had begun to like the monster.

When they entered, there was someone sleeping there.

Addy shook her head.

The next thing she remembered was seeing Tate on the floor, reaching for her. For a moment she'd been so happy to see him alive, but then he had left her again. Just like Daddy. Just like Korin.

As she had said good-bye to Tate, the monster had picked up something from the other side of her brother and handed it to her. She couldn't see what it was, but she'd taken it all the same. It was warm and wet.

225

Before she could get a good look at it, the door opened and someone was there. For a moment she'd thought it was Korin, and she was so happy. After he had stepped into the cabin, she saw it wasn't Korin, but Davis. Addy became scared. Korin would be mad at her if he found her in the cabin with his brother, so she ran away.

And now she had no idea where she was or where she was going.

Tears streamed down her face and she started to wail. Not paying attention to what was in front of her, she tripped over a root and tried to catch herself on the wrist the monster had broken. Pain shot up her arm and she screamed. The object she was carrying dropped as she fell to the ground.

Addy lay on her side in the snow, clutching her injured wrist to her chest. She was so tired and hungry. She was in so much pain.

In front of her on the white snow was what she had dropped, and she stared at it hard. It was what she wanted. It was what she needed. Addy stared for a long minute, fixated on it, before reaching out and drawing it closer to her.

Off in the distance, the wind carried the sound of barking dogs and calls for her and the Perrins. No one called out for her brother.

She ignored them. What was in front of her was more important than anything.

She rolled to her stomach and reached out for what she had dropped. When her hand touched it, she dragged it across the snow to her. In its path, it left a dark red trail.

The calls and the dogs were coming closer.

Addy didn't care. Everything was drowned out by the pounding of her heartbeat in her ear and her stomach crying out in hunger and loneliness.

Addy brought the object to her lips.

Oh, how she loved her brother. She was so afraid of being without him.

"I'll keep you forever," she whispered as she bit down on the raw heart.

Acknowledgments

Writing my first book has been an enlightening and exhilarating (if not stressful) experience. This was not a solo adventure and I had a large group of people who helped bring this book to life. A heartfelt thank you to all my friends and co-workers for your continual encouragement and support. To my ladies of the Leaser Lake Hive and the members of the PA Chapter of the HWA / Mid-Atlantic Dark Fiction Society, I am eternally grateful for your words of wisdom and guidance.

Thank you, Steve, Amber, and Sally for the support over the years and the chance to publish this story. An additional round of thanks to Amber for always keeping me well fed when in Vermont (because I get hangry when I write). To Dave, Colin, Ken, and Ben: Thank you for believing in this book, the monsters, and the publishing opportunity.

My deepest gratitude to my parents, sister, and family for the encouragement to be "my true self" as an author… even though I write creepy and disturbing stories that you may not want to read.

And to Professor Karen Blomain (1944 – 2012), I wouldn't be where I am today without your blunt and honest words of "You are a writer. Don't you dare question that again."

About the Author

With a love of scary stories and folklore, Amanda Headlee spent her entire life crafting works of dark fiction. She has a fascination with the emotion of fear and believes it is the first emotion humans feel at the moment they are born. Most of her work focuses on dark fiction associated with folklore and cosmic horror. By day Amanda is a Program Manager; by night she is a wandering wonderer. When she isn't writing or working, she can be found logging insane miles on her bike or running the backcountry of Eastern Pennsylvania. She's one of those crazy people who compete in long-distance endurance races. You can follow Amanda on Facebook, Instagram, Twitter, and at her website: www.amandaheadlee.com.